# Back to Williamsburg

## Kerry A. O'Brien

**O'BRIEN BOOKS AND PUBLISHING**

Published in the United States of America by O'Brien Books and Publishing

Copyright © 2008 by O'Brien Books and Publishing

ISBN **978-0-6151-7526-3**

Printed in the United States of America

*To Aislinn Elizabeth, Kristin Alexandria*

*and the new little one yet to be born.*

# Chapter One

*Courage and perseverance have a magical talisman, before which
difficulties disappear and obstacles vanish into air.*

**John Quincy Adams (1767-1848)**

She never really became aware of its presence until much later in
life when she ventured to meet the world. Of course, she had peeked
at the world from her own backyard, met its people, peered at all
different kaleidoscopes of life, in school and neighborhoods, in the
small town of Colonial Williamsburg, on various trips to New
England, New York and the mid-West to see friends and relatives, in
various trips to South and Central America, even in various career
paths after college, but it wasn't until she really voyaged on a search
for some unknown life meaning that she discovered its presence.

Sometimes it was magical. Other times it was haunting. But it
simmered beneath the surface, soothing, beckoning, calming, and

luring her. But this presence was difficult to name. It existed. It breathed. She tried to name it by discovering what it was. But even still, she couldn't quite put her finger on it. Perhaps social class had something to do with it. She wasn't quite sure.

Her sister had always talked about social class, mainly as a peripheral commentary on her one true passion—the issues of racism in American culture. She had dedicated her life to such practices, and became a college professor to kids wet behind the ears in the "real" happenings in life—like interstates built through African-American neighborhoods in the 1940s and 1950s, and real incidences of racism and sexism that happen beneath all of our noses--- like the glass ceiling in the workplace or traditional patriarchal models of marriage. God grant her patience for such a task -- how do you attempt to open one's eyes to such a world, from the haven of a classroom? Many people may say that experience is the world's best teacher. She would teach them, in a brief moment in their lives, in the hope of planting a seed, or enlightening a mind to the racial prejudices and injustices still afloat in the world.

The two sisters differed in a lot of ways, but one thing is for sure is that they always built off of each other's ideas, which is all we can really hope for in this world---the building of ideas and minds.

But on this one evening, in the summer of 1991 in Williamsburg, Sarah, a bright fifteen-year-old, with short blonde hair, lay on her bed in the dark, as it was close to the midnight hour. She had been lying in this bed for the past month, and only in the last two weeks did she begin to leave the bed to go to the bathroom which was across the hall. She loved her bed, as most fifteen-year-olds do, but to spend a month in it, staring at the same blue curtains and the same stucco paint on the ceiling was more than any teenager could take.

The frilly curtains lay lifeless on the three windows. The four poster double bed was situated in one corner, and her step-sister's wrought-iron twin bed was situated in another. Both girls had decorated their respective walls with swim team ribbons, magazine photo collages, knick-knacks and posters. Two antique dressers, two closets and a table which held a record player were snuggled amid the blue-flowered comforters, pillows and window accents.

8

Sarah was a social girl. She loved her friends, she loved to go out and laugh, and make other people laugh. She loved to be around other people. School didn't matter much to her. Her grades were always half an attempt of what she could really do, because her social life meant more to her. But, by some stroke of luck, she enrolled herself in a literary magnet school in high school. It interested her because the school marketed itself to teach much more than the average curriculum of English literature. Many times this class clenched her interest in school, as not much else held her attention. She was bright, but untapped. At least this class allowed her to write, to compose music, to create.

She was a born leader, even though she took on the role of follower with her sister. Her sister was the school choral accompanist and an over-achiever in all subjects. If the younger one would have applied herself to her studies, she would have been more like the older one, but such is the case that she likened herself with social living, while living and playing hard. She had a passion that the older sister did not. Or rather, they both possessed a certain passion but Sarah's was led by her emotions. This can be heavenly, or dangerous, depending on the situation. The older was a little more pragmatic about her passion, and to the younger, sterile.

The older sister wasn't always like that. When she was younger she let her creativity run full reign, and led the younger on numerous daily projects. The older composed song lyrics and poems from age five onward, and the younger just perceived this as normal daily life. Certainly the older was a born teacher, as she had been teaching the younger her whole life.

But on this one evening, as Sarah lay there, with a cast on her leg that started from the tips of her toes and ended at the top of her thigh, you can imagine how tortuous this must have been for a fifteen-year-old girl who relied on her social life outside of the family home to give her pleasure. Her older sister had left the home a year before, as she was dating an African-American boy, which their mother and step-father did not agree with, so she left the house to live with their father and step-mother in Massachusetts. With this new change in the family dynamic, the younger had thrown herself into her social life, her boyfriend, and tried to spend as much time away from the home as possible. It was summer, and things were a bit freer. There is something in the air of summer which calms the weary souls and becomes a blanket of relaxation. The day's events included going to the pool, hanging out at a friend's house or throwing an occasional party.

Summer for a young girl in Williamsburg was as close to heaven as one could get. The options for activities were limitless: Water Country, Busch Gardens, Colonial Williamsburg, friends' houses and the neighborhood pools. While the temperatures rose and one felt the heat of a true Southern summer, an aura of laziness and relaxation permeated the air and nestled itself like a blanket upon the town. Most of the neighborhoods were only a few miles apart. The roads were canopied with shady pines and leafy oaks that seemed to encase the town in its magic. Summer mornings and afternoons were spent traveling in air-conditioned cars back and forth to friends' houses, pools and various events. There were no cares, no worries. Life was good and sweet.

But one month before summer ended, on one of her summer-filled jaunts with friends, she was hit by a car, thus the full-length cast.

It was not your run-of-the-mill car accident, as she was struck by the car of one of her friends! Strange as that may be, it seems absolutely fitting now, as the "friend" changed schools the next year and was never heard from again. But we will save lessons, and the lessons learned, for much later. But this is what happened:

Sarah and two other friends, Tracy and Susan, spent one lazy afternoon visiting their various friends around town who were working summer jobs. Tracy had just gotten her driver's license--- and she was the first in the group to do so—so, the idea of driving around town had a certain appeal and sense of freedom. They drove to Merchant Square---the small area of shops which helmed the infamous Duke of Gloucester Street in Colonial Williamsburg.

Colonial Williamsburg was the foundation of the town, as it drew families and historians from all over the country. But it wasn't just a tourist attraction. It was a living and breathing entity that transported its visitors back to a time when our country was first founded.

Costumed interpreters roamed the grounds performing their various daily tasks—gathering brush, blowing glass, mending hats and shoes, designing clothing. Hundreds of Colonial Williamsburg employees walked the historic campus chanting cheerful greetings to each other along the cobblestone streets, as if they were living in the seventeenth century. And while the living museum maintained its seventeenth century romantic aura, the people of the twentieth century town of Williamsburg ensured it kept afloat.

Merchant Square was situated at the helm of the street across from the oldest building on the College of William and Mary's campus—Wren Hall—which was also the building that faced the original country's capitol at the opposite end of the long, cobblestone street. Within Merchant Square in the early 1980s was a theater/playhouse, the historic pharmacy complete with a diner counter which made the most delectable lunch sandwiches, the upscale women's and men's clothing stores, Binn's and R. Bryant, the Colonial Williamsburg Silversmith, Master Craftsman, Laura Ashley, the infamous four-star fine cuisine restaurant, The Trellis, an investment firm, the old toymaker shop, a collectible's shop, an upscale department store, Casey's, the Williamsburg Post Office, a large fast-food eatery with upscale flair called, of all things, "A Good Place to Eat," and last but not least, the Wythe Candy Shop. Many tourists made their annual trip to Williamsburg solely to stock up on Wythe fudge or candy treats—and the shop owners insisted that the workers give a steady supply of free samples of fudge—and most of these workers were Sarah's friends.

The fudge kitchen was set up behind eye-level sheet of plexiglass so that all the tourists could watch the magic happen. It was as if one had stepped into Willie Wonka and the Chocolate Factory. And of course, the owners of Wythe lived in town. Most of the candy workers were fellow high school students and friends of Sarah and their group, hailing from the only two high schools in town, Somerset and Montier.

Twice a day, the sound of the marching fife and drum corps floated through the open door of the candy store as the group of young children and teenagers who formed the corps marched along Duke of Gloucester Street, or Dog Street, as it was affectionately known by the locals. It was an honor to be part of the corps, as it was a competitive process to gain selection. Many parents enrolled their children on the waiting list to be a part of the corps at birth. By the time they reached the appropriate age to play, a spot was available. Often times this process took five or ten years—or more. Many of the Wythe candy employees' brothers were members of the corps, and to hear the steady beat of the drums and patriotic whistles of the fifes were a constant reminder to the whole town that families ensured Williamsburg's magic.

So, on that hot, summer afternoon in August, Sarah, Tracy and Susan planned to visit their friends working in the candy store in Merchant Square.

Tracy pulled her car into the back parking lot of the Williamsburg Post Office, and Sarah and Susan got out of the car while Tracy looked for a parking space. As Sarah walked around the back of the car, the front bumper clipped Sarah in the side of her leg, which sent her sprawling onto the concrete in a daze. Tourists and Colonial Williamsburg employees in full costume, alerted by the commotion, approached Sarah, who sat with her leg outstretched in the middle of the parking lot. An ambulance was called, and a full-length cast put an end of Sarah's afternoon jaunts for the remainder of the summer.

So, as she lay there, in her bed for one month, the mere loneliness and solitude began to wear on her. She had Leo Tolstoy to keep her company, as Anna Karenina, was one of the assigned readings for the summer in the Literary Magnet School, but even Tolstoy, with his mass of indistinguishable names and list of characters, was not enough to keep her sated. She craved interaction. She needed to know who was going out with whom, who had been to her boyfriend's apartment, which had become the central meeting location for that particular summer, and any other news that kept the social circle in motion. Eighteenth century Russian life – either elite or peasantry, which Tolstoy illuminated quite well – was not enough to satisfy Sarah's need for sociality.

So, Sarah devised a foolproof plan to find out the night's events after each night. Tracy called Sarah's house near the hour of midnight, allowing the phone to ring once, and then, hung up. Sarah then called Tracy back. This plan was devised because Sarah was not allowed to receive phone calls after the ten o'clock hour. 'Tis remarkable how ingenious this fifteen-year-old was. So, this carried on for about a week. The phone ominously rang, and Sarah, with the phone in the bed, called Tracy to find out the latest events, as she knew her friend was home from the night's adventures. Sarah talked at a whisper, so as not to wake her sleeping step-sister.

But, this one night, in the later days of the August warmth, was the last night that the phone rang throughout the house. Just as the phone rang on the previous nights, it rang this night, and Sarah waited a few minutes to pick up the receiver to make the nightly call. Finally, after a few minutes, she picked up the phone only to hear her stepbrother, John, and his girlfriend in mid-conversation. She was confused. How did this happen? The line was free only thirty seconds before, as Tracy had just called. How were John and his girlfriend in mid conversation at this moment? She hobbled with crutches to John's room right next door.

Sarah's family became quite big after her mother remarried. It was not just Sarah and her sister anymore where creative pursuits abounded without constraints. There were now four other children – Italian, at that, with an Italian father who had retired from the Navy years earlier. In all honesty, Sarah's oldest sister probably received the best education out of all of the children, because she had her mother's undivided attention and precision that only a first-born child receives. And as more and more children were added to the pie, her mother's attention and ability to create conditions for free creativity were spread thin.

John had always been a wayward dreamer, from whose room Beatles lyrics and songs were heard. He had a great singing voice and a special knack for the guitar, so Sarah was happy her room was right next to his. Her bed was closest to the wall of his room, so she heard what music he was listening to, what songs popped into his head, and what guitar riffs he was perfecting. She walked into his room one day-- it must have been about a year earlier, when he was practicing a bass riff from a song by Cream. She had gone into his bedroom for a purpose, but he sat her down and taught her the Cream bass riff he had been playing for the past hour. So, she sat with the guitar in her lap, and perfected a Cream riff, on a whim. Out of all of the stepsiblings, John possessed an easiness and sureness of himself that the others didn't have. He had to, almost as a calming mechanism for his younger siblings, and he would prove in later years to keep senses and sanities afloat despite difficulties.

So, she hobbled next door to her step-brother's room, knocked and entered.

"I'll be off in a few minutes," was his reply to her entrance. She had not said a word.

Sarah hobbled back to her room, resumed her position in the bed where she had taken residence for the past several weeks, and listened and waited until she could no longer hear his voice. Perhaps she dozed off, perhaps she was not listening intently enough, but the next sound that sprung her to awareness was the sound of the ringing phone. She instantly reached for the receiver, as if in a panic. How did she not hear when John got off the phone? And why didn't he tell her? And why was the phone ringing again this late at night?

Surely, when Tracy had called the first time and didn't receive Sarah's response, Tracy thought that perhaps Sarah didn't hear the signal, so she called again. Perhaps she called several times throughout John's conversation, and he didn't answer the call waiting. It is futile to make theories and guesses now. But it is common, as this would be the night that would change her entire life, seal her fate, and nudge her out into a world of various experiences---experiences that she never even dreamed of. She never stopped, hasn't stopped, since that night, forging ahead, doing things that needed to be done, experiencing the world. She never does stop until she receives brief moments in life when she can reflect on such experiences. But such is life, her life, in that, another great experience comes and forges another path, to form her destiny.

# Chapter Two

*And even in our sleep pain that cannot forget falls drop by drop upon the heart, and in our own despair, against our will, comes wisdom to us by the awful grace of God.*

**Aeschlyus (525-456 BC)**

Sarah quickly picked up the receiver, and heard a dial tone. It could not have been anyone other than Tracy. Sarah lay there for a moment in the dark, petrified of some looming thing, something that she couldn't quite explain, if she had to in that moment. It was a fear that simmered in her soul. It was an unfathomable fear that only her spirit and soul had some recognition of---- Sarah didn't know what it was. She just knew that she had never felt something like that before.

Her stepsister, in the bed across the way, hadn't stirred. But she heard movement and it was coming toward her room. She had no time to plan how she was going to call Tracy back; she only had enough time to perceive that angry footsteps were coming toward her room. She lay in the dark, with a full-length cast, petrified of the next moments, when all of the sudden, the bedroom door burst open, and her step-father came lunging toward her bed. He did not turn on the light when he entered, but the light from the hall provided enough light for both of them to see the contents of the room. At that point, she could see better than he, since she had been laying in the dark for quite some time, and her eyes had grown accustomed to the darkness. Plus, she knew her room. God knows she had spent enough time in it. She knew every stucco paint crevice on the ceiling, and she knew where every piece of furniture lay, and could maneuver herself very well in the dark, as she often went to sleep after her step-sister was already asleep. And there seemed to be an unwritten rule that no one should disturb someone who was sleeping. So, it only made sense that her stepfather did not turn on the light either, even though his footsteps and presence conveyed an intense anger. He was just as scared as angry, as any psychologist will tell you that anger is a mask for fear, and he headed into that dark room where Sarah lay upon the bed with the phone close to her body. The phone was an important symbol in her life, and it was her connection to a world outside of her family life. She had struggled for years to be allowed to have one in her room. And this struggle came after the initial struggle of phone calls which lasted more than five minutes, even in the day light hours. This was a rule for both of the sisters, as they were the only ones, really, to ever use the phone. Phone calls, no matter who they were talking to, could not last for more than five minutes, and if either of them extended their phone conversation past the five minutes, an ominous hand appeared and just clicked on the receiver, severing the two people on opposite ends of the phone line. Sarah and her sister's friends, after a while, grew accustomed to severed phone conversations. They just accepted that sometimes in mid conversation with one of the two, they might receive a dial tone. Most of them learned not to take it personally, nor to be alarmed of any danger. But the five-minute rule existed years before the current situation. Sarah had struggled and won the privilege now to have a phone in the room, and at this moment, she literally hugged it to her body, as it seemed to be the only unconscious comfort in the room at this time.

She seemed to lose all awareness of her leg in a cast at that point, and awareness of everything around her for that matter except the figure which stood before her, as the light from the hall shone on the left and back side of his body. The fear that she had experienced was standing right before her. Sarah was not afraid of her step-father, per se, but the series of events that came about because of this precise moment in time. Her step-father was just the catalyst. Of course, at the time, she had no way to know of the future events, she only recognized the intense fear that shook her bones and quietly rumbled within her being. Her step-father was just as scared as Sarah was, but it was his house, and she was his step-daughter, and he was angry.

"Give me the phone," he demanded. He still could not see Sarah lying in the bed in the dark with the cast on her leg.

Sarah did not respond, but moved slowly and meticulously to unplug the phone from the wall. The fear had gotten hold of her tongue, and she could do nothing but move slowly with caution and precision.

Sarah's step-sister awoke, and John, in the next room, was listening intently to the ruckus that began to ensue in the next room.

"I'm tired of your friends calling here at all hours of the night," boomed her step-father's angry voice.

He had every right to be angry. He was trying to sleep, along with the rest of the kids in the house. He had to work the next day. The last thing he wanted to hear while he was trying to sleep was a persistent ringing phone. He did what any step-father or father would do: nip the problem in the bud.

Sarah's mother was downstairs in the kitchen doing God knows what. Their marriage had begun to fall apart at that point. It actually began falling apart shortly before Sarah's sister left, and her departure was just something to further the chasm forming between them. Her step-father was accustomed to going asleep alone while Sarah's mother remained downstairs. There was fated doom in the house, and this was only the beginning. Her mother had already lost one child because of his strict rules. But she still continued to try to maintain a running household, since Sarah was still fifteen, and the younger twin children were eleven.

As Sarah handed the phone to the looming figure, she could not hold her tongue, which had always been her way. Her fear, just as his fear, was unleashed. She didn't know where her words or her courage came from. She just knew she could not give him her phone without something to say.

"I wish you'd stop blaming my damn friends for everything!" Sarah yelled.

Curse words were not tolerated in his household, let alone a disrespectful child. And the amount of time that Sarah spent with her friends had always been a bur in his side. But most of Sarah's friends came from good neighborhoods, good families, achieved high marks in school, and were not the type to influence her in any disagreeable way. But the age of fifteen is one of the most critical ages in the forming of a person's life, as any parent can attest to. But what could her stepfather do? He was not her father, and her mother had turned a blind eye on this strange behavior. Her mother mainly concentrated her energy on her own problems downstairs in the kitchen, where she spent the majority of her time drinking wine bottle after wine bottle to escape her pain. Time and distance would reveal the logic of her mother's behavior——not that it was right-- as her mother had done it and her mother's mother had done it, so it was all she ever knew. The raising of children was not a primary concern, personal survival was.

But Sarah's last statement was a direct contradiction to his authority. So, he did what any scared and angry man would do, he lifted his hand and began hitting, in the dark, Sarah, who was in the bed in a full-length cast. He didn't know what else to do at that point, as he was angry before Sarah's last comment, her words and disrespect pushed him over the edge. He unconsciously transferred all of his angered energy into his hand - - which made direct contact with the fifteen-year-old girl.

The blows hurt her, she must admit, but not entirely. Fortunately, her broken leg was the left one, which was furthest from his body, so the right side of her body received the majority of the blows. He hit,

18

open-handed in the dark, so her side and the side of her thigh received the brunt of it. If he had hit the broken leg, the pain would have been much worse as the leg was just beginning to heal. But still, any slight touch to it was painful. But as it were, the pain of the human touch was not the action that produced the magnitude of fear in her, but rather, the unleashing of his anger at such an intense rate and abundance which was transferred to his swinging arms. His utter helplessness with what to do at that moment, at such a refuting nature to his power, unleashed a physical anger that sent his arms flailing. The phone, the culprit of his anger, was in his hands, but what disturbed him the most, the icing on the cake, so to say, was the final straw, her final words as she handed over the phone.

Sarah's step-father was a black-belt in karate. Once a week, he gave lessons to others in the family garage. The sport commands much respect, as it is based in Chinese philosophy, and practices, to a tee, the blending of self-discipline of the mind and body. Oftentimes Sarah watched him, in the garage, perform hundreds of push-ups on his knuckles, sometimes, he would perform a few on one arm; she laughed with glee when he chopped a piece of wood with his bare hands, and begged him when he was finished to do another. She had never seen anyone break a piece of wood with their bare hands, except maybe in the movies. But she was much younger then, and anything out of the ordinary impressed her.

She watched as kids from the neighborhood asked to receive lessons from him – even adults – and they all lost interest because his methods were so strict. Certainly, karate, and any other marshal art, or any form of practice that requires self-discipline should have a fair amount of strictness involved. For who can excel at mastering the mind and body if they don't have the self-discipline to stick with a strict teacher? Strict teachers are normally the ones who can teach the most---if one has the courage and wherewithal to stick with them.

Sarah had had her own lessons in self-discipline in other areas like piano and gymnastics. The two seem totally at odds with one another, as gymnastics is body based and the discipline of piano practice is mind-based, but the two formed a good foundation in her soul, and served as a much needed discipline which every human being should receive.

So, it seemed so peculiar, that the moment when her step-father had the opportunity to practice this self-discipline of the body and mind in real life – when the bubbles of anger and fear rose to the surface, a life-time of self-discipline was no where to be found, and his anger was released on Sarah, who was technically, already beaten up by her own carelessness. The two acts--- self-discipline and uncontrolled violence-- cannot easily be reconciled, but life reveals, in time, that its events are always a mystery.

At such an intense unleashing of anger, she felt all of her defenses release. Her words, her fear, her innocence, all mingled together and flowed from her in the form of urine on her bed sheets. She could feel the wetness between her legs as it seeped deeper and spread under her boxer shorts. She couldn't stop its rush, as he continued to hit her in the darkness. The urine continued to flow, and she lay there helpless, unable to move. She had no other choice but to endure the beatings and feel all of her self-dignity flow from between her legs.

John, hearing the blows from the next room, rushed to the side of the bed and shouted at his father, "It was Lilah who called. It wasn't her friends."

John just wanted to stop his father from hitting Sarah.

Sarah, at this point, could feel nothing more than embarrassment for the massive amount of urine which saturated her bottom and sheets. Should she sit there in it, or get up? Movement was a bit of a struggle at this point because of crutches and a full-legged cast.

Sarah remembered at that moment, that many years earlier, her stepfather hit their family puppy in the same way. He said that it was a form of training. Snuffy also peed in the same way whenever his hand touched the dog. She felt like that dog that had lost all sense of self-dignity, when his hand touched her in that forceful manner. It seemed strange that a man, who wanted desperately to exert his power and have his own man-made kingdom of submissive children, should choose little helpless children as aggressors. Granted, as children become older and grow into adults, they realize that there are certain battles they must fight in the world, and there are two important rules: Number one: You can win a battle without using your hands, and number two: Never fight with a person who does not match your strength, mentally.

John's shouts alerted Sarah's mother who was downstairs in the kitchen. Sarah continued to lie in the puddle of urine, surrounded by her step-father, her step-brother, and her step-sister, who was in her own bed across the way. The sound of her mother rushing up the stairs spurred Sarah to take some kind of action.

Sarah thought, "Well, I have already lost all self-dignity. No use in hiding it now."

So, she lunged for her crutches, and began to frantically make her way to the dresser for a new pair of underwear and boxers, while her step-father and step-brother argued about the phone call. Sarah's younger step-sister, sat upright in her bed blinking innocently at the event in front of her eyes.

"What's happening?" Sarah's mother yelled as she lunged into the room. She had already lost one daughter, and was barely holding her wits about her in the merciless regime of her husband, so the look on her face expressed years of concern, regret, questions and doubts.

As Sarah searched her drawers for dry clothes, she didn't really know what she was looking for. What did she need? What was she going to do? Where could she go to escape what had just happened? She only felt the wet urine on her legs.

"He hit me again," Sarah said to her mother.

# Chapter Three

*The glow of one warm thought is to me worth more than money.*

**Thomas Jefferson (1743-1826)**

This was not the first time he had hit her. He had hit her about ten months earlier, on her fifteenth birthday, to be exact.

It was a crisp October in Williamsburg. The leaves had begun to change their colors of bright greens to deep reds, oranges and yellows, reminiscent of the spectacular autumn shows in New England. All of the town's families adorned their front doors with harvest cornstalks, autumn leaf wreaths, and homemade miniature scarecrows with straw hats of rusts and green plaids. Families gathered outside to rake the leaves and to set-up autumn showcases of bails of hay and large cornucopias in the front yards. Fathers and sons lazily tossed footballs and Frisbees, and practiced game tactics, as the football season had begun its course. Sweaters were unpacked from attic boxes and chests, and parents held meetings to plan the year's events of concessions and volunteers, Parent Teacher Association events, town meetings and carpools. The town had come alive again after a successful tourist summer and the children and parents who had worked at the various outlet stores, Colonial Williamsburg markets and shops, Busch Gardens, Water Country, and four-star restaurants and hotels to accommodate the summer tourists connected again as families who were involved in their children's school activities. The hours of the various retail markets were cut back, and the only cars seen on the streets were local ones with Virginia license plates and "Welcome to Williamsburg" pineapple bumper stickers.

Sarah's birthday party was a haunting night – another one of those nights that Sarah had planned to be a festive occasion yet ended in tragedy and pain. Sarah and a close friend, Patty, whose birthday was close to hers, decided to throw a joint birthday party at Patty's house. Sarah's parents never would have allowed the kind of birthday party they were planning, nor would Sarah even think about asking them. Anything and everything was a struggle for Sarah and her parents. If Sarah wanted to do anything or have a friend over to spend the night, she'd beg for days, clean the entire house, wash the windows, vacuum the rooms, dust the furniture, wash the walls-----all for a night out with friends, or to have a friend over. Of course, her friends never knew this. So, Sarah knew that even asking to throw a theme birthday party was out of the question. Well, perhaps they would have complied, but it would have just been a party under the restricted regime that dominated the presence of the house, so it would not have felt like a party at all to her. Her parents would have outlined a written list of rules---do's and don'ts and time schedules. Sarah could not see this happening. Moreover, Patty's mother was always conducive to her daughter's plans, and was agreeable to the two girls' idea to throw a toga party for their birthdays. Both birthdays were in October, and it was a fine time to throw a party, as school had just begun in September, and football games and other such spirited activities were underway. So, it only seemed fitting that the two girls would supplement such activities with a theme party. They had heard about toga parties at universities and colleges, but to two fourteen-year-olds, ready to be fifteen-year-old girls, those parties were a distant enigma. So, they decided to create their own.

Patty lived in Abingdon Cross, a newer neighborhood just a few miles away from Sarah's neighborhood, Earlham Estates. Their neighborhoods actually bordered each other on their back sides, and were separated by a thicket of dense woods, and a small stream--- which was Sarah's backyard. The only road that connected the two neighborhoods was located off of the main highway, and was about two miles in distance. Sarah could easily walk the one acre of wooded path, crossed the log that connected the two banks of the trickling stream together, and emerged on the cul-de-sac road which ended the very back of Abingdon Cross. But it was just as easy to pop in a car for a ride.

The party attracted a lively crowd, and most everyone complied with the toga requirement. Members of all classes- freshman, sophomores, juniors and seniors- were in attendance. Both Sarah and Patty were proud of their party, as they were only sophomores at the time. There was no alcohol at the party, or at least, none was supplied. It was just good fun, and a different place to get together as friends. They were given full reign of the house, which was quite large, so there were different types of activities happening in each room. A boy and a girl were making out in one room on the sofa, in their togas. Others were watching movies in the living room. Others were outside in the front yard visiting with friends. Others were in the kitchen munching on party snacks and sodas. And most flitted between all the different areas where people were congregating--- as wearing nothing but a bed sheet was new, exciting and out of the ordinary. Nothing got out of hand, and everyone was in good spirits. Patty's mother kept a relatively low profile, as she knew that most teenagers would have their fun without many problems. And if anything did happen, Patty's mother had the good sense to talk to someone to figure out the problem and resolve it without much mayhem.

Patty's mother was a good woman, a good mother, a hell of a good driver, and an agreeable friend and confidant. She was a petite woman-- she couldn't have weighed over one hundred pounds, but she was strong. One could sense it in her presence. She was never over bearing, always agreeable with any plans that arose, spoke to her daughter and her daughters' friends with a kind heart and with soft eyes. She had a mass of curly, wiry hair, which was short and full, at

24

the top of her head, and she thrived on the interior decoration of their new house which they had recently designed, built, and adorned. She had impeccable taste in interior decoration, and coordinated all the colors quite well. This little perk was one of the concessions to appease both Patty and her mother for having to uproot their happy lives in Delaware, as they had just moved to Williamsburg the previous summer. But their sadness of leaving their Delaware hometown was never talked about. They both seemed to embrace their new life in a new neighborhood with new friends, in a new town, quite well, and immersed themselves into whatever was before them.

But you could see the unhappiness deep down in their eyes.

Patty's mother drove a black Saab, which Sarah always associated her with, as she handled that car like she had known it her whole life. Sarah had never seen such a small, petite woman---much less a mother--- handle a car like Patty's mother. Sarah was used to seeing her own mother maneuver the 1971 gold Volvo station wagon like a boat. And most of the other mothers in town drove big station wagons with wood paneling on the outside of the car, and sticky vinyl seats on the inside. And most drove their big boats on wheels cautiously, slowly and deliberately. Patty's mother's Saab was black with tan leather interior, and a delectable moon roof, that both Patty and Sarah occasionally fit both of their bodies through to experience the open air of the road. These were the simple pleasures in life that soon-to-be-fifteen-year-olds partook in. Sarah was thrilled to experience such an open display of enthusiasm and lack of abandon around a parental figure. That type of behavior was foreign to Sarah, as one never acted like oneself in front of parents. They were taught to be reserved and curb their appetites for rushes of adrenaline.

In all honesty, Sarah did not think that Patty acted in this fashion before she and her mother moved to Williamsburg. Sarah sensed the stiffness in her mother's demeanor at some of Patty's decisions and movements, but she never said anything to her daughter, and if she did, she couched it in the most careful and cautious terms, as if scared of what might ensue. Patty had a temper. Sarah never saw it, but it bubbled beneath her surface, always waiting to blow. It came from the energy that was emitted from her. The energy was somehow artificial and too stiffly energetic that it somehow indicated an anger that stirred beneath. Patty's mother had seen it before, and curbed her language and actions in such a way to avoid ever seeing it again. Sarah had heard that she once got so mad at a girl at her previous Delaware school that Patty stabbed a pencil into the girl's cheek. This was all hearsay, as it happened before Sarah had met Patty, but these kinds of stories were not taken lightly.

Patty left her boyfriend behind in Delaware, and she always held resentment toward her mother for allowing the move to happen. Patty's mother was following her husband's job, as any good wife would do, but one could sense that she felt a stronger loyalty to her daughter, as she never saw her husband anyway. She certainly wanted her daughter to be happy and the idea of moving to a new town with new friends, a new school, a new house, away from her boyfriend and everything she had ever known was not particularly appealing to a fourteen-year-old girl, nor was it appealing to a mother who only wanted her daughter to be happy. What is a mother or a wife to do? Does one choose the happiness of one's daughter, or does one fulfill the duties of a wife? Perhaps the change in environment would be good for Patty. Certainly, living in the town of Colonial Williamsburg is an opportunity of a lifetime for opening doors and chasing dreams.

In the end, after many tears, struggles and fights, the whole family moved. Patty got her own large room, which she could decorate herself; her mother received a brand new Saab sedan, and a new house that she could decorate to her liking. So, the two seemed to survive together. Patty talked about the boyfriend whom she left behind with such passion, happiness and longing. They had an intense and loving relationship, for such a young age, and Patty talked about it as if it would always be there. Even once, a few months earlier, Sarah traveled to Delaware with Patty and her mother to see their old stomping grounds, meet their old friends, see the images of Todd which Patty had vividly created in Sarah's mind, but the life and the people seemed dead and sterile. They had moved on, as most teenagers do, and in retrospect, Patty was able to embrace and accept her new life and friends in Williamsburg. So, all the struggles, tears and fights were futile. The move was actually good for both Patty and her mother.

To tell you the truth, Patty is probably the better for it, as she was removed from a dead-end Delaware town, spent a year in Williamsburg, where she began to bloom and gain her confidence, and then the next year, Patty's father was transferred again, this time, to North Carolina. So, the house just served as a buffer or a transition home. It was a symbol to keep the two girls, mother and daughter, busy. And the house still stands today-- built, designed and decorated to filter the feelings of a displaced life, to create a new one, and to move on once their strength had been gained. But that's not usually the case. Once families move to Williamsburg, its charm and unique spirit usually hold them close, as if to protect its character.

Patty's father had moved to Virginia for work, as he was one of the top executives for Owens Brockway, the glass bottling company that provided bottles for other Williamsburg companies like Anheiser-Busch and Pepsi-Cola. Many families in Sarah's school came from Delaware in the same fashion, as the Brockway, Delaware company, also had a large plant in Toano, a small town about five miles from Williamsburg. Years before Sarah arrived to Williamsburg in 1983, there was a mass exodus of Brockway lay workers, plant workers and factory workers, to the Virginia location, and they all, including their families, moved to the same neighborhood, Harrison Hills, which was just across the street from Abingdon Cross. There was a distinctive delineation between the two neighborhoods. Patty's father was an executive for the company, and thus, lived in Abingdon Cross. The others were factory workers, and thus, lived in Harrison Hills.

Harrison Hills, a small neighborhood with the houses built closely together, kept the Owens Brockway workers, the neighborhood paper deliverer, the high school basketball coach, Anheiser-Busch plant workers, and other blue-collar like jobs. It was built about twenty years before Abingdon Cross, and reflected the culture of rural Williamsburg in the 1960s and early 1970s. The houses were one-story ranchers and two-story box houses with quaint front yards with a few plots of daffodils and pansies. The houses usually had about three to four cars parked out front with a makeshift basketball net on the black-tarred driveway. In the 1960s and 1970s, all of the driveways were gravel, and when the 1980s arrived, paving one's driveway in black tar was the newest trend. Plus, it cut down on those pesky stones in the tires. Sarah's stepfather had refused to have the driveway paved, only because he saw it as an unnecessary expense, and said that others were merely spending money like water.

Sarah's house didn't sit on the street. It wasn't even built parallel to the road. It lay sideways, as if jutting out from the magic of the woods that thrived behind it. And as they turned right onto the driveway, a small incline gave way to a longer descent that poured the driver into its shady grounds. The front yard was a large expanse of oaks, beeches, pines and holly. There was no grass to mow. There were just tons of leaves to rake in the autumn months. They did try to plant grass in a small plot of land to the right of the front door, but the ground was like clay. Sarah and her friends, when younger, half expected to find old Native American or colonial settler archeological remains in the clay. And Sarah never lost her imagination of finding these treasures in her own yard.

Patty and Sarah worked at the same athletic shoe store in the first outlet mall in Williamsburg. Williamsburg, famous also for its mass of discount outlets, built the first Outlet Mall just down the road from the Williamsburg Pottery shops. The Pottery, an expansive warehouse of vases, pottery, ceramics, decorative silk flowers, wall hangings and frames, mirrors, Oriental rugs, garden adornments, lamps, house-wares, glasses, crystal, baskets, china, wood sculptures, candles and other household accessories, was a special cornerstone of the town. It was started in 1938 by John McMahon, who originally started the business by selling salt-glaze reproductions at discount prices. Over the years, the business expanded to include products from all over the world, and attracted shoppers from all over the world. The entire business now covers over two hundred acres of land about a mile down the road from Earlham Estates, Harrison Hills and Abingdon Cross. McMahon's two twin grandchildren lived in Earlham Estates, a few houses down from Sarah's house, and attended elementary and high school with Sarah and friends. The McMahon's built an indoor gymnasium next to a large field and allowed all the kids from town to use the gym and fields for basketball, football or any other activity. The small area became affectionately known to the kids as "Swampy Bottom," and when the juniors and seniors of Sarah's high school bragged to the younger freshman and sophomores about the coolness of their "Yacht Club" and activities to support the school sport activities, the McMahon grandchildren and friends of Sarah's class retaliated by forming the "Swampy Bottom" group for a little competitive rivalry. Every year, the kids hosted a Yacht Club/Swampy Bottom Bowl on the McMahon's land for good measure. And today, the McMahon grandchildren are running the Williamsburg Pottery for their grandfather.

Both Sarah and Patty worked for The Starting Line, one of the only athletic shoe outlets in town. The manager was a responsible young man, about thirty-four years old, with bleach blonde hair. He had an easiness that was catching, and he was secretly, but not entirely so, in love with the assistant manager, who was a junior at Virginia Tech. She told a story with precision and utter animation that listeners often found themselves mesmerized by her language. And the stories. Sarah and Patty heard about their nights of parties at college, and their nights of drinking at the only two bars in the town, Paul's Deli and The Green Leaf. The two bars were situated on the corner, in the heart of the College of William and Mary, across from the football stadium, and one block from Merchant Square on Dog Street. And anyone who knew Williamsburg knew these two places. The Green Leaf was often touted as the better of the two, as it contained an old world charm that seemed to accompany the College quite well, and occasionally hosted local bands. The tap-house was lined with exposed brick walls, stained glass windows, dark wooded bars and bar stools, and sturdy wood tables with green-painted captain chairs. It opened its doors in the mid-1970s and served as the college's and town's celebration house for parties after games, parties after concerts, a gathering place for law and business students, and a meeting place, particularly on Christmas night, to connect with old friends over its extensive list of Belgian and microbrew bottles.

Sherry, the spitfire assistant manager of the athletic store was a senior at Virginia Tech, and grew up in Williamsburg. She attended Montier High School, and lived with her family in the premier neighborhood across town located on the James River, called Queen's Point.

None of Queen's Point's residents attended Sarah's high school, as it resided in the James City County district, while the others, like Earlham Estates, Harrison Hills and Abingdon Cross were located in the York County district. But that didn't mean that everyone in Williamsburg didn't know about Queen's Point. It was the only gated neighborhood in town, and housed one of the best golf courses in the nation. Of course, today, Williamsburg is the home to more than ten gated communities.

Queen's Point was a planned community and a pilot project by Busch Properties, Inc., a branch of the Anheiser-Busch companies, whose plant created and packaged most of the American beer sold throughout the United States. In 1969, August Busch II, president and Chief Executive Officer of Anheiser-Busch at the time, sent his son August Busch III to Virginia to scope out land for a new brewery plant site. While he had his sights set on Newport News, Winthrop Rockefeller, then Chairman of the Board for the Colonial Williamsburg Foundation and Governor of Arkansas, convinced Busch II to purchase thirty-six hundred acres from Colonial Williamsburg on the James. As part of the real estate agreement, Anheiser Busch agreed to build a theme park on the land, similar to the Busch Gardens theme parks in Florida and California to help boost tourism in the Williamsburg area.

Engineers and developers were hired and through their survey work, it was suggested that Anheiser Busch acquire Camp Wallace, a one hundred and sixty-acre Army base along the James River. In exchange, Anheiser Busch gave the government a larger portion of land which increased the Army base at Fort Eustis, and agreed not to develop the land for a period of years. Queen's Point's Resort's Woods Course is on its site today.

The brewery plant opened for business in 1970, and shipped its first barrel of beer in 1972. In 1970, Busch Properties created a master plan for a planned community with large multi-family parcels. The plan called for keeping forty percent of the area green spaces in effect today, which has increased the property's value tenfold. Homes in the new Queen's Point community began to sell in the year nineteen hundred and seventy-three, and signaled a new era for Busch Properties.

The neighborhood now has about five thousand retirees and families, many of which are the original owners from the early 1970s.

The community contains a world renowned golf club, a marina facility, offering outlet to the James River and the Chesapeake Bay, a tennis center, a conference center, a sports center, a spa and four restaurants. It was also home to the Michelob Championships on the Professional Golfers' Association tour.

Sarah knew about Queen's Point from various swim meets in the summers, as it had one of the strongest teams in the town. And Sherry, the assistant manager, and her family lived there. Her father was one of the dentists in town.

Sherry opened the store in the mornings after such nights of reckless abandon in the summers, and recounted the night's events in detail to the two fourteen-year-olds who were fresh from their dreams of family homes. Sherry's best friend, Laura, was also a Starting Line employee, and a junior at Radford University, and her party habits were just as animated. The two fed off of each other, serving as each other's memories when the night's events became foggy. Laura was also a former cheerleader for Montier High School and took a liking to both Sarah and Patty, as both were cheerleaders for Somerset High School, and they talked about their plans for half-time shows and pep rallies. Laura had competed in national cheerleading championships, and she began to attend their summer practices to teach new cheers, dances and spirit moved to Sarah and Patty and their Somerset squad.

An occasional customer entered the store, and in between stories, the group of workers and friends learned the ins and outs of athletic shoes and products. Because the Starting Line was the only athletic supply store in town, most of Sarah's classmates and school athletes came into the store with their parents and siblings to purchase their necessities for the year's game schedule. Outings into the town were done as families.

Patty was not an only child. Patty had a brother, and Sarah met him once at a family dinner. He didn't live at the house, and seemed to be a bit of a wayward soul. He was in his first year of college at North Carolina State in Raleigh. But what struck Sarah strange, when she met him that first and last time at dinner, was he spoke with a British accent. Both he and Patty were big Pink Floyd fans, and Sarah thought, at the time, he was just mimicking their way of talking. He did it with utter seriousness, though, and no one seemed to question the switch. She was too young at the time to determine if it was a good or bad accent, but she could distinguish it as British, nonetheless. He also sat at the table, drinking beer from the bottle, as the father was not present. He was, no doubt, living up to the role of his father would have played, had he been present, as the loss of a father as a presence in anyone's life, by divorce, by work, or by death, has immense repercussions. In retrospect, Sarah's soul cringes because he was hurting and blamed his mother for not keeping his father there. Mothers certainly receive the brunt of their children's pain, in all respects, as they are, in many respects, always torn between their children and their duty as a wife. Certainly, a father has his attachment to his children, there is no doubt about that, but he feels that his first obligation is to provide for the family, and if that means being away from home for the majority of the time, then he is still fulfilling his role as a good husband and good father.

After dinner, Sarah asked Patty, "Did your brother live in England?" as Patty never talked about her brother.

"He has just returned from a trip there," was her reply.

"Oh. How long was he there?" as she was curious how long it takes for one to develop the accent of a foreign country. She was expecting an answer like, six years, eight years, perhaps.

"Twelve days," was her reply. She said it with all seriousness. And Sarah thought it was a bit strange that one could acquire a British accent within twelve days, but kept her opinion to herself. Who was she to judge family idiosyncrasies?

So, Sarah and Patty's birthday party began in the later parts of October---on a cold and brisk night in the middle of the changing leaves and landscape. It was the first night that her step-father ever hit her. And he swore it would be the last time.

# Chapter Four

*Twenty years from now you will be more disappointed by the things that you didn't do than by the ones you did do. So throw off the bowlines. Sail away from the safe harbor. Catch the trade winds in your sails. Explore. Dream. Discover.*

**Mark Twain (1835-1910)**

Sarah's mother arrived at the toga party, and walked to the upstairs bedroom where Patty's mother sat. They both looked out of the window that overlooked the front yard where party attendees were coming and going, and chatted. Sarah's mother usually didn't have time to sit and chat, but because the younger twins, Sarah's younger step-brother and step-sister were in bed, she decided to hop over to Abingdon Cross to help Patty's mother chaperone. Both Patty's mother and Sarah's mother seemed to talk freely and naturally, and Patty's mother was quite surprised at the naturalness of Sarah's mother. The two women had not spent much time together, as

Sarah's mother was quite busy taxiing the other five children to baseball practices, tee-ball games, band practices and swim practices. So, they sat in the open air of the upstairs window with the crisp October air wafting through the screen, and learned about each other as mothers and as wives.

About the same time that Sarah's mother arrived, Sarah's crush from the football team arrived, scantily clad in a Snoopy toga. He was a junior, and Sarah had quite fancied him since they had met each other the previous year in Biology class. Derrick, a full back for the football team, was not an A student, and struggled to even pass. But he had the looks and the charm to win a young freshman's heart from the beginning. And Sarah applied herself in her studies when love was involved. Let the record show that she received all A's in this particular Biology class, as a freshman, among all sophomores and juniors. Sarah had met Derrick one year earlier, so she had a history with the charming young football player. But their lives had never quite coincided. She had always hoped for more, but he had higher hopes and a need for a good grade in Biology. Sarah didn't quite see the difference at the time, but at least she received a straight line of A's on her report card in the encounter. Their paths always crossed, as he was a football player, and she was a cheerleader, but never to the extent that she had hoped for. So, when he arrived at *her* birthday party, she was attentive as any sophomore cheerleader would be to a junior fullback football player---never mind the fact that the high school won one game in the season. Sarah had been gleefully flitting between each room of the house exchanging commentaries with Patty on the success of their party, and how everyone seemed to be having a good time. They checked the Chex-Mix bowls, made sure drinks were a-plenty, and took part in the conversations of each room.

When Derrick entered the house, Sarah's heart flittered for a moment, and he approached her, and asked, "There's no alcohol at this party?"

Sarah had never wanted to appear as a young girl in his eyes, as he seemed to take more of an interest in older women---or at least with the girls in his class or above---juniors and seniors. So, anything he said seemed to be a direct assertion to her youthfulness and immaturity. She knew that Patty had a few beers hidden in her room.

34

They had purchased them a few weeks earlier for another party, and Patty preferred to keep the remaining three beers in a glass-mirrored box that served as a corner decoration for her black-and-white room. She couldn't exactly keep them in the refrigerator, since Sarah and Patty were both fifteen.

Patty's room was decorated with mirrors and posters of Pink Floyd, Marilyn Monroe and Sting, the floor was covered with diagonal black and white tile, the couch was black leather, and the comforter for her large bed was black and white checks. Her room was tastefully decorated, and rightfully so, as she had nothing else to concentrate her efforts on when they first moved from Delaware.

Sarah had almost forgotten about the hidden beer in the mirrored chest but remembered as Derrick asked about the presence of alcohol at the party. Not wanting to have a displeased party attendee, Sarah told him to wait outside and she would bring it out to him. She smuggled the beer out of the house without much commotion. But, little did she know, her mother and Patty's mother sat in an upstairs window with full view of the procedure. So, as Sarah blissfully complied with Derrick's requests and attempted to appease her "young-ness" in his eyes by producing a "mature" drink of choice, her mother walked downstairs and confronted her in front of all of her friends.

Now, this wasn't a discreet confrontation, where a mother might tactfully approach a daughter to make her aware that what she was doing was wrong, rather, it was a direct confrontation, an accusation, an admonishment. Sarah didn't know what to do.

Sarah's mother didn't know what to do either. She was embarrassed, in front of another parent, that her daughter would provide beer for a party attendee. Sarah's mother's first thought was: What would Patty's mother think about her as a parent? So, Sarah's mother did the only thing she knew how to do: to confront the problem with full force.

Sarah would stand nothing of the sort, as self-dignity was paramount, in front of her friends, who for all intents and purposes, were her family. Sarah's home life was not the most stable environment, and Sarah involved herself with as many activities as she could so she would not have to be around her home and her family, except perhaps to sleep. She had formed her own family of friends and they were all standing outside in togas watching her mother admonish her.

So, she did the only thing she could think to do: she walked away from her mother. She didn't know where she was walking---she just wanted to avoid the public display of discipline, particularly in front of the mature boy in the Snoopy toga.

She walked toward the darkened street to escape the group of friends who had walked outside to observe the commotion. Patty ran up to Sarah and expressed her anger that Sarah took the beer without asking. Sarah explained to her that it was not her beer, but merely kept in her room for safekeeping, since they had both purchased it.

"But you entered my room, and took it from my things," Patty persisted. It was indeed interesting to Sarah that the friend with whom she had shared everything with, including clothes, cheerleading activities and the vast majority of their free moments outside of school, was now separating the delineations between what was Sarah's and what was Patty's. Did that mean that Sarah's clothes that were hanging in Patty's closet were Patty's? Sarah became an outsider, at that point, from Patty's house, and she walked toward the dark road, in her toga, without a direction, nor an idea of where she was going. Her one ally, her mother, berated her in from of all of her friends, and she felt she had no one.

In reality, this was the first time that Sarah felt this sense of aloneness. She had always been a part of a family, a part of friends, a part of teams, of classes, of groups, of events, of activities and people. And the only thing that felt right at the time was to walk away from it all. This is the first time in Sarah's life that she walked out into the unknown. She walked away to save her pride. But she didn't know that she'd do it many times after this moment, as she grew into a woman, and embarked on a search for herself, and the meaning of what it meant to belong to something, to give and to take to and from something without being ashamed of discipline or embarrassment in front of loved ones, family and friends.

As Sarah walked on the open rural road, she heard her mother's van approach from behind her. Her mother got out of the van and pulled her by the hair to force her into the van. This desperate attempt at violence stung Sarah to the core, and she broke free of her mother's hold and ran toward the darkness. She ran into the woods, which her mother would not enter, and she soon drove off. Sarah's mother was desperate. The only thing she could think of to do at that moment was to physically force her daughter into the car, and even that didn't work.

When Sarah felt safe enough to emerge, she began walking again on the open road, trying to formulate a plan. Where could she go at such an hour? She was fifteen-years-old, barely, and felt she could not go home. As she walked a little while further, a car's lights approached and slowed to a stop at Sarah's side. She saw it was one of her friends from the other Williamsburg high school, Montier, behind the wheel, whom she had first met over the phone.

His name was Rafael. He was a few years older than Sarah and her friends, and attended Montier, which housed about four thousand students. Much of its students were black, as the county had been redistricted in the late 1970s to funnel the black folk into another high school. Sarah's high school, Somerset, held about four hundred students, a magnet school, Extend students, and several other accelerated programs which delineated the two high schools in the same town. Sarah's school had its share of black folks, and they comprised about forty percent of the school's population, but they were a different sort than the other school. The other school was traditionally more violent, harder on the edges, and contained less of the academic standards that Sarah's school possessed. Somerset High School was located in York County. Montier was located in James City County, although the two schools were only a few miles apart. And York County had become known to be the best school district in the state. It was a selling point for families relocating to the county. So the redistricting to make sure the certain classes stayed within James City County, and not York County, was not entirely random and uncalculated. But, because of the larger student population, the James City County high school students excelled more readily in sports and band performances. This is a generalization, of course, but one that was commonly known among Williamsburgers.

And because of the two schools rivalry, not many Montier students associated with Somerset students. But Sarah and Rafael were friends.

So, Sarah was relieved to see Rafael's face as he drove up on the darkened street.

# Chapter Five

*Such is the state of life, that none are happy but by the anticipation of change: the change itself is nothing; when we have made it, the next wish is to change again. The world is not yet exhausted; let me see something tomorrow which I never saw before.*

**Samuel Johnson** (1709-1784)

Sarah officially met Rafael over the phone at Belle's house. Belle, one of Sarah's friends from the sixth grade onwards, had short strawberry-blonde hair, was a bit plump and a brain. Belle's bedroom became a secret haven for both Belle and Sarah, to talk about dreams, history and wishes.

Belle was a dreamer. Both of her parents graduated from Duke University. Her father's parents hailed from Texas. And her mother's parents held a fair amount of land in the foothills of North Carolina---good Southern people. Her father had just retired as a

Colonel in the Army and quickly learned the real estate business in their blossoming town. Her house was interesting, as it was bizarrely shaped, with rooms and staircases that seemed out of alignment, like a M. C. Escher drawing. Sarah never knew where another door would lead. And in the basement was another apartment where Belle's grandmother from Texas lived. She was a quiet sort, kept to herself, as she felt out of place and out of sorts in the basement of a Virginia home, far away from her home grounds. But in reality, she was lucky to have a son who would create an apartment for her instead of whisking her off to some assisted living or residential centre where some folks' wit and spirit tend to wither away without the daily interactions of family.

Belle's house was a grand voyage, and her family, year after year, displayed the most spectacular Christmas tree with thousands of presents underneath. The dining room was never used except on Thanksgiving and Christmas, but housed a majestic table and china hutch which overlooked the sliding glass doors that led to a view of the lake. Belle's bedroom, where the girls spent the majority of their time, was decorated with her oldest sister's artwork, posters from New York City plays, operas and Broadway shows, a small twin bed, fine Oriental rugs and two closets full of clothes and shoes from the top designers. Belle had a large collection of perfumes and Sarah loved to pick her favorite of the day and adorn herself with the smell. Sarah's step-father would not allow her mother to spend money on such luxuries as perfume. So, perfume was a special treat.

Belle was one of her closest friends, as she often spoke to her soul. Belle dreamed, as not many people could and articulate well, and she talked about the things that her parents had taught her, about the Vietnam War, about their trips to New York City, about Kansas, where they had lived before moving to Williamsburg, about the Army, about different countries where their family had lived, about Colonial Williamsburg, where Belle's mother was a trained, costumed interpreter. Belle's knowledge extended far beyond what students were taught in school. She had the presence and the know-how that indicated that her parents took the time to teach her about the world. And she hailed from a military family, which is a world of education in itself.

Williamsburg was the hub of military activity, as well as a tourist haven, with Central Intelligence Agency training quarters at Camp Franklin, practically right in their high school's back yard, and Fort Eustis, Cheattam Annex, Langley Air Force Base, National Aeronautics and Space Administration, and the Naval Shipyard. Children who come from military families tend to have an education and a knowledge that cannot be taught in schools. It is a sense of worldliness, of duty, of honor and courage, all wrapped into one.

Belle knew quite a bit about the peace movements in Vietnam and the music revolution that surrounded it. Even though Sarah's father served in the Navy during Vietnam, and Sarah's mother was attending Boston College during Vietnam, neither parent discussed their personal perspectives of the era. Sarah's father didn't talk about that era of his life, because of the harsh realities of his coming of age in a foreign country, and Sarah's mother usually occupied her time with making sure that homework times, bath times and bedtimes were all on schedule. So much for the country's bi-national struggle.

Both Belle and Sarah were born in the mid-seventies, so it was a bit odd that Belle knew so much about the war----the military side and the peace movement side, especially since her father was a top official in the United States Army at that time. Her mother must have provided those teachings, as no high school classes at that time taught about the peace movements of the 1960s. And no high schools teach it even now — at least not the social aspect of it, or how the nation formed a band of solidarity to fight for peace.

Belle magically produced the old record player, with vinyl 1960s records, and they listened, in the haven of her room, to the music of a time gone by. A time before their time, but preserved by vinyl records and the music generation of a courageous group of youth and celebrators of peace.

"Listen to this," Belle said to Sarah as she placed a record on the record player.

"This is one of my favorites!"

So, both Belle and Sarah sat within the protective haven of Belle's insular bedroom and learned about the 1960s peace movement through old records. They sat in an upscale neighborhood, one of the best in their time, in a house with nooks and crannies, and doors and decks, and basements and patios, and split level stairs, and a view of the lake. Belle talked of the imagery of neighborhoods with little pink boxes all in a row whose families, mothers and wives waited for their fighting sons and husbands to come home from war. She didn't speak about class delineation, but she seemed to know it, and to feel it, and the effects that it had on the war. Belle told her about Joan Baez, Bob Dylan, and Peter, Paul and Mary, and the efforts of the music generation. And she spoke about her future, and her hopes. She spoke with such confidence and power.

Sarah loved those moments in Belle's room. They were never the type of friends who connected on the phone, only face-to-face, and only when they talked about dreams and talked about "seeing" the world.

They met in the sixth grade, and their friendship was a roller coaster, as is such with two people who hold an immense amount of passion. Passion can be heavenly, but it can also be too intense, if unleashed with unchecked emotionality. And they had the right ingredients to connect, and to clash, at various moments in their lives.

But it was there, in Belle's wonderfully aesthetically pleasing house where the circumstances for meeting Rafael occurred.

It was Sunday, and Belle and Sarah were bored. The house was empty, so they somehow ended up in the parents' bedroom to make a phone call, as Belle did not have a phone in her room. She normally kept the cordless phone in her room, but the electricity was out, as this happened often in this particular neighborhood, King's Gate.

King's Gate, the neighborhood on the other side of town from Abingdon Cross, Harrison Hills and Earlham Estates, was situated on the one-mile long fresh water King's Lake and King's Creek, the small tributary that led to the York River, and eventually led to the Chesapeake Bay. King's Gate embodied more than a community association and neighborhood. It was the magical talisman that preserved the charming character of the town of Williamsburg. While the other neighborhoods and pockets of family homes existed, it was King's Gate that stood at the helm of the town.

While Queen's Point protected its residents behind gates, and adorned its guests and homeowners with golf courses and restaurants, King's Gate slowly and meticulously cultivated a mythical and enchanting community of people with spirits that kept the historic presence of the town alive. With only four hundred and fifty homes, the community was nestled snugly amid great maples, white oaks, poplars and dogwoods that served as the marvelous homes to the morning calls of the towhees' 'wick-er-chees.' The spring and summer breezes rustled the stillness of the beauty surrounding the lake that served as the protective home of a pair of mated white swans, as well as large-mouth bass, croaker and bream.

In the late 1950s and early 1960s, a community sensed the magic that encapsulated the area of King's Gate and joined the wildlife, nestling itself along its banks.

Belle's house was just a small part of this magical community. King's Gate served as a haven for many other families, teachers and mentors that helped to shape the unique character of its children--- the future of the town.

It was early afternoon, the sun was beginning to break through the clouds, and the house was quiet and tranquil. They made a few phone calls to friends, but alas, no one seemed to be home. So, they began calling random numbers (this was before the days of caller identification), and asked random, riddle-like questions to the parties who answered. These were normally joke-like questions, and they readily provided an answer with a joke-like laugh. The party on the other end, usually stunned by such practices, either hung up, or shouted some obscenity and asked them to stop calling, but in much more terse terms. It was all in good fun, as they saw it, and they were just passing the time on a lazy afternoon. They were not harming anyone and they only asked rhetorical questions like, "Have you seen my refrigerator?" and then, "Where did you MOOOOOO-ve it?" and other such childish antics. Such a call would be a delight to some people who only receive phone calls from creditors, or to a lonely soul who doesn't receive phone calls at all. They called numbers at random, and when the novelty of such a practice began to wane, as it always does, Sarah called one last number and asked, almost half-heartedly, "Have you seen my refrigerator?"

"Yes, I have it here," was the reply on the other end.

Sarah was in a state of shock at such a quick and witty response. She didn't quite know how to respond, but kept the conversation going, as she was now curious.

"Why do you have it?" was her next question.

"Because you left it here," was the response. Belle drew closer to Sarah, eager with anticipation as to whom she was talking to. Did she know the caller? Her face seemed more alive, more alert. How could she have such a conversation with someone?

After a few more lines of spontaneous and interactive conversation about a missing refrigerator, he asked, "What's your name?"

And a friendship with Rafael, the African-American athlete from the other high school, was born. The more they spoke, the more they realized they had mutual friends, acquaintances and interests. He became a part of their group, in many respects, showed up at parties, lent an ear when any of the girls needed an objective perspective, and kept a watchful eye on all of them whenever he was close. If any of them needed a big brother, or just an extra pair of eyes at that point of their lives, Rafael seemed to appear at the right moment.

So, Sarah was thankful to see Rafael driving down that dark road with Belle riding shotgun, and Lucy in the back seat, clad in togas.

Lucy had shoulder-length natural bleach-blonde hair and a large build, as she stood five feet and seven inches, which towered over Sarah's five feet and two inches frame. She was one of the forward players of the Somerset field hockey team, in the top six seats of the women's tennis team, and one of the editors in the school's yearbook staff. She was outspoken and passionate about her beliefs, and equally as determined on the field hockey field or tennis court. Sarah first met Lucy in the fourth grade, as they shared a group table on the first day of class. But their teacher, Mrs. Crowe, who lived three doors down from Belle's family in King's Gate, quickly separated Lucy and Sarah because they seemed to take more of an interest in talking than anything else.

During that fourth grade year, Mrs. Crowe pulled Sarah's mother aside on parents' night, one month after school started.

"Mrs. O'Higgins, I must tell you that Sarah is such a pleasure to teach!"

"Oh, well, thank you, Mrs. Crowe, I hope she doesn't cause too much trouble in the classroom."

"No, not at all, "Mrs. Crowe replied, "But I will say that I have never had a student spend so much time planning her birthday party. It's the only thing she has talked about since the first day of class!"

"Well, that's Sarah!"

So, since the fourth grade, Lucy and Sarah had graduated from Brownie's to Girl Scouts, swum on the King's Gate swim team, and spent hours of their summer days at the pool inventing imaginative games with lifeguard whistles, childhood teddy bears and other pool items in the pool house like boogie boards and flippers. Sometimes, they were the only ones in the pool---so the lifeguard, a graduate of Somerset, who worked as a summer lifeguard before beginning his college career at John Hopkins for the medical program, took an interest in their imaginative games, even though he was almost a decade older than them. But his younger brother was friends with Sarah's older sister Meghan, and he was good friends with Lucy's older brother, Gary. So, everyone was family in the town of Williamsburg. Everyone looked out for one another.

Lucy leaned forward from the back seat to get a good view of Sarah, walking down the dark street.

Rafael was not wearing a toga, and Sarah did not expect it, as Rafael seemed to carry an air about him that he was above sheets and olive branches. He was a senior at the time, but his actions and demeanor seemed to portray a man much older and wiser than his age. Sarah never knew much about his story and background. Ironically, he became closer to the other girls, as Sarah was the point of contact. Sarah always saw him, heard about him, from the others, but never nurtured the relationship herself. He seemed to have his hands full with the others.

Lucy asked, "Why don't we take you home?"

"Okay."

Sarah hopped in the car with Rafael and instructed him to take her home, as this seemed to be the only feasible place, at this point, to go.

In the meantime, Sarah's mother had left her daughter in the thick of the woods, as she didn't know what else to do. She couldn't leave her car in the middle of the street to run after her daughter. And she had her own image to uphold. There she was in front of all of her daughter's friends, and her daughter's best friend's mother, and she had taken beer from the friends' room and run off into the woods. What would they say about her as a mother? Would they say that she couldn't control her daughter? What would they say? She didn't know what to do, but luckily, they were far enough away from the din of the party where most could not see either of their actions, so she did what any rightful mother would do: she drove home to get the male parental figure, Sarah's step-father. Sarah's mother was at a loss, and needed help. She had even tried to use physical force, and even that didn't work. Her only ally at that point, she thought, was her husband.

So, she drove home, retrieved her husband and drove back to Patty's house. As Rafael, Lucy and Belle drove to Sarah's house, her stepfather and her mother drove to Patty's house. The two cars passed each other, no doubt, with neither of the two cars' occupants aware of the other. Rafael dropped Sarah off and left. Her two best friends, Belle and Lucy, said a bewildered and confused goodbye to their crying, toga-clad friend, and Sarah walked into the house.

The house was dark and empty, which was a relief to Sarah. She went upstairs, changed into her pajamas, and went to bed, wanting to escape and forget the situation altogether. She knew she would have to face it, but for the time being, she only wanted to sleep. She lay there and heard from her upstairs bedroom the back door open downstairs and the word, "Sarah?" was shouted throughout the house. The tone of that one single word seemed to possess a bit of concern along with anger, so Sarah was at least, a little hopeful at that point that the next moments of her life would not be as severe as she would imagine they could be. She arose out of bed, walked to the top of the stairs, and replied, "I'm here."

"She's here," the stepfather echoed to someone downstairs. At the time, she believed that person to be her mother, but her mother had stayed at Patty's house just in case Sarah showed up there. Sarah's stepfather was talking to John, who had taken an interest in the hot pursuit.

Tis strange how John always seemed to be present in all of these severe situations of Sarah's youth. His presence was somewhat of a combination between help and a prodding curiosity. He always seemed to keep his father's anger in check at a critical moment, but still seemed to support whatever the father was doing at the time. Tis fitting that John became a newspaper reporter, loved a good story, and was a damn good writer.

Sarah stood at the top of the stairs as her stepfather made the phone call to Patty's house to inform Sarah's mother that she was at home. Sarah waited at the top of the stairs, listening, and after the phone was placed in the cradle, the stepfather angrily yelled, "Get down here!"

At that point, John passed her as she descended the stairs toward the dungeon of doom, and he walked to the safety of his bedroom, or at least to the safety of the wrought iron banister that formed the top of the stairs, which always served as a good listening post to all of the actions that happened in the downstairs portion of the house. Who could blame his curiosity, as such a confrontation and family unrest is of high interest to any party, much less a journalistic-budding brother.

"Sit down!" he yelled, as he pointed to the captain's chair that piloted the head of the kitchen table.

The kitchen table was quite large, as it served as the daily dining place for a family of eight. The stepfather had made the table with his own hands. It was made of pinewood. Sarah helped to sand and stain it. It had removable leafs, and a decorative post at the bottom that supported its egg-like shape. It sat in a large bay window that overlooked a large wooded drop off into the thick of woods, stream and lake that separated Sarah and Patty's houses. In the large, pane-less center window of the bay window was a large stain-glass window that Sarah's mother had found in an antique shop in one of the family trips to Illinois. It served as a window in some old house long ago, and the original wood frame supported the beautiful stain-glass centerpiece. The stained glass was simple, and made with four distinct colors, but the prominent centerpiece was the simple heart that branded the middle. When Sarah's mother saw it in the antique shop, she knew it belonged in their kitchen, in that bare, large window that overlooked the lush back yard. Sarah's stepfather refused at first, as the window was large, and they didn't have a lot of room in the family Volvo as is, with eight people and a car full of luggage. They certainly didn't have enough room for a breakable item that may or may not have been the perfect centerpiece for their kitchen. But Sarah's mother was convinced. She insisted. And she eventually won that battle. And it was perfect. It belonged in that window.

Sarah noticed all these familiarities and the memories that each item evoked as she was ordered to sit in the captain's chair. She had no idea what would happen in the next few minutes, but she used her imagination and memory to transport her to another time. This was another technique she used quite well to escape the realities of the present.

The captain's chair that Sarah sat in was acquired in Missouri from an old riverboat from the Mississippi River. It was a beautiful chair, and one that the stepfather always claimed as his proud and joy. It was a subtle reinforcement that he was captain of the house, and everyone seemed to respect it and revere it. It was rounded on the edges, and made of a dark wood – strong and sturdy. But it was aged, and had a character and look of an old weathered friend. It creaked with glee and contempt, and Sarah always tried to sit in it at the dinner table.

Dinner was quite an event. The seating arrangement was always the same: the four step-children sat in the core of the table, the two boys, John and the younger, Joseph faced each other in high sturdy-backed chairs that belonged to the family kitchen table before the two families combined, and before the new dinner table was built. The two youngest, Jacob and Fanny, the twins, faced each other as well. And on the ends of the oval table were Sarah's mother and Meghan on one end, and Sarah and Sarah's stepfather on the other. Sarah directly faced her older sister on the other end of the table, and Sarah's stepfather faced Sarah's mother, with the four stepchildren as the nucleus. Meghan sat in a chair that was originally part of a childhood desk set that she had acquired as a birthday gift far before the families combined. The chair was made for a child, but Meghan continued to use it as her dinner chair even as she grew to be a young woman. She never complained. She never attempted to change chairs. In fact, her presence was never much noticed at the table, as I believe she dreaded it just as everyone else, and mustered enough energy to receive her nutrients, and depart for the rest of the evening. She never spoke much, even though she was a genius, and always sat a bit lower than the rest, because of the smallness of her chair. Sarah's mother's chair was another sturdy-back straight chair with four wide rungs across the back, but her seat was never occupied. Somehow, throughout the marriage, Sarah's mother had developed the habit of never occupying her chair to eat during dinner. She seemed to busy herself with other things in the kitchen. She also watched all six children to ensure that everyone was holding their forks right, that no elbows were on the table, that everyone was not avoiding their vegetables and that everyone "shopped around their plate," or didn't eat too much of one thing.

On the opposite end were Sarah and the stepfather, and the captain's chair served as one chair, and another chair was pulled from the dining room, which was situated right next to the kitchen, and contained a set of six mahogany, ornamental dining chairs. Sarah normally sat in the captain's chair, as it was easier to push the heavy chair toward the window, and pull the dining room chair from the other room, as Sarah was usually the one who helped to prepare and set the table. But the chair was technically Sarah's stepfather's.

So, it was strange that Sarah sat in the captain's chair at that moment after her toga party. Her stepfather paced the kitchen, not knowing what to do or say about the night's events. Before Sarah's mother came home, he was watching television, preparing to fall to restless sleep when his frantic wife entered the back door into the family room, and requested his urgent help. He didn't ask to get involved in this situation. He should have been asleep at that moment, and there he was, pacing in front of Sarah.

Both parents had made a pact long ago that they would only discipline their own children. But somehow, in the last year, since the Meghan had left, the channels were crossed and Sarah's mother began disciplining the other four children. Sarah's step-father always expressed his displeasure with this, but Sarah's mother felt as if certain activities of the stepchildren were accepted as okay, whereas activities of Sarah and Meghan were not accepted. This, of course, was escalated by the stepfather's interference with Meghan's interest in dating African-American boys. Sarah's stepfather actually forbade it, which left Sarah's mother in an awkward position. Should she support her daughter or her husband? Her husband had provided for her children, had taken her into his home when she struggled to make ends meet, as she worked on her master's degree at the University of Maryland, and worked for the United States Government in Washington, DC, and tried to raise two young girls. Her husband had appeared at a critical time and supported her efforts for seven good years. But what about her daughter? This was the daughter whom she had taught the foundation of the Bible. This was the daughter she had taught to follow her heart, and to see no differences in skin color. This was the daughter whom she watched compose lengthy poems at age five, contemplate the vastness of the universe, achieve straight A's, accompany the school's chorus on piano, score extremely high on the Scholastic Aptitude Test, and compose school songs. At that moment, as Sarah rebelled to all wits end, Meghan had been gone almost a year, because Sarah's mother's husband forbade her daughter to date an African-American boy. What was a mother to do? Follow her daughter, or stay by her husband? Where would she have gone if she had left her husband to support her daughter? She was only working part-time as a reference librarian and could hardly support two daughters.

When Sarah's mother and step-father met, Sarah's mother was working on her master's degree in library science. She finished the degree, but quickly became a full time mother to her own children, as well as four more. In all truth, she had always wanted to be a stay-at-home-mother. She grew up in the sixties where this was expected of a mother, and she only wanted to thrive in this role. So, she finished her degree with the intention of becoming a reference librarian, but never went to work. As the marriage progressed, certain items that Sarah's mother bought for Sarah and Meghan were scrutinized and judged by Sarah's stepfather. He questioned every pair of pants, put a five dollar price limit on a pair of jeans, and questioned any other expenses that incurred through extracurricular activities. The other children participated in extracurricular activities, but not at the extent that Sarah did. Sarah played the piano, and took piano lessons from one of the best, and cheapest, teachers in the town. She took gymnastic classes. And cheerleading expenses always took a toll. After a while, the daily scrutiny of money spent on Sarah grated on her mother, so she decided to get a job working part time at the local library where she could own her own money, manage her own check book, and pay for things for her daughters without much supervision.

Sarah's mother could not have left when Meghan left because she was also a mother of two younger ones, the twins, who she practically raised from birth. She could not render them motherless at such a critical age, as they had already been through so much, as they did not have their own mother with them. Sarah's mother was already going through a bastion of emotions after losing her first daughter, and Sarah was now rebelling to high hell. She didn't know how to handle it. What would possess a child to act in such a way? She felt she had no control over her daughter and asked for her husband's help in discipline. This was the first breaking of the pact, and gave the stepfather full reign on the rebellious teenager. No one can blame the mother, she felt helpless, and felt at that point, that her only ally was her husband.

So, there Sarah sat, in the captain's chair, alone in a house of foreigners. Her mother was not there. Her sister was not there, and her stepfather stood before her, pacing with excitement, anger and power.

What should he say? How should he begin? He was in the power now, his wife, the mother of the poor helpless fifteen-year-old who sat before him, in the captain's chair, had given him the okay to discipline the child in front of him. She had no reason not to trust him. He had never hit her children before, so why would he do such a thing now?

As Sarah sat alone in the kitchen with her stepfather, her mother tried to make amends at Patty's house by talking with Patty's mother and smoothed out any wrinkles her daughter had caused. The party had dissipated at that point, and many people had left for home. Patty was left dejected that her party was ruined, and darted evil glances at Sarah's mother, as if she had caused the unrest. Patty's mother offered to drive Sarah's mother home, and she accepted as she was somehow pleased and relieved with the knowledge that her daughter was safe at home, and not in the woods somewhere.

But far from safe she was! Sarah sat in boxer shorts and a tee-shirt in front of the pacing figure and waited for the blows – in whatever form they would take. She had no reason to believe he would hit her, but was still petrified of the looming scolding, as his oral punishments always made her cry.

"What the hell were you thinking?" were the first words from his mouth, which were followed by a long soliloquy of other accusations and angry assertions under the pretence of her mother's permission. He ranted and talked as if they were a team now.

"How dare you treat your mother like that!"

This last statement bothered Sarah because who was he to defend her mother when he forbade Meghan to date an African-American boy and watched as she left her mother's wing to live with her father in another state? He clearly was not concerned with the best interests of his wife, as he smugly watched one of her daughters leave his house. Who was he to defend her mother when his actions and demeanor spoke clearly against her?

52

"It's always you causing the trouble around here. Every time something goes wrong, we can always find Sarah as the culprit," he ranted as he continued to pace the kitchen floor.

She listened to his long and useless speech, and decided to listen and nod, as now was not the time to be mouthy. She only wanted to go to her bed and forget the whole night had ever happened. He said that he and her mother would decide together what the punishment would be. Finally, she thought she was nearing the end of that horrible evening. But then he said something that struck a chord with her and she couldn't contain herself. Perhaps he was a little agitated that all of his words were not rendering an action or a response from her. Perhaps he wanted to see how far he could go. Who knows why he said the next sentence. But Sarah's response shot out of her mouth almost as a defense to his foundation-less accusations.

"And those friends of yours aren't friends at all. They are nothing but thugs and tramps."

"You don't know shit about my friends." She heard the words leave her mouth, but barely registered their meaning. They were just defense reactions. He had no idea what her friends were about. He had no idea what kinds of homes they came from, how their families talked to their children, and asked their opinions, and told them about history and politics, and talked about the latest news at the dinner table. These were Sarah's friends, and her stepfather called them thugs and tramps. To a young girl whose life revolved around her friends and social life, this was a direct blow to her heart. Her friends were not only her confidants, but also her teachers in many ways, and many of their families had willingly taken her in on school afternoons or Saturday afternoons. How dare he!

With an objective eye, how tragic this situation is. The anger in both of the two figures, the years of competition, and anger, and issues of power, seemed to culminate in that moment. Talking, negotiating and discussing were all foreign words to the two of them. Sarah was never taught how to talk, how to discuss, how to negotiate, she was taught to defend with the only weapons she knew how to use, and those were words. She had learned, through sheer survival, to use language as weapons to defend against such attacks that simply needed to be pacified. But she was a teenager. And it is the job of every good parent or teacher, to teach the younger how to use language to positively affect any situation.

"You don't know shit about my friends!" came before she realized the words had escaped and the next thing she knew, Sarah's step-father lunged at her with all of his power, and began hitting her repeatedly with all of his force. She turned her back to him and crouched down toward the floor, to try to escape the severity of the blows, but it did not help much. He hit with his left hand and swung from the side, hitting the young girl against the left side of her head and ear. The tips of his fingers hit her left eye repeatedly as each blow increased in severity.

She sat crouched on the floor and endured the beating. She yelled, "Stop," through broken tears, but it was a weak and helpless attempt beneath all of the anger and strength that loomed above her. Her words were useless. John came running downstairs from the upstairs banister, where he had stood post, and yelled, "Dad," to break the beast out of his fury. The voice from his eldest son was enough to break his angered trance, and he ordered Sarah to go to bed, and they would deal with it in the morning.

She was happy to be rid of everything that the night entailed. She heard her mother enter the house a few moments later, from the darkness of her room. She did not expect her mother to come to her room. They had all endured enough for the night, and Sarah was quite certain that the beating was not spoken of. Sarah fell asleep, dreaming of all things that would take her away from such ghastly circumstances.

# Chapter Six

*Belief consists in accepting the affirmations of the soul; unbelief, in denying them.*

**Ralph Waldo Emerson (1803-1882)**

Sarah's mother had met Sarah's stepfather, Casp, after she had been divorced from her first husband for four years. Sarah was two, Meghan was six, when their parents divorced.

Sarah's mother suddenly found herself as a single mother, without work, and the dreams of a happy family scattered in Newport News, Virginia. The O'Higgins had lived in Newport News because Sarah and Meghan's father had been stationed at the Naval Shipyard, as he worked in nuclear energy for the United States Navy.

Newport News seemed as if it was an accidental town which was born as a midpoint between Virginia Beach and Richmond. Most of its citizens were military families awaiting orders to be transferred elsewhere. And it served as a transitory town with make-shift strip malls, bars, restaurants and used car lots. Apartment complexes and doctor offices sprung up to accommodate the young transitory families. Newport News was technically a part of the Hampton Roads corridor that stretched as far north as Williamsburg and included Norfolk, Suffolk, Virginia Beach, Portsmouth and Chesapeake. And it is not as if Newport News had no attractions. It actually had wonderful museums, colleges, festivals and history sites. But to the people that grew up in Williamsburg, Newport News was the place to go shopping, or to go to a different restaurant.

After Sarah's parents' split, Sarah's mother found a part-time job in circulation at the law library at the College of William and Mary in Williamsburg to help support her two young daughters at home. And because she was no longer tied to the area with her husband's Navy obligations, she decided to obtain her master's degree in library science from the only university in the area to offer the degree: the University of Maryland.

Through her connections at the College of William and Mary, she obtained a job in Washington, DC working at the United States Department of Justice, and attended the master's degree program in the evenings. The three girls, mother and two daughters, relocated to Maryland and lived life the only way they knew how: surviving, because this is what Sarah's mother did.

The two young girls continued to excel in school. Meghan wrote school songs for her new surroundings, won school spelling bees, and Sarah skipped a grade despite her young age. Although Sarah's mother spent a lot of time away from the girls, she was providing for them, while securing her career for a future. Babysitters and neighborhood friends helped out, cooking a meal here and there, phoning to check on the girls in the afternoons, and participating in birthday parties and home-spun dance recitals. Sarah's mother continued her involvement with the church and church retreats.

On one of the weekend church retreats, Sarah's mother met Casp, who had been recently widowed, with four children, two of which were newborns. The two connected and decided to get married, combining their families. Casp entered Sarah's mother's life at a critical time and supported her efforts for seven good years.

As the years of being a combined family flew by, the delineations between the discipline of *her* children versus *his* children began to fray. The fabric of their family began to unravel. It first came about with the little things.

Sarah played the piano, and took lessons from a young woman in town who made her living by playing piano in cocktail bars and elegant hotel lounges in the evening, and giving lessons to children in her home during the day. She received her degree in music from the College of William and Mary, and lived in an apartment complex on the narrow strip of road that led to the only grocery store in town in the early 1980s. Her Steinway grand piano, electric keyboards and computer equipment filled every possible square inch in the small space.

When the income from her daily piano lessons afforded a decent down payment for a mortgage, she purchased a home in York Gardens. York Gardens was a neighborhood situated across the street from James Gardens, an equal and comparable neighborhood located in James City County. Both were located on the King's Gate side of town. One road separated the counties---the children from the west side of the road attended Somerset High School, King's Gate Middle School and Randolph Elementary School in York County; the children from the east side of the road attended Montier High School, Spotswood Middle School, and Daniel Custis Elementary School in James City County.

The homes of York Gardens nestled themselves next to each other, on small plots of land, where the side windows of each one-story house could easily see in the neighboring house. Some lawns were meticulously manicured with well-trimmed bushes, simple potted flowers, and brightly colored children's toys scattered about. The piano teacher's new house was a small two-bedroom quaint house with two gabled windows at the top.

While Sarah's friends from school attended piano lessons in the homes of the King's Gate colonial charmers where its occupants were instructed to behave themselves with perfect etiquette—back straight, shoes off----Sarah was able to be herself in her piano teacher's home. Her instructor cared about her sound, and her movement with the piano keys. Sarah watched television in the den until the prior student finished, and played with her two cocker spaniels that were happily curious of any of the house guests, particularly the younger ones. And because of Sarah's ease with the instructor at her side, her skills increased at an immense rate. By the fifth grade, she had won a finalist seat for the Exchange Club talent show, and accompanied a classmate while she sang the popular song, "Heaven" by Bryan Adams for the school talent show. By the eighth grade, she was playing Frederic Chopin's "Polonaises" in the town talent show at the Williamsburg Regional Library.

"Who do you take lessons from?" Sarah's friends' mothers asked.

"Sandy Jones," Sarah replied, adding, "She lives in York Gardens."

But most mothers who lived in King's Gate did not take their children to homes in York Gardens, regardless of a piano instructor's talent. Sarah didn't understand the reason at the time. But that was the way it worked in Williamsburg.

Sarah also took gymnastics classes. And cheerleading expenses always took a toll. After a while, the daily scrutiny of money spent on Sarah grated on her mother, so she decided to get a job working part-time at the Williamsburg Regional Library where she could earn her own money, manage her own checkbook, pay for things for her daughters without much supervision, and finally to use the degree she had worked so hard to achieve.

Williamsburg Regional Library nestled itself on Scotland Street, one block from the two college delis, one block from the first African-American church, one block from the train station, one block from the College of William and Mary, one block from Merchant Square, and one block from Colonial Williamsburg.

It was the only library in town, so school children from both districts came to check out children's books, attend story-time

58

readings, research school projects, read up on used car and magazine material, peruse the new acquisitions sections and socialize with the rest of the town they saw at Parent Teacher Association meetings, school plays, church, town hall meetings and holiday festivities. The library was the place to be-----for both children and their parents, alike. And many of the town's parents worked there, including Sarah's mother, at the reference desk. She was also the one who visited the study tables if the kids became too rowdy during their studies.

"SHHHHHH! Here comes Sarah's mom," was heard from the rowdy tables when the kids became too noisy for the hushed environment. At least they knew her.

Because the town of Williamsburg was like family, parents were parents anytime of the night or day, and they looked out for one another's children. Any child that came within Sarah's mother's reach, either at the library, at church, or any other town function, was like her own. She was able to teach and to mother them at any given moment. This was the Williamsburg way. This was Sarah's mother's way.

The Library began serving the community residents of the City of Williamsburg in 1909, and the James City County residents in 1926. The library was first housed in the front hall of the St. George Tucker House (now part of Colonial Williamsburg) and relocated several times before moving to the Scotland Street building in 1973. In 1977, the City of Williamsburg and James City County established a mutual agreement that formed the Williamsburg Regional Library, and each jurisdiction contributed funds for its operations based on population and circulation. York County also started contributing to the town's library. The building and institution became an anomaly because it allowed the mutual agreements of all three governmental jurisdictions for the benefit of the education and community awareness of its people.

It was a haven of activity and education. Nationally renowned poets stopped in for readings. The counties conglomerated on talent shows for the town's youth, local artists' works were displayed, concerts were held, educational movies like, "Little Women" were shown in Saturday and Sunday afternoons, professional storytellers gathered children around them to illustrate the author's magic with their voice and animation, and circulation staff members carefully stamped each book and asked, "Oh, yes, and how is Bob doing?" and the like, and the town shared their successes and troublesome times with each other. The library was just one of the places where the town supported each other, like a family.

# Chapter Seven

*The important thing is not to stop questioning. Curiosity has its own reason for existing. One cannot help but be in awe when he contemplates the mysteries of eternity, of life, of the marvelous structure of reality. It is enough if one tries merely to comprehend a little of this mystery every day. Never lose a holy curiosity.*

**Albert Einstein (1879-1955)**

The next morning Sarah awoke to the sound of the announcement that the whole house needed to go to church. It was Sunday morning, and the morning seemed to hold a degree of gaiety and rebirth. The sun was peeking its way through the blue-curtained windows. The trees had begun to change their colors, and the vibrancy of their annual cycle occurred right outside of Sarah's window. The oranges, yellows, reds and browns reflected the sun's rays in autumnal grace. Sundays felt different. And they always started with church.

Sarah had slept well, without stirring much in the night, and was pleased to awake to such a sound of familiar voices. She swung her legs to the side of the bed with the usual, "Do-I-have-to-go-to-church?" feeling, but she always knew the answer. She loved Sunday mornings, as the house was fresh and her mother could be heard singing a happy song like, "Good morning to you!" or other types of beautiful morning songs. Sarah's mother's demeanor was no different this morning and the events of the previous night seemed to have been forgotten by all, including Sarah. Sarah walked to her dresser with the tilting mirror that she was so fond of, and looked at herself. She noticed something a bit strange with her left eye, but she still did not remember the previous night's events. She peered closer to get a better look at her bruised left eyelid, and the events of the previous night came tumbling back.

About the same time that the memories of the horrible circumstances came flooding back to Sarah, her mother peered into the door next to Sarah's dresser where she was standing, and began singing, "Rise and shine and give God his Glory, Glory." It's quite a catchy tune actually, full of spirit and youthfulness, and one of the many graces that Sarah's mother never lost. Even in adulthood, and even with the grey hairs she received from her two daughters, namely the youngest, she never lost that youthful spirit. She always whistled, and sang, and had an extra bounce in her step that other people have always admired, even envied. She had a beautiful heart, and a youthful soul.

As she peered into Sarah's room, Sarah could say nothing but, "Yeah, sing that tune to your husband who gave me this last night." Sarah closed her eyes and pointed to her bruised eyelid.

"What are you talking about?" her mother asked. She clearly had heard nothing about the beating, which meant that Sarah's stepfather had felt no remorse or guilt, which is, in itself, worse than the actual act of hitting a helpless child. It would have been one thing to commit such an act, and then confess the remorse to the poor creature's mother. If he had felt any guilt afterwards, or felt that he had lost his senses in some way because he was so overpowered by anger, that would have been one thing. It would have shown that he had some conscience, and humility, but he couldn't even do that! His

62

wife, Sarah's mother, would have appreciated even that gesture, and probably would have understood. But he didn't. Sarah's mother discovered his anger, and his inability to tell her about it, by a mark on her child. She didn't know what to do at that point. She looked closely at it, as Sarah recounted and demonstrated the several beatings that she took while she was crouched on the floor of the kitchen, near the trashcan, underneath the wall phone and message board. Her mother couldn't believe it at first.

"What? Why didn't you tell me?" her mother gasped in disbelief.

"You were mad at me."

"Alright, we'll talk about this later. Get dressed for church."

"I'm taking a picture of it."

"Fine," her mother said as she walked toward her bedroom to get ready for church herself.

The event was not spoken about for the rest of the morning, as Sarah's mother had to worry about ushering the whole family to church by ten-thirty that morning. But Sarah took the photograph of her closed eyelid, dressed for church, and joined the family as they drove in the van to the Catholic Church on the other side of town. Her step-father drove while her mother sat in the front seat, like any normal day. The events of church with the other town families ensued and the previous night was brushed beneath daily living.

St. Bede's Catholic Church was founded as the Catholic population began to grow in the early 1900s. Priests had always traveled to the town in earlier years, but had conducted Mass and services in people's homes. In 1932, the Bishop in Richmond approved the construction of a college chapel, located on a plot of land donated from a woman who lived in the Appalachian Mountains of Central Virginia. The land just happened to be next to the College of William and Mary, nestled between pines, oaks and the large, brick colonial charmers that lined the main thoroughfare: Richmond Road. So, the church was developed as the Colonial Williamsburg foundation began to develop as the center of the town. It thrived in a pale-brick church, adorned with religious artwork brought over from Europe. After WWII, the church purchased a fraternity house from the college to help with the displaced servicemen and homeless and needy people of the town. Later, the colonial house became the church rectory where the priests lived and often held receptions with doughnuts and orange juice after the ten-thirty morning Sunday services. And as the town's population began to grow, an intramural college gymnasium located directly behind the brick church was purchased as the Church's parish center, for the more informal gatherings and worships. And it was in the parish center where Sarah and her family attended church every Sunday. And it was no different the Sunday after her step-father hit her.

The next week, Sarah's mother filed a report with the county social services, as she didn't know what else to do. A couple of weeks later, Sarah, her mother, and her stepfather met with a county social worker. The social worker said that the account had been documented and asked Sarah's opinion. At that moment, Sarah believed that she was a rebellious, hellion teenager who deserved such a response for her lack of respect to authority, and said as much to the social worker. At this point, the social worker could do nothing. Sarah believed she deserved the beating. Nevertheless, she said the case was documented, and that, if it happened again, the stepfather would face charges.

This appeased Sarah and her mother's hearts for a time, as they felt they were somehow protected. But this protection vanished the second time his anger was unleashed, unfettered, in that dark bedroom, with the cast on her leg, and the mysterious caller in the night.

Before that night, word had spread to Sarah's friends and parents of what was happening in Sarah's home. As Sarah frequented many of the friends' houses, parents knew her well from sleepovers, Girl Scouts, Brownies, swim team, and all of the countless activities that friends share throughout elementary, junior high and high schools. One mother, in particular, Brownie, who was Lucy's mother, had boldly approached Sarah's mother some time after the first child abuse case and said, "You know, if you ever feel unsafe, you can always bring Sarah here."

64

Brownie had mentioned it to Sarah once when she was visiting Lucy, but she didn't think much of it, as the need didn't seem too urgent by all standards. But how bold and courageous this mother was to foresee such a complication, and risk the feelings that may arise from another mother who could have felt threatened by such an offer. Did Brownie feel that Sarah's mother was not doing her job as a mother?

Brownie wrestled with the decision as well. Would Sarah's mother hold a grudge if she made such a suggestion? Would she feel as if she was taking her daughter away? She wrestled with the scenario at all angles and decided that the well being of the child was much more important than any harbored feelings of imagined resentment, so she decided to take the liberty to say something to Sarah's mother. Sarah's mother was thankful and felt as if she had an ally in the struggle with her husband. Here was a woman who saw the situation, understood its implications, and expressed her ability to help in some way. How beautiful this woman was, as no other friend or acquaintance chose to come forward, even though the struggles of this particular family's house were beginning to permeate the town gossip.

Brownie's suggestion was a welcome relief as other friends and families in the neighborhood and elsewhere saw other things. Sides were taken with Sarah's mother or Sarah's stepfather. If the tensions were not already enough within the family, Lord knows they did not need the petty squabbles and loyalties of the town to add insult to injury. More and more folks began to side with the stepfather, and Sarah's mother felt herself losing a downhill battle. The friends whom she had cultivated from the times before her daughters were even born seemed to lose interest in her life now, the time when she needed them most. A few steady stalwarts kept their ground, but the majority of her friends turned a shaded eye to the happenings in their home. The time when Sarah's mother most needed an ally and a friend, was a time when the ones whom she most trusted were nowhere to be found. Sarah's mother didn't see this when it was happening, and truly appreciated the few moments of attention they *did* manage to spare in later years. And when Sarah discussed these friends much later, as the events of the situation lost their power,

Sarah's mother still defended them with a stalwart loyalty and love. And that, my friends, is true heart.

So, Sarah's mother continued working at the reference desk in the library, but she could feel the stares and she could hear the whispers.

"Doesn't it bother you that the friends whom you thought were your friends do not support your decisions?" one of Sarah's mother's friends asked one day.

"I have faith in God. I always have. Perhaps people have their reasons for doing what they do. The only thing I have in this world is my own confidence for the decisions I make in life. If I worried about what everyone thought of me, I'd crumble."

Sarah's mother was one of the strongest women in town, unbeknownst by many.

So, both Sarah and her mother had the knowledge of this option of going to Brownie's house at the point of the second beating, but this thought did not quite enter Sarah's mind as she stood, leaning on her crutches, in front of her dresser, as she grew more and more aware of her urine-soaked bottom. As Sarah's mother's concerned face continued to repeat, "What happened? What happened?" Sarah managed to muster, "He hit me again."

A crowd of concerned children had formed outside of Sarah's door, and her stepfather walked toward his bedroom on the other side of the banister. Sarah somehow managed to find dry clothes, although she had no idea about fashion, color matching, or coordination at that point. Her only requirement was that they were not soaked in urine. She was in a panic, in a state of flux, what was she going to do? Her mother began to yell, "I'm calling the police," in a desperate attempt to help a situation which she still did not fully understand. She just saw the face of her daughter, and the urgency that it evoked. She ran back downstairs to the phone.

Sarah just wanted to change and rid herself of such degradation. She could not change in the privacy of her bedroom, as it was now a spectacle of onlookers. She could not go across the hall to the

66

upstairs bathroom, as that seemed to be too close to the foreigners, and too close to her predator, too close to curious onlookers of the family, and surely, they would all see her wet bottom as she hobbled through them to get to the location across the hall. She felt ashamed and desperate. Her only option was to hobble down the stairs where her mother was and hope to find a place to change downstairs. She began the descent quickly, with wobbly crutches, when she heard from above her head, "She is nothing but a tramp."

At the sound of these words, she wanted nothing but to escape the added torment of words. It was one thing to endure the physical pain, suffer the pure humiliation of losing one's bladder control, and be observed as a cripple with a cast trying to make her way downstairs. But to add the word, "tramp" to the situation was the tip of the iceberg. She hadn't spoken a word since the incident, except the few words she was able to muster to her mother to alert her to the graveness of the situation. So this word came as a final stab to the creature he had already destroyed. And with that word, one of the ends of her crutches slipped off the side of the stair, but because she was trying to get down the stairs at such a rapid pace, she shifted her weight forward to the crutch that had no leverage, and Sarah went sprawling down the first level of stairs. Her mother, who had begun to go to the phone to call the police, came back to the steps to see what the falling disaster was. Sarah had begun to pick herself up to mount her crutches again, as she was now sprawled on the steps with urine soaked boxers and a cast, and the stepfather looked downward on her with a smug smile. Sarah did not look at him, she couldn't bear to see his face, but picked herself up as quickly as she could and proceeded down the stairs.

"She's only faking it," was the stepfather's response to the fall.

Sarah began to tune all else out at that point, and even began to forget the wetness in her bottom. It was not a time to be overcome by feelings of shame and emotion, as she needed to decide what her next steps were going to be. She blocked out all awareness of the situation in front of her, a tool she had begun to utilize quite well, and a tool that served her well time and time again throughout her childhood, as some situations were too grave to mentally handle. She looked directly in her mother's eyes and said, "Take me to Lucy's."

They both knew the implication of such a statement. She was not going to Lucy's for a sleepover, or to talk about the latest gossip of their school. She was not going to Lucy's to share a coke and a laugh. She was going to Lucy's, and leaving their house for good. Sarah's mother knew in her heart that this was the only option, but she didn't want to believe it.

"Take me to Lucy's," Sarah repeated, as if to reassure her mother that there was no other option at that point. If her mother had had any doubt in her heart about taking her daughter to another family's home, Sarah dispelled it quite quickly by repeating her statement.

"Okay," was the only response that Sarah's mother could muster. They didn't talk about what the next steps would be, but they both knew. You could hear it in their voices, in their hearts.

# Chapter Eight

*Love alone is capable of uniting living beings in such a way as to complete and fulfill them, for it alone takes them and joins them by what is deepest in themselves.*

**Pierre Teilhard de Chardin (1881-1955)**

Sarah changed her clothes while Sarah's mother called Brownie in King's Gate. Brownie was expecting the call at some point, and she could tell from the sheer desperation and lack of discretion in Sarah's mother's voice that this was real, and that a new family member would be coming to their home.

"Hi, Brownie. It's Louise," Sarah's mother's voice cracked.

"Hi, Louise. How's everything?"

"Ummmmm . . . ."

"What is it, Louise?"

"It happened again."

"Oh, God. What do you need? What can I do?"

"Oh, shit, Brownie." Sarah's mother's emotions and desperation flooded the airwaves. She didn't even know how to begin to describe the circumstances that had just taken place in her home. She didn't know how to ask her for what she needed. She couldn't find the words to express what she was about to do.

"Oh, dear Jesus, what do I do?" her voice sobbed with dry tears.

"Bring her here." Brownie said without a moment's hesitation.

"I've tried everything. I've already lost one daughter and I just don't know what to do now. I simply can't …."

"Bring her here," she repeated.

"Is this the right thing….." Sarah's mother began.

"Bring her here." Brownie reassured her. "You'll have plenty of time to figure it out later."

"I don't know, Brownie."

"It's just for a night or two. Bring her here," she repeated again.

"Alright," she replaced the phone in the cradle and turned to Sarah.

"Pack your clothes."

What was she supposed to pack? How long would she be gone? Would she ever return?

At this point, the onlookers had retreated to their respective rooms, Sarah's stepfather had retired to his bed, and Sarah felt safe to enter her room again. How was she to decide what to pack when she knew she was leaving for good? This parting was symbolic of everything that would come in her life. She thought she had lived a full life up until then, but what about the events to come? She had no clue what this hegira had in store for her. This hegira would change her life forever. She was leaving her childhood. She was leaving her mother. She was leaving the blue curtains, and the white stucco ceiling. She was leaving the woodpecker that pounded on the side of the cedar house near her bedroom window every morning. She was leaving the backyard of woods and streams where she had invented so many adventures of exploring the world. She was leaving her childhood dog, who she watched grow from a puppy to an adult. She was leaving the piano that she played everyday, and practiced the great masters' fugues and sonatas. She was leaving her bedroom, which she always decorated with her latest interests: her ribbons from the swim team, her display of beautiful dresses from the Jessica McClintock advertisements which laced all the Seventeen and Glamour magazines, the display of Swatch advertisements that were equally as fashionable. She was leaving her closet, with shelves of childhood games and adventures; she was leaving her stuffed animals, her blue-flowered duvet which always served as such a comforting peace to her. She was leaving her collection of books and gifts her father had given her. She was leaving the familiar smells of home, and the little rituals she performed as she walked throughout the house. For instance, on the wall, leading up the staircase, was a bronze-raised print of John's hand and foot when he was first born. She touched this engraving as she walked up or down the stairs. When she walked to the living room to play the piano, she greeted the four busts of the four piano greats – Chopin, Bach, Mozart and Beethoven – which her father had given her and her sister, before she played. And if she was having a good day, she turned Beethoven on. His bust was a bit different, he was all white, and served as a music box of the Ninth Symphony, as well as a stalwart onlooker of her progress. That would be no more. Everything she had cherished, everything that had established her being and her routine, was being left behind, abruptly and with haste. And this was just a precursor to the long line of similar events that would follow her life.

She packed her clothes, by throwing them into a large trash bag. This was not a vacation where she carefully planned the outfits and requirements of the trip. This was not a holiday where she prepared a list of items and coordinated daily outfits weeks in advance, and checked them off as she meticulously packed her suitcase with the little green ball that her grandmother had given to her to identify her suitcase on the baggage claim on one of her frequent trips to Massachusetts.

She hobbled back down the stairs. Since her both of her hands were used for her crutches, she threw the large trash bag to the foot of the stairs.

"Let's go," she said as she hobbled toward the back door.

"Oh, Jesus," her mother muttered as she scanned the kitchen for the car keys.

"Don't worry, Mom," Sarah said as she looked at her mother through the picture window that connected the family room and the kitchen. Sarah was leaning on one crutch as she held the black trash bag over her shoulder.

"Oh, Jesus," she muttered again as she looked at her daughter waiting at the back door.

"Are you sure you want to do this?" Sarah's mother asked her as she walked to the door.

"It's not a big deal. We'll figure it out later," Sarah said, oblivious of the future implications. She was just happy she was ridding herself of the events of the night.

Sarah lopped the trash bag of clothes and her crutches into the back seat of the Volvo. Her mother started the engine and backed the car out of the garage into the crisp October night.

When does parenthood train a mother for such a moment? There are no handbooks or manuals that talk about this sort of thing for mothers with teenagers.

72

Sarah's mother drove silently.

Sarah talked as if everything was normal.

"The Junior Ring Ceremony is on the twelfth. I'll be playing the piano for it. Oh, and also, my school pictures are in, so I'll need to order those."

Sarah's mother was silent.

"Oh yeah, and I think the cheerleading squad needs some help selling buttons for the Homecoming game, so I'll be staying after school for that." Sarah was unable to cheer that year because of her broken leg.

"Am I doing the right thing?" Sarah's mother thought. She didn't even know exactly what happened in her daughter's bedroom, as everything from her perspective happened so quickly, and without much notice. She was confused, and just acting at this point, which is all any of us can hope to do in a situation as grave as this. Was she supposed to keep her daughter in a situation where her health was in danger? Was she supposed to take her daughter out of that environment, with herself included?

Surely, Sarah's mother felt a loyalty and responsibility toward Sarah's stepfather who had taken her in nine years earlier, and she also had an obligation to the younger twins who were still in elementary school. She could not, in good conscience, leave at that point. She felt confident in Brownie, Lucy and her family who lived just a stone's throw away. The situation would buy Sarah's mother enough time to think about the situation and assess it with a clearer head.

Sarah has much respect for her mother for going back into the pit without an ally. That takes a courageous and brave woman, but time would soon tell that such an arrangement began to eat away at the kind woman's soul. The goodness that permeated her very being, and the liveliness and youthfulness that always charmed the hearts of others, began to make way for a new type of living: living among those not of her kind.  She was outnumbered, and the friends that she had spent a lifetime cultivating were nowhere to be found.

# Chapter Nine

*Love sought is good, but given unsought is better.*

**William Shakespeare (1564-1616)**

Sarah cringed at the thought of some of her mother's pleadings, her efforts to try to get them to see the truth, but all were not so convinced by a woman who seemed to have lost her self-dignity. How else would a good woman react if she felt she had no allies, if she felt, in her core, that she had been betrayed and not believed? True, these types of grave circumstances can drive a person to do many self-destructing things. The same stepfather that hit Sarah also forbade Meghan from dating an African-American boy. Meghan was then watched like a hawk, and put on countless restrictions to ensure that she would not fraternize with black folks. As a result, her first-born daughter, whom she had loved and nurtured to perfection, felt that her only option was to leave her mother to live with her father. Keep in mind also, that Sarah's mother was living with a man who beat her second-born daughter, twice. The first time, he left recognizable bodily damage, and the second time, he hit her while she had a full-length cast on her leg. Keep in mind also, that Sarah's mother felt an obligation to remain in his house, with his children, because it was her duty as a wife to support the man she married. She had always believed this, even from her first marriage, and all she ever wanted was a loving husband whom she could support, for her entire life. Her first marriage ended because her husband left. He was unfaithful and felt the need to be free. He later tried to patch the marriage, but Sarah's mother would hear nothing of the sort. She believed in the true foundations of marriage, the ones that came from the Bible: if one is unfaithful, it is a sin against God. What is amazingly brilliant about this woman is her resilience, and her incredible hope in the face of adversity. And she brought Sarah to live with another family.

Weeks before Sarah's father left her mother, she had been working with the local church to prepare a special Easter program for the children's liturgy. It was to be a special event, and Sarah's mother was excited about involving her daughters in such a project, as well as leading the production for the whole congregation on Easter morning.

The program was to involve the idea of the transformation from a caterpillar into a butterfly as a symbol for the resurrection of Jesus Christ. She had planned to make tissue paper and carpet cleaner butterflies for all of the children to keep and display on Easter morning. And she had planned to involve her daughters in the massive project. She knew it was an enormous undertaking, but felt confident that it was worth the work, as she needed something to occupy her mind, as her husband had been a bit distant. But on Good Friday, as she sat in front of the television with the movie, "Jesus Christ," twisting butterfly carpet cleaners, she discovered, after her two girls were already in bed, that her husband was not coming home that night, and would not be coming home on any future night. So, on Good Friday, two days before the production in front of the church about Hope, Resurrection and Transformation, she discovered that her husband was leaving her, and her two children. How was she supposed to tell her two daughters that their father wasn't coming home? Meghan was six and Sarah was two. How was she supposed to go forward with a planned church production about Hope and

Resurrection, when she had just discovered that her husband had left her?

But she did it. Amazingly enough, she did it. And she put on a smile every morning for her two daughters, even though she didn't know what she was going to do. She explained to the two girls that their father would not be coming home.

"Sometimes," Sarah's mother explained, "two people who love each other very much cannot see eye to eye with many things. Sometimes, two people who love each other very much need a break from each other."

The two girls did not understand her words.

"Surely, Daddy will come home when he knows that I baked a cake for him," Meghan said as she lovingly began to collect the ingredients for a special cake. She stood at the kitchen counter, on a stool, and baked a "Welcome Home" cake for her father.

That cake sat on the kitchen counter untouched for weeks.

But somehow, Sarah's mother made it through the roughest times. She moved her two girls to Maryland, where she worked on her master's degree in library science, while she worked part-time for the United States Department of Justice in Washington, DC.

She was a woman of strength, determination and perseverance. When life served her lemons, she made lemonade. That was the only way. And throughout it all, she kept a positive attitude for her two children.

Sarah's mother met her second husband at a time when she wasn't looking for one, at a time when she seemed to be making it just fine.

At the time, Casp, Sarah's soon-to-be-step-father, was married to his first wife who gave birth to twins a few days before Christmas in 1979. The twins were delivered an hour apart, which was rare in those days for twin delivery. In most cases, twins emerge into the world within minutes of each other. The doctors began to worry about the long delay. Finally, when Jacob decided to emerge from the protection of his mother's womb, the doctors were so relieved that the babies were healthy and fine. As the celebration ensued, the doctors did not notice that Casp's wife's health began to deteriorate. She was not responding and she slipped in and out of consciousness.

Casp was worried. The twins were carefully wrapped and placed in the newborn room, and Casp knelt by his wife's side as the doctors tried to figure out what had gone wrong.

An internal infection was discovered and she was flown by helicopter to the Medical College of Virginia in Richmond from the hospital in Newport News. Richmond's doctors and nurses were better trained in her condition. Casp stayed by her side the entire time while the newborns were tended to at the hospital in Newport News, and his two older sons, John and Joseph, were looked after by family members who had flown into town when they heard the news.

After five days of fighting the internal infection, Casp's wife gave up the fight, and Casp was left with two sons at home, and two newborns not yet taken home from the hospital. Family rushed to his side, arrangements were made, a permanent nanny was hired, and weeks later, Casp returned to work as an aerospace engineer for the National Aeronautics and Space Administration. Needless to say, his mind was not concentrated on work.

Friends persuaded him to become involved with the Catholic Church and attend various single retreats and faith seminars to meet other people and talk about his situation. And it was at one of the weekend faith retreats where Casp met Sarah's mother.

It was a match made in heaven, and thus, the new marriage came to be.

So, one can see Sarah's mother's loyalty and her reluctance to leave such a man who changed her life, when her own daughter, Sarah, was physically abused by such a man. His youngest children were a little over one year old when they were married. So, Sarah's mother was the only mother they had ever known. She could not leave the decaying pit of a family that the house had come to represent.

So, she stayed and continued to drink more and more wine. Meghan was in Massachusetts, and Sarah was in a friend's house across town.

Meghan, who reached the legal age of eighteen halfway through her senior year of high school in Massachusetts, came back to Virginia to finish her senior year with her friends, and in a familiar surrounding.

She had worked three jobs while in Massachusetts, while attending high school, and cheered for the school's winter sports teams, and had saved enough money to rent an apartment to finish out her high school she had grown to love in Williamsburg.

As her other friends and classmates went home from school to their family homes, and traveled to college campuses with their parents to decide on the colleges that they would attend the following year, Meghan went home to her own apartment, where she slept on a mattress on the floor. She advertised for a roommate to help her cover the expenses. One roommate, who stayed with her for a few months, slept on a foam pad on the floor, and ushered in a slew of male companions for the evenings. The other roommate was promising, as she purchased new furniture for the apartment on loan. But she never paid the bills, so the furniture disappeared one day, with the promising roommate and two months worth of rent.

Nevertheless, Meghan maintained her impeccable grades, worked to make sure she could pay the expenses for her apartment, and caught rides to school from friends.

She chose to live in the only apartment complex that was located in York County so she could legally attend the York County high school, but this complex was a foreign place to a girl from her background, and a foreign place to all of her friends who came to pick her up there. The buildings were brick with four apartments in each building. The dark staircases that led to the upstairs apartments smelled of cigarette smoke from twenty years ago and years of fresh paint---layer after layer----which revealed the years of tenants. The stairs were lined with plastic coverings and the banisters usually hung from one screw. The buildings were square and boxy, without much character or life. Many single mothers raised their kids there, as small plastic and metal swing sets and toys were scattered around the small plots of grass and asphalt around the apartment buildings.

Meghan did not concentrate much on her surroundings. She worked to pay the rent. She worked to maintain an A average. She lived. She survived in the life that had been thrown her way. She was just happy to be back in Virginia, and able to finish high school among friends and the town that had helped to shape her-----the town that made her into an author and university professor of race and class consciousness, the town that had expelled her at the end of her college years, and welcomed her again as a sociology professor.

The fact that she was the only one of her classmates that was living in an apartment complex on her own was trifling. She still participated in the same state math competitions, attended the same basketball games and pep rallies, and spoke fluent French with her classmates.

At that time, Sarah was still at home and had completed her freshman year. The family achieved some sense of normalcy again during this period, because even though Meghan was not in the same house as Sarah and her mother, she was close enough now that they could see each other on a regular basis. They were attending the same school, which was the first time in both of their lives where they shared the same school. Because school had always been a respite for both of them, the grounds offered a greater incentive to attend because they were able to see each other on a daily basis. School was a way for the sisters to connect with some normalcy. It was a chance to concentrate on studies and their lives that extended beyond what they experienced at home. School offered the only hope, joy and peace alive in their worlds.

Meghan traveled along with Sarah to all of her cheerleading events, and the two supported each other despite the tumultuous circumstances of their respective lives. School became their place to connect. They shared a locker, as Meghan was never assigned one by the school since she only enrolled halfway through the school year. They saw each other between classes. They hugged each other in the hall, as the novelty of seeing each other in a safe surrounding never wore off. In the five minutes between each of their classes, and during the breaks at lunch, they found each other to fill the other with enthusiasm and strength.

They had both grown accustomed to clinging to each other throughout their whole lives, as they were all they had. They were there for each other during their mother's first divorce. They were there for each other on the afternoons and evenings when their mother was at work or studying at the University. They were there for each other when they found themselves in a new home with a new family. They were there for each other while they played the piano. They were there for each other when they traveled to see their father. Events in their lives----whether good or bad---- did not take place without the other one present.

They had built each other up again in the darkest moments, and provided a beacon of light in the darkest corners of their worlds. They had the same history, the same knowledge, the same light of surviving and doing well in the world, but they never talked about these things with one another. It was their lives, and they were just there for each other. There was no need to talk about it. They knew.

After Meghan graduated from high school in Williamsburg, she went back to Massachusetts to begin her freshman year at the University of Massachusetts. Meghan got an apartment, visited her grandmother, who lived in Northampton, every day, attended classes, and worked three jobs to pay the rent and college expenses and to afford the monthly trips to Virginia.

Sarah became close friends with Patty and threw herself into her cheerleading activities. She studied Entertainment and Sports Programming Network (ESPN) tapes of cheerleading performances, studied dance routines on Music Television (MTV) videos, choreographed dance routines, created cheers, squad formations and pyramids, and loved to teach these new creations to her squad. She mixed music tapes for dance performances, making sure to appeal to all sorts of music tastes for the school population, created banners for the school halls, created construction paper encouragement buttons for all the football players' jerseys and lockers for game days, ensured that the cheerleaders had a fresh supply of plastic megaphones to throw out to the crowd and all of the countless other duties that a cheerleading captain must perform.

Meghan, despite her far distance, drove down the Eastern seaboard for each pep rally, making one just in time before the two o'clock bell, just to see her youngest sister cheer.

Sarah will never forget that day.

It was basketball season of the eighty-nine/ninety school year. Sarah had spent months creating a choreographed dance routine for a pep rally that combined several dance riffs from a Sting video, In Living Color, a popular television program during that time, a Janet Jackson video, and other cheerleading competitions that were aired on the Entertainment and Sports Programming Network.

She taught it to her squad of twelve girls, and she was nervous about performance day, as the dance involved chairs, and a fair amount of movements and gymnastics that had never been done before.

She had talked to her sister the previous night from Massachusetts and she assured that she would be there to see it, and would leave at three o'clock in the morning to ensure her arrival by two o'clock in the afternoon. But the two o'clock hour came and her sister was not in the audience.

Sarah was nervous.

The cheerleaders assumed their positions on the basketball court, the crowd hushed to watch the performance, and Sarah stood at the helm of the squad formation, with her hands on the chair in front of her. She moved her head downward, looked at the floor, and waited for the cue of the music to begin.

The swirl of the crowd bobbed around her. The freshman, sophomores, juniors and seniors were all in their respective places in the bleachers. Many waved pompoms; many guys painted their faces or their chests to show their green and gold spirit, friends shouted to one another, and the festive school support weaved itself within each one of the students.

As the cheerleaders assumed their positions with their heads pointed toward the floor, the students in the bleachers hushed. The music blared out of the speakers throughout the gym: "Here the juice, time to get loose," BOOM, BOOM, BOOM, BOOM, and her movements began. Just the sound of those beginning words was enough to start the crowd in a roar. When Sarah heard the music, and the sounds of the cheering crowd, she lost herself and could feel nothing but the music, and all the hard work she had done over the past few months, all leading up to this moment. Her movements came easily, as she had practiced them time and time again, in front of her squad. "We came here to knock some boots," was the next line, and her stiff and powerful movements, swung her body around to the front, where she finally, and dramatically lifted her head up to see the cheering crowd, and right, in the front row, was her sister, who had rushed in and was sitting on the edge of her seat beaming at her younger sister. It was a moment Sarah will never forget.

It was moments like these that made them sisters. It was moments like these that made them understand they spoke an unspoken language. It was moments like these where they understood that they spoke with their hearts.

# Chapter Ten

*To live in this world, you must be able to do three things: to love what
is mortal; to hold it against your bones knowing your life depends on
it; and when the time comes, to let it go.*

**Mary Oliver (1935-   )**

Winter led into spring, and Meghan transferred to Virginia
Commonwealth University in Richmond, Virginia. Sarah felt
relieved that her sister was closer again.

But things worsened at home. Sarah became to involve herself
more and more with her extracurricular activities, as that kept her
away from the house where the daily arguments and screaming
matches were the norm. Sarah dealt with it by ignoring it. If she
didn't see it, it didn't happen. It didn't exist.

Summer came, and Meghan moved to Newport News, which had cheaper apartment living options, and she commuted to Williamsburg for work. She worked three jobs in the summer to pay for school, for her car, which took her back and forth to school and her jobs, for her rent, and for the countless expenses that surmounted for each.

No one really noticed the pains that Meghan was going through, and Meghan didn't complain about it. This was just a part of living for her. She was determined to dedicate her life to something bigger than herself, but she never talked about this with other people. As she lived her life and surrounded herself with the harshness of life out of necessity, she studied the impacts that race and class had on culture. She studied it in books, and lived it in life.

As she worked, and planned to attend the College of William and Mary in the fall, she learned that Sarah had been hit by a car and bed-ridden in the house that she tried to relentlessly avoid. Meghan did not see Sarah much during this time, as it was too painful for Meghan to go back to the home full of hate and contempt, even if it did mean that her only sister was there.

Williamsburg represented something different to Meghan. The town was the place that gave birth to the parameters placed on her life due to racial prejudices. The town represented everything conservative, antiquated and right-winged. The town represented the place where its citizens judged each other by the color of their skin, rather than what was in their hearts. This town was what shaped Meghan, but she didn't know that the racial prejudices existed in most small towns across America. She wouldn't learn that until she dedicated her life to its study in college.

She began her sophomore year at the College of William and Mary, and concentrated on her studies, as that seemed to be the only viable way out of the life she was living. She reconciled that the only way out of her daily struggles was to get her bachelor's degree, master's degree and doctor of philosophy (PhD) and live her life according to the principles that were right in her heart. Because Casp had forbidden her to even speak with black folk, she dedicated her life to fighting against people who perpetuated those injustices, namely, people like Casp. She wanted to teach it. She wanted to write about it. She wanted to open people's eyes to the wrongness of it. And she would struggle to do it.

As Meghan sifted through her first semester at the College of William and Mary, Sarah moved to Brownie's home across the town of Williamsburg.

Meghan had planned to move to Williamsburg when she had saved enough money as the cost of living was slightly higher than Newport News, but the need was now greater, as Sarah needed a place to live to finish high school. Surely, Sarah could not live with another family for too much longer. It was an imposition and awkward situation at best. So, Meghan planned to get an apartment in Williamsburg by Christmas, so that her younger sister could feel safe and finish school comfortably.

Sarah's sixteenth birthday came and went in Lucy's family's household, and her leg began to heal. She was given a smaller cast in the middle of September, which made things a lot easier for movement. She could not receive her driver's license as most of her other friends did at age sixteen because of her cast, but was thankful for the rides that Lucy always provided. Lucy and Sarah were very close during that time period, as Sarah now lived in her brother's room, down the hall. He was completing his junior year at the University of Virginia.

Sarah's classes still entailed her literary magnet school, and Lucy always went along with Sarah's goofy projects. During the autumn months of 1991, one of Sarah's classroom projects was to deliver a presentation on Japanese drama and the No Theatre. No is a very old form of traditional Japanese theater with its origins in the fourteenth century. **By tradition, No actors and musicians never rehearse for performances together. Instead, each actor, musician, and choral chanter practices his or her fundamental movements, songs, and dances independently or under the tutelage of a senior member of the school. Thus, the tempo of a given performance is not set by any single performer but established by the interactions of all the performers together. In this way, Noh exemplifies the traditional Japanese aesthetic of transience.**

Sarah had planned to put make up on her own face with the theatrical drama that displayed the exaggerated expressions of the theatre. So, the night before the day of her big project, she had an idea.

"Lucy, I've got to make sure this looks right since I've got to put this make-up on my face tomorrow in front of the class. Want to be my model?"

"Okay," Lucy said. What's the harm?

So, Sarah made Lucy look like a true geisha girl with white powder make-up, large arching black eyebrows, and small, pursed red lips. With a kimono, and her blonde hair pulled away from her face, no one would have been able to tell that she was not Asian. As Sarah painted her face, she tried to remember all the facts she had read about the No theatre and its importance to Japanese culture. She gathered together her presentation as she practiced on her friend.

And Sarah received an A on the presentation the next day. She never would have had the time or space to practice those presentations in her former home. No one there really cared about grades anyway. Homework was always enforced, but it was enforced as an item on the check-off list from a mother who was trying to run a six-child household successfully. Cooking, table set-up, dinner, table clean-up, homework and baths were enough to do a mother, and her six kids, in for the evening. The content of the homework was peripheral.

"Did you do your homework?"

"Yes," was always the response.

No one really cared what the homework was, or what kinds of creative ways she was illuminating it. Her mother had other things to worry about, like arguments that erupted from an upstairs room, or an argument that erupted over the remote control, or the entrance of three neighborhood friends at the backdoor, or a constant string of phone calls each night, or whose turn it was to feed the dogs, or which child's turn it was to take a shower. And this all happened while she was trying to make dinner for eight.

This had not always been the case. Sarah's mother's change was gradual. Her impatience and feeling of drowning didn't come all at once. It was a character change that couldn't truly be noticed by the people surrounding her on a daily basis. She didn't even notice it herself. When her children were just Meghan and Sarah, she initiated creative projects and took a proactive role in any life lesson, whether it had to do with church, school or play. By her seventh year of marriage with four extra children, her creativity was buried beneath the suffocating din of her husband's idea of a household, and the jugs of wine she used to cover it up.

Homework was handled much differently in Brownie's household. And since Lucy and Sarah, many times, were studying the same things, they were able to talk about the assignments together.

Sarah's grades improved and she was introduced to a new type of life.

Brownie's household was a bit different from the one Sarah was used to in many more respects. Firstly, it was encased within the realms of King's Gate, protected by the nestled houses and trees, and the familiar faces and friends from school and other activities around town. Her classmates' brothers, mothers, fathers, pets, friends from church, swim team, and softball games were all around. While each family maintained their own household, there was an unspoken communication between all the families that they all were family. It was a sensation felt when one entered the woody, shady streets with trees that hardly let in any sunlight on long summer days because of their prolific greenery. Secondly, neither Brownie nor her husband ever shouted. In fact, there wasn't much language at all, just sentiments that needed to be communicated----about after school practices, homework assignments, etc. There were no fights, accusations, rumors or peals of laughter. The only laughter that entered the home came from the upstairs bedroom when Lucy and Sarah studied together. Studying with a friend was a whole different concept for Sarah. It wasn't something that had to be done, but rather, something enjoyable, as Sarah could find a joke to make out of anything. Her jovial nature was a way for her to compensate for others' lack of enthusiasm. She never understood why people didn't laugh or have fun with whatever they were doing.

Brownie made breakfast for the girls every morning before they went off to school and ensured that each one received their proper vitamins. At the time, the two girls joked that the mountain of daily vitamins would soon overtake them, but they swallowed each one with their morning glass of orange juice, and left the tranquil house to partake in a day of school. Lucy drove a Chevy Blazer at the time, a big car, to ensure her safety, and it was also a loyal, sturdy car to haul numerous friends around town. It developed a personality for the girls, and they made songs about their trusty friend in their free time – The Blazer, Life Saver, Hell Raiser, It's the Blazer! These were just childhood songs, something to pass the time, but everything had meaning, particularly in teenagers' lives where the mind and actions are unfiltered, and not quite at a stage of adulthood where many of the intrinsic thoughts and perceptions are repressed. The childhood rhyme about the trusty car was much longer- a gay little jingle - but it conveyed everything of their relationship, minus the car.

Sarah, still clad in leg devices, but with a removable brace, waited for Lucy after school, until she finished field hockey practice, which lasted until the dinner hour. The two girls then proceeded "home," where dinner was usually near finish. On the free days, when Lucy did not have practice, the two girls came home after school to feast on snacks and watch television from the armchair by the window. The cats were let in and out as they pleased, and the television was turned off far before the dinner hour.

Sarah received phone calls at her new household, primarily by her boyfriend, as Lucy and Sarah shared the same friends. They even had a piano in the living room which Sarah played occasionally, but in this house, the living room was Lucy's father's space. This new arrangement was new to Sarah, as the living room in her house had been primarily her territory, as no one else played the piano, nor frequented the "good" sofa and winged-back velvet chairs. But the living room was where Lucy's father retired after dinner. Lucy and Sarah walked upstairs to do homework, and Brownie cleaned up after dinner.

Lucy's father was a stable figure in the house, but he was quiet and kept a reasonable distance from the family. He was always there in case anyone needed him, but he didn't feel the need to talk much. He was an accountant for one of the largest companies this side of Richmond. The company's headquarters were in Richmond, so his long commute every morning and evening gave him ample time to unwind from the corporate business life of Richmond culture. He liked his home. He felt comfortable in it, was pleased with his wife and children. His oldest son would soon graduate from one the best universities in the state of Virginia and his only daughter was heading in the same direction. His wife had a part time job, was active in the community and Parent Teacher Association, kept the house clean and orderly, raised two fine children, and provided active and stimulating conversation. He had every reason to be happy.

But Brownie was another story. She had a spirit that merrily bubbled beneath the surface of her seamless life. Her spirit shone brighter than the reserve of her responsibilities. Perhaps that is why she connected with Sarah. She knew how to have a good time, and maintained her youthful heart despite the responsibilities that adulthood, marriage and motherhood required.

But she was a spitfire in her heyday. She was an only child, daughter of a wayward sailor who had an adventurous spirit. He told her of adventures and tales of the sea, and in the time he was away, she spent her alone moments as a little girl, dreaming of far away jaunts and adventures. She buried herself in the great literature of the past and invented stories of her own to fill her time.

She had a spirit and a soul that her mother didn't have, nor could see. So, she learned to keep her dreams to herself and foster such stories and adventures in her head while playing with her dollhouses and old antique trinkets from days gone by.

Brownie's father had that spirit – that glow of a dreamer -- and she longed to share that connection with him, but he was a father of that time, a parental figure of stalwart sureness. He gave his only daughter a spark of such feelings, and Brownie polished them to perfection. She was always a doer, a seeker of a new challenge, always one to seize an opportunity. She always made friends easily, and her outgoing personality always won a group of friends, hands down. She had a knack for planning a trip, an outing, a party, or any other excuse to get a group of friends together. Brownie usually

90

found herself in a leadership role of neighborhood activities, swim team, Girl Scout activities, Parent Teacher Association meetings, town meetings----just because she could catch the ball and run with it. She had the enthusiasm and drive to ensure that an event happened, and with grace. Her mind was razor-sharp and she involved herself in the political movements of the time, actively serving on the League of Women Voters, and wrote frequent letters to the editor to comment on the current events covered in *The Daily Herald* and *Virginia Journal.*.

She grew up in Pennsylvania, attended a Friends school, and received a good education. Even in her adulthood, she remembered the strict teachings of one of her English literature teachers, Mrs. Finkley, and boy, did Sarah and Lucy hear about Mrs. Finkley! She was almost like another visitor in the house. Sarah liked to talk about literature with Brownie as she seemed to be an adult figure that knew the literary stories that she talked about and took an interest in things like symbolism, characters, family scandals and adventures. It was not as if Sarah's mother did not have the time to brood over Fanny's heroine characteristics in Austen's *Mansfield Park*, or Bronte's search for love in *Jane Eyre.*

And with these conversations, Mrs. Finkley's voice (may she rest in peace) entered every conversation. Sarah felt as if there were no time barrier between her and her friend's mother – they talked of literature and characters from centuries ago, they talked of Mrs. Finkley from Brownie's own high school days in the early 1960s, and they talked of Sarah's current high school literature class with a teacher who lived one street over from Brownie's house in King's Gate. Oh yes, not only did King's Gate house the families, it housed and protected the teachers of the families.

King's Gate nurtured the inhabitants of the town. Its shady trees and hidden streets protected its people, and nourished the families and Williamsburg citizens who gave back to the community that cultivated a legacy. The people, the children, and the families that emerged from these woods, had been transformed. King's Gate was not just a neighborhood in Williamsburg. It *was* Williamsburg. It breathed life into its streets. It pulsed oxygen into its veins. It thrived and provided the magical town with the necessary manna for growth, sustenance and rebirth. It wasn't a place. It was an enigma.

While physically, it was not the only neighborhood in town, for all intents and purposes, it was one of the only places within its parameters that embraced and nurtured its character.

But there would be a time when its foundations were tried. There would be a time when its sustainability was questioned. But that proliferation and determination to fight for its survival had much to do with the people and families that inhabited it. Sure, it was a neighborhood, but only its people made it what it had become.

# Chapter Eleven

*Neither a lofty degree of intelligence nor imagination nor both
together go to the making of a genius. Love, love, love, that is the
soul of genius.*

**Wolfgang Amadeus Mozart (1756-1791)**

Mrs. Cliff was a middle-aged woman with brownish-gray hair that
wisped around her head with healthiness. Her two front teeth were a
little larger than the rest, but they fit her face perfectly, as that was the
mouth that would lovingly teach her students about music, culture and
literature.

She was the newest teacher to the literary magnet school.

Sarah had begun taking classes in the second year of its inception
when the demand of students only required one teacher. Once Sarah
enrolled in the magnet school her freshman year, she made a

commitment to stay with the program for the remaining four years of her high school education.

The magnet school was similar to etiquette school, in that, it taught culture, drama, opera, ballet, literature, symbolism and art. It taught its students to look at the subtleties of art and of life. Its contents breached far beyond the subject matter taught in regular English classes or art classes, and since the classmates formed a bond based on their enrollment in the program, the school was able to foster an environment where creativity abounded.

The classes were comprised of fifteen students at most, and they hailed from all over the county and lower part of the state. The largest class was Sarah's second year when the school allowed one student to come from the other high school in Williamsburg, and allowed a senior from another York County school at the end of the county near the York River.

Sarah was a sophomore at the time, as were most of the other students, so the added students and seniors offered new perspectives and experiences to the classroom. Most of the students were chosen by their ability to create and by the backgrounds and experiences that they could contribute to the classroom experience.

During Sarah's sophomore year in the program, she formed friendships with people from other schools and counties, and learned that her circle of friends could include others outside of the ones whom she had shared her childhood with.

Her classmates were smart, creative and acted freely, which always guaranteed an engaging moment. The program allowed students to create without inhibitions, which was an innovative concept in the traditional public-school setting. Sarah didn't find many experiences where all of her senses were ignited and activated, but this environment, this period of two hours every day, where students were bussed in from different parts of the county and state, provided a universe within itself that opened Sarah to the world of literature, to the world of the great masters which her father only had enough time to touch on, was the only place that offered an outlet for her sensitivities.

This was the year that the magnet school hired Mrs. Cliff. There were two teachers, Mrs. Cliff and Mrs. Crumble, the latter of which Sarah had in her first year. In the first year, her classmates and her were all freshmen, and did not know quite what they were getting into. Either did Mrs. Crumble, as the school was new, and she had taught for many years in a traditional classroom where the classes were shorter, and only English literature was taught. She was not accustomed to teaching young freshman, as she had spent most of her years in the upper echelon of English classes and students.

Mrs. Crumble was nearing retiring age, and thought much about it, as she wanted to concentrate on other things herself, like writing and traveling, but the former superintendent of the York County school system, who had previously been principal to the high school, and was now principal to the magnet school, asked her to teach these classes.

Mrs. Crumble felt obligated, as her and Theo, the former superintendent, had been good friends for many years. They both lived in Yorktown, and had grown together as administrators and teachers as the school system evolved into one of the best public school systems in the country.

Yorktown was the nucleus of the county. It sat on the banks of the York River, and was about twenty miles south of the town of Williamsburg. Yorktown housed the county municipal buildings, the courthouse, the closest beach, and the football field in which Somerset High School played their games. To get there, one would take the Colonial Parkway, a cobblestone-like paved, unlined, sleepy road along the York River which was frequently traveled by Somerset busses carrying athletes, cheerleaders and athletic supporters. And throughout all of these places in which the town folk of Williamsburg spent their time, the unspoken and sublime influence of the historical impact of the environment weaved its way into their lives.

So, Mrs. Crumble decided to take the new position as a teacher for the Magnet School with the hope of renewed spirit in teaching. Sarah's class was a challenge. The students were very young, very immature, and Mrs. Crumble's gentle spirit allowed much of their antics and enthusiasm, which often bordered on recklessness. But lessons were taught, and Sarah learned about points of view and perspective. This began to open a world which she had only read about but didn't quite know how to analyze. Her father had talked about such things in periphery, but her father had always talked to Sarah like a fellow philosopher, which would serve her in later years, but at such a young age, seemed to be a conflux of tangled words. She could only assert enough energy to hold herself above water when he talked. But she did, and as these ideas began to surface at a slower rate in the classroom, the context of her father's teachings illuminated and supplemented her classroom revelations.

But something very peculiar happened to Sarah in this first year of Magnet School. Near the end of the school year, about the same time she became more enamored with Derrick, the football player, she began to get very behind in her assignments. She felt overwhelmed with projects and papers; she couldn't handle the workload, and turned to her older sister for help. Meghan was a senior in the same school during this time, as she had transferred from the high school in Massachusetts to finish her final semester in Virginia. There was an essay contest in the local newspaper about abortion, as that seemed to be a hot political debate at the time of Governor Wilder's re-election. Sarah was not too interested in politics, or abortion, at that time, but knew that her sister always had a strong political opinion involving women or minorities. Sarah trusted her sister and normally agreed with the opinion that her sister took. Mrs. Crumble had assigned such an essay for the entire class. The winner of the essay contest would have their essay written in the paper for all Hampton Roads newspaper subscribers to read. This abortion essay was just one of the assignments on Sarah's long to-do list. She knew that Meghan had a passion for such an assignment, so she approached her about it. Sarah saw her sister in the hallway between classes.

"I need your help, Meg."

"What's up?"

"I'm up to my ears in assignments and I need to have an essay on abortion written by tomorrow. Either pro or against."

"Yeah, I just wrote the same essay for Advanced Placement English."

"Oh good! You know about it!"

"Fine, I'll write another one. But the first one will be better."

"Fine. Thanks! I just need to turn something in. I don't care if it wins."

"When's it due?"

"Tomorrow."

"Fine. I'll print up a draft and give it to you in the morning. You'll have all day to make changes if you want."

"You're the best sister in the world," Sarah squealed as she hugged her sister. She felt her load lighten.

"I know. Good thing I'm your only one."

The bell rang, and the two sisters found their respective classrooms by the second bell. Life was good.

Meghan jotted down a second essay without much effort, as naturally, she wanted her own, the one she had worked so hard on, to win. Sarah put a few final touches on the essay, typed a final draft, and turned in the effortless essay to Mrs. Crumble the next day. She didn't care much about the contest or winning, she was just relieved to have one more thing to scratch off her to-do list. And she didn't care much about the subject matter. Again, she knew her sister was passionate about the subject, but Sarah hadn't quite formed her own opinion about abortion. She just trusted her sister.

And the two sisters felt confident in their little arrangement..... until a few weeks later when the newspaper announced the winner. Naturally, it was Sarah, a freshman in the Literary Magnet School. The Magnet School was so proud, as they relished any chance to have one of their students published anywhere, using the name of the school. Because the school was so new, and needed continual funding from the county government, they wanted to prove to the community, and the people who cut their pay checks, just how gifted their students were. And in all actuality, Magnet School writers *were* published more frequently, and the content of their writing was more complex and imaginative. But this particular situation was not supposed to happen. Shortly thereafter, *The Daily Herald* contacted Sarah and wanted to interview her for a newspaper article. Sarah wanted to crawl under the covers.

"That was the worst essay I have ever written," Meghan said when she found out Sarah had won.

"I can't believe it!"

"I wrote that thing in ten minutes."

"This wasn't supposed to happen."

"Good thing you're my sister."

"I'm going to tell Mrs. Crumble you helped me with it," Sarah said as the guilt began to rise to the surface.

"Whatever, it's just an essay."

Shortly thereafter *The Daily Herald* contacted Sarah and scheduled a time to interview her for a newspaper article. The ball continued to roll, and unfortunately, Sarah was attached to it.

Her picture appeared in the newspaper, with a list of personal information about her, like her favorite food, favorite movie, hobbies, where she wanted to go to school, her family members, etc.

The newspaper featured people from the community like this every Thursday.

The interviewer asked the last question.

"What's your worst fear?"

Sarah thought for a moment about this question, and then answered truthfully.

"Injuring myself so that I could not participate in sports."

"Well, thank you for your time. The article will appear in next week's *Your Neighbor* section."

"Okay, thank you."

Sarah was still in a daze as she hung up the receiver. Little did she know that exactly one year later, her worst fear would come true.

# Chapter Twelve

*Love does not consist in gazing at each other, but in looking outward together in the same direction.*

**Antoine de Saint-Exupery (1900-1944)**

Mrs. Cliff, the new teacher for the Magnet School, and a resident of King's Gate, was a lover of art. She did not have the years of experience that Mrs. Crumble had but she had a patient spirit, a love of children and an unfettered enthusiasm, and a desire to proliferate art and literature in any form.

She attended South Carolina University and began teaching shortly after college, but soon married a brilliant scientist, had three boys, and dedicated her life to being a mother. She played cello for the town symphony in her free time, and was the steady female figure in a home of brilliant, male mathematicians. She decided to work for the Magnet School as her youngest son was nearing the age of finishing high school, as he was one year below Sarah. Mrs. Cliff felt the need to fill her time with purpose. Her soul and spirit had not been tainted by years of teaching and she brought much enthusiasm and spirit to the classroom.

Sarah always admired her, as she seemed to be comfortable in her role, but contained enough playfulness and easiness to keep her flexible. She taught Sarah her sophomore and senior years, and observed from a distance the traumatic circumstances that were happening in Sarah's life. When she taught Sarah in her sophomore year, Sarah was living in a relatively stable environment, she contributed much to the classroom, even composed the tercentennial celebration song for Yorktown's celebration of the last battle of the Revolutionary War where America claimed her Independence from the British, and she played and performed while the class sang the lyrics. During this time, Mrs. Cliff observed Sarah taking an invested interest in the class field trips, particularly to Colonial Williamsburg to study different types of period architecture in the buildings and churches, as well as the landscapes and gardens. It was one thing to live among the remnants of the past with Colonial Williamsburg in each of the town's families' backyards, but it was quite another to study the history of each architecturally-designed building and piece of landscape. The origins of each Palladian window and Japanese latticework porch were studied and traced back to the architect's heritage and cultural influences from his travels abroad. Each mound of land was studied and its importance was identified for its historical significance during the Revolutionary War. Each pew and gravestone at the Bruton Parish Church was studied and scrutinized for the significance of each historic figure who graced its wood or soil. The students were treated like true academic historians by the costumed interpreters and the staff historians. Sarah brought her camera to each outing and snapped pictures of the details she studied. These were the subtleties that tourists and town folk passed on a daily basis. These were the subtleties that were manna for Sarah's heart.

The literary class traveled to New York City to study paintings, architecture, operas and plays they had only explored in the haven of their classrooms in Williamsburg. Vincent van Gogh's Starry Night spoke to Sarah with its vibrant blues and yellows in the halls of the Museum of Modern Art. And the architectural theory and placement of buttresses and rose windows only came to life when Sarah walked through the entranceways to cathedrals and Cloisters. **The Cloisters house the Metropolitan Museum of Art's collection of art and architecture from medieval Europe. Best known for the beautiful tapestries on display, the Cloisters also offer architectural installations, a series of special programs, and fantastic views of the Hudson.** She felt as if she was living a dream.

Mrs. Cliff had a soft spot in her heart for the young girl with tragic circumstances, so it broke her heart to have Sarah again in her senior year, after she had moved to a friend's house, an apartment complex in a shady area of town, and then in another condominium community when her mother mustered enough courage and bravery to leave her husband. And her grades reflected it. Her projects lacked creativity and spark; her attendance fluctuated, as most of her energy was spent on surviving. She always kept her positive spirit. Many people who did not know the circumstances never would have guessed her background. She hid it well, with a smile and a joke. There were some that saw her behavior as reckless and judged her by this image, with eyes that had an inability to look deeper – to look underneath – to look at the circumstances behind such a lifestyle. Sarah did not blame them, as she chose not to reveal it to most. But those who read her writing, namely Mrs. Cliff, knew Sarah wrote plays and children's stories, essays and novellas, and they all seemed to reveal the pain that Sarah concealed quite well. She wrote poems about masks and mirrors. She wrote illustrative essays about joyful moments in her youth, perhaps when she sat and listened to her father play the piano.

This was one of Sarah's favorite things to do. She could do this for hours, and she could describe her father's movements and mannerisms to a tee. Her father left when she was two years old, so she didn't have much recollection of him. So, the summer and winter visits were gems to both her and her sister.

Sarah's father was a classic pianist. He was a Music Major at Boston University when the mandatory draft was instated during Vietnam. He had begun playing piano when he was five years old. He was always around the finer things in life, as his mother was a governess for a prominent German family in New Hampshire.

The family came from a long line of musicians, and the German musician met a lovely opera singer in Paris. The two married and moved to America to start a new life during the booming music scene of the 1930s. The woman sang for the New York Opera while her husband taught music at various universities. She also raised dogs, kept an impeccable kennel and had two children, a boy and a girl. Sarah's grandmother looked after the children, helped the lady of the house with the accounting books for the kennel, and traveled extensively with the family throughout Europe to various musical engagements. When the two children were old enough to shed the need of a governess, Sarah's grandmother met an Irish charmer who worked for the Massachusetts Railroad. The Jerner family finally rested their laurels in Northampton, Massachusetts at Smith College, where Dickinson, Margaret Mitchell, Betty Friedan, and Gloria Steinam, among others were graduates. Sarah's grandparents were both older, and unmarried, when they finally tied the knot, which was very uncommon for this time during Franklin D. Roosevelt's presidency. Sarah's grandfather was a stoic type, kept his peace, watched the horse races like a hawk, and kept his sure-fire Irish charm in his back pocket, only releasing it to a few trusted souls. He smoked an occasional cigar, teased his wife with a few flirtatious jests, and always donned a woolen Irishman's cap. He told stories with a charm and hyperbolic wit that only Irishmen can do, and he reveled in his son's pursuits, as he seemed to take on the dual role well: macho, muscle-bound basketball player and sensitive, mathematical piano player. He had never been able to do it, so he enjoyed living vicariously through his son. He kept a close distance, as his wife seemed to dote over their son's every move, and he didn't want to suffocate the poor boy. That kind of attention from one parent is enough!

Sarah looked forward to the moments with her father, as both sisters did. And the frequent airplane trips and car rides were the starting point of Sarah's adventurous spirit. She loved to travel, as she always associated traveling with something pleasurable, as her father was always on the other end of the journey. She reveled in the special treatment she received from the airline personnel, as she traveled along or with her sister, under the age of twelve. Many of the airline stewardesses in their crisp and neatly pressed uniforms accompanied Sarah through the long, bustling hallways. And always, exactly before they boarded the plane, Sarah and her sister always asked to see the cockpit. She was curious about the mysterious men who flew these massive pieces of machinery, and loved to see all the instruments and gadgets that lay in front of the two men with the equally as crisp uniforms and pilot caps. They were always so kind and delighted in the presence of two curious children heading into the skies. Sarah always sat by the window, and looked out into those clouds and dreamed. She let her imagination run wild in a world of sunshine, blue skies and rainbows. She always delighted in the fact that no matter what the weather was like on the Earth, she could simply travel through the clouds and there, above the darkness, were blue skies and sunshine. You always hear the cliché that although it may be cloudy, you know the sun is always shining behind the clouds. And her plane rides were living proof that this cliché was real.

Her father had remarried shortly after the divorce was final with Sarah's mother. He wasn't entirely sold on the marriage, but things had been happening so quickly for him ever since he had decided to leave Sarah's mother, and he asked this spunky new college classmate to marry him, on an instinct, on a whim. They had only known each other for a few months, but she seemed like the right woman. He had a feeling about her when he saw her after class one day at the local community college in Newport News. She was in her car, and they had agreed to meet somewhere after class. He was following her in his little Morris Garages (MG) sports car, and saw a banana peel fly out of her car window, followed shortly thereafter by another. Lunch.

Health had always been one of the most important things in his life – and this little indicator was enough to prove to him that she could share his healthy lifestyle for the rest of their days. She accepted his proposal, with the same, "What the hell?" attitude, as she had recently divorced her first-husband, and had two budding teenage boys to think about. So, they married, and she soon became the wife of a Navy seaman with two young daughters somewhere in Newport News, Virginia. But the two girls were too young to know what was happening at the time. It was 1978.

# Chapter Thirteen

*This is the miracle that happens every time to those who really love;*
*the more they give, the more they possess.*

**Rainer Mara Rilke (1875-1926)**

Sarah's father had a spark. He had always had it since he was born, and his life experiences polished and shined it to perfection. He had the same Irish wit that his father had, but he possessed a gentleness and sensitivity that he only revealed to the women in his life. He was a perfect gentleman, trained and bred by a prim-and-proper, doting mother, and polished by the Navy. He always involved himself in athletics – basketball teams, racquetball, tennis – he even weight-lifted for some time, and earned the title of the strongest man in one of the small towns in Massachusetts from a weight-lifting competition. Surely, this title was more for his ego, more than for any other purpose, as any man cannot help but admit that being the strongest man alive is a boyhood fantasy that often extends to adulthood. He was a vegetarian, read all of the new literature about natural and healthy eating that surfaced in the early 1970s and even raised his first daughter, Meghan as a vegetarian. Sarah and Meghan's mother was always a good sport and became vegetarian with him. He jogged, and took care of his body. But he also spent hours at the piano, playing the latest James Taylor or Chopin, whatever struck his fancy, and took well to married life. He knew that he harbored a freedom that would soon manifest, but for the time being, he was in the Navy, all of his other Navy buddies had wives, and it seemed like the thing to do.

He was content with his newfound role of father and husband, but something – something that is so difficult to name – itched the back of his heart. Maybe this role of father and husband, with the dog, and the new house, and a new account at Sears and the new set of bedroom furniture – maybe this wasn't his place. He harbored the dreamer inside of him as well, and it was lost beneath all these expectations that surrounded him. He threw himself into his work, his buddies, his piano, his sports, but the uneasiness grew.

About the same time, the second daughter, Sarah, arrived, and the marriage barely stood on two feet. Sarah's mother was in Northampton, Massachusetts with his parents, while he was in Norfolk surveying the area for a suitable house to live, as he was being transferred to the Hampton Roads area. His second daughter was born and he raced up the Eastern seaboard to see his new daughter, and raced back down to report for duty. Sarah's mother felt like a foreigner in her husband's parent's home shortly after giving birth, plus, she was feeling ill and overwhelmed by all of the events. So, Meghan stayed with the grandparents, and Sarah's mother took her newborn daughter to her own mother's house across the way in another town in Massachusetts. Her mother was not exactly welcoming, as she had never agreed with her daughter's marriage from the get-go. So, Sarah's mother tried to nurse herself back to health, after giving birth to a ten-pound baby who was delivered ten days after the due date (and during one of the most famous World Series in history, at least from a Boston Red Sox fan's perspective, in 1975), while nursing this newborn. She had always believed in natural childbirth, including the naturalness of breast-feeding, but came close to giving her newborn a bottle, as she was so sick herself.

106

She felt alone, as her husband had to report to duty, and she had long since separated herself, emotionally, from her mother, as she didn't approve of her daughter's choice of a husband. Who wouldn't? The woman must have been off her rocker, as Sarah's father was every Irish schoolgirl's mother's dream!

She spent a few days with her mother, and quickly reunited again with Meghan, as Meghan was eager to play the role of Mommy's helper and big sister to Sarah. The three joined their father in Newport News, settled in a new house, and began to form their new life in the South.

Sarah's father spent more and more time away from home, and Sarah's mother began to suspect that there were other women involved. Even if there weren't, Sarah's father was beginning to nurture the seed of freedom, which began to grow within him.

Both were raised staunch Catholics, and Sarah's father even played the organ in the town's church every Sunday for Mass when he was a little boy. It was something he was proud of at first, but then became more of a show-off piece for his mother, which lessened his pleasure in the weekly practice. At age eighteen, when he graduated and moved to the big city of Boston to attend college, he was happy to put his organ playing days behind him, much to the dismay of his mother, and the church parish.

But even though they were both staunch Catholics, Sarah's father began to question the foundations of his spirituality and began reading much spiritual literature of the day about the cosmos, which offered a different view of religion, much different from the rigid rules and structures that the Catholic Church represented for him. His seed of freedom was now blossoming into a full-grown tree. He tried to share some of his revelations and enlightenments with his wife, but this new man scared her. She saw these new ideas and philosophies as a direct threat to her marriage. These new ideas about the universe and our place in it were far too much for her at the time. She was worried about diapers and dinners and casserole recipes and storybooks. It was not that she was incapable of comprehending such ideas, but she just wasn't ready for them at that time. He seemed to be so enthusiastic about this newfound knowledge, and she only saw it as something that took his attention away from her and their children. The more indignant she became about his interest in this new life philosophy, the more inward he became, as he didn't have anyone to share it with. The more and more he withdrew, the more desperate she became, as she felt she was losing him. She suggested that they attend counseling together, and he did it for her, but they met with a Catholic priest, as Sarah's mother began to turn more and more to the Catholic Church for comfort and peace. But this Catholic priest and counselor almost seemed like an impostor to him at this point, as he questioned the faith in which he was raised, and from the standpoint from which this priest in front of him now stood. Everything seemed to happen so quickly for him, and he wanted nothing more but to share these open-ended philosophical ideas with someone. Even the Navy began to lose its spark to him, as he began to read more and more about the universe, and the great masters who had asked the same questions about existence which he now seemed to harbor. He had begun the universal search that many take.

But there was a problem. He now had a wife with two children, who were still centered in the life that they had started many years ago, and it seemed as if he was growing by leaps and bounds, but his wife wasn't. But she couldn't, at that point, as she could only think about raising two children. Motherhood was something new and extraordinary for her, and she was embarking on her own new discoveries, and at that time, she was incapable of questioning the cosmos. She wanted nothing more but to share her new discoveries of motherhood, crock pots, Tupperware and fondue plates with her husband, and her husband was contemplating his existence and the universal energy that runs throughout. Certainly, they were in different worlds.

But he felt like he was ready to burst. He needed out. And so, he left on Good Friday, two days before Easter. It was a symbolic blow against the Catholic Church, against everything he was raised upon. He wasn't sure where he was going but he needed to feel free.

A few months passed, and Sarah's mother threw herself into Church. She participated in a weekend retreat that offered a supportive network of friends in a faith-based setting. She formed special friendships on this De Colores retreat that would form for life.

These were some of the friends who would prove their loyalty, and lack thereof, even in the break-up of Sarah's mother's second marriage.

But there was one in particular, Cinda, who saw a golden opportunity to help Sarah's mother in her first marriage. Cinda and Sarah's mother had been acquaintances for a few weeks. They were about the same age, attended the same church, and Cinda had a daughter who was about Sarah's age. Sarah's mother was desperate for support and companionship at this point in her life, as her husband had just left her with two small children, and she felt as if she had no one. She was in a state where she had no family, and she had alienated her mother by marrying this man, so she felt as if she had no one. She had estranged herself from her family, as they had their own problems, and she was eager to start a new life of her own. This church retreat felt like a safe place for her and she felt comfortable talking about her recent problems, as she didn't know what to do. And, to boot, her husband had recently called with a softened heart and wanted to try to patch things up and come back home. She didn't know what to do, as she had been so wounded by the act of him leaving, that she didn't know if she could accept him back so readily. Plus, she had her pride as well.

She explained her dilemma to the group, and one friend in particular, Cinda, listened intently and recognized the problem. She approached Sarah's mother after the meeting and swiftly took her under her wing.

She suggested that she should see a lawyer to settle the matter all together. Her husband was the perfect lawyer to see. Sarah's mother met with Cinda's husband, and he suggested that in order to have the divorce meet her favor, they needed to prove that he was cheating on her. Somehow, Sarah's mother knew where her husband had been spending the night. Cinda's husband placed an egg behind Sarah's mother's husband's car at eleven o'clock in the evening. He went back to check it the next morning, and the egg was still in tact. In those days, this was proof enough that Sarah's mother's husband was cheating on her, and gave her grounds for divorce.

No mention was made that he had wanted to work things out. Cinda's husband proceeded with the paperwork, and Sarah's parents started their lives again, apart.

# Chapter Fourteen

*The harder the conflict, the more glorious the triumph. What we obtain too cheaply, we esteem too lightly; 'Tis dearness only that gives everything its value.*

**Thomas Paine (1737-1809)**

Sarah's mother had grown up in a small town in Massachusetts. She had gone straight from her mother's lap to her husband's, and now she was charting waters on her own. She had to trust the lawyer with the credentials in front of her, especially because he was the husband of a church-going woman. She had no other choice, and a trusting heart.

So, the next time Sarah's father called to make apologies and attempt some kind of reconciliation, Sarah's mother said that she had a lawyer and was filing for divorce.

He was stunned. But there was nothing he could do at this point. The deed was done. She had made up her mind.

Things were happening so quickly and he couldn't seem to stop them. He was taking a few classes at the local community college in Newport News, where he was able to find a haven for some type of academic discussion. And it was about this time when he met Sally, the petite, banana-eating spitfire who chucked banana peels out of the window of a speeding car. She seemed like a good, free-minded woman, she was healthy, able to take and accept his ideas. Why not marry her? So, he proposed, and Sarah then acquired a stepmother, and two new stepbrothers, Timothy and Thomas in 1978.

But the year 1991 was a different story. Sarah adapted to her new life at Lucy's house well, and Brownie provided a conducive environment for the girl who had already been through so much. Sarah quickly forgot the events of the past few months, and threw herself into her studies and her classes. Her friendship with Lucy grew by leaps and bounds. But Brownie noticed that Sarah was always sick, and stifling a sniffle and a cough. It was soon passed to Lucy, while Sarah recovered, but then passed back again to Sarah, while Lucy recovered, and this cycle continued to take its course. Brownie attempted to load the girls with vitamins and healthy foods, but the persistent cold continued to be passed back and forth between the two girls. They didn't seem to notice it much, but to a concerned mother, this was torture. Finally, in conversation over breakfast one morning, Brownie discovered that the two girls had been sharing the same toothbrush. In Sarah's mad rush to leave her family house in the dark of the night, she had forgotten to pack her toothbrush in the black trash bag, which served as her suitcase. As Sarah did not want to be more of a burden to the already burdened mother, she kept quiet about the lack of a toothbrush, and Lucy seemed content in sharing such an item with her best friend. They had grown to share everything else, why not a toothbrush? Brownie was horrified to discover the deficiency! A new toothbrush was bought for the newcomer, and the cold slowly dissipated, and two healthy girls soon emerged.

Sarah almost forgot the horrors of her past life in this tranquil environment. She didn't hear much from her mother, and Sarah didn't make the initiative to call either, as she wished to forget that life altogether. Her mother drove her to her doctors' appointments for her leg, and Sarah noticed that her mother was different. Sarah's mother managed to ask a few questions about Sarah's new life, but Sarah could tell that she didn't ask the questions to hear the answers; she asked the questions to fill the air. It was not that Sarah's mother didn't care; she just didn't have the energy to provide interest. She actually felt comfortable and somewhat safe in her daughter's presence, and used this time to recover from the atrocities that were happening in her own home. She was just happy and relieved that her daughter was safe. She didn't talk about the events of the past, but only talked of the happiness of the present, which warmed her mother's heart. It took her out of the world that was her reality back home, the reality that consumed all of her energy and spirit. She was happy that her daughter was no longer a part of it. She didn't talk about what was happening back home, as things got much worse after Sarah left.

Meanwhile, Sarah lost herself at Lucy's house. She almost forgot about her real family until the ninth day of November, the day her grandmother died.

Grammy was the only grandmother Sarah really knew, as she lived longer than her mother's mother. And what a spirited Irish lass she was! Sarah only knew her with a head full of snow-white curly thick hair, but was told she had a mane of flaming red curls in her heyday. She was a beautiful Irish lass with an iron disposition. She lived in Northampton, Massachusetts faithfully from the day she married her husband during Franklin D. Roosevelt's presidency. She and her husband, as a wedding gift, received a set of Irish linens from a prominent shop in New York City. Sarah discovered this box, years later. The linens were unused; the tissue paper from the 1940s still in tact, and the box contained an enveloped business card with the name Henry Morgenthau, Jr., Roosevelt's Secretary of the Treasury, printed on the front. On the back of the card was a quick note: "To Harry and Helen on their wedding day. Best wishes, Henry." Sarah still hasn't solved the mystery, but time will tell.

Sarah's grandmother always harbored the wish that Meghan would attend Smith College, the college situated in her front yard. The family's patriarch, whose children she raised, was a music professor for Smith College after the family settled down from their travels and musical jaunts through Europe, after the Lady retired from the New York Opera. The College even named their Music Library after him after he died. But Smith College just wasn't in the cards for Meghan, much to her grandmother's dismay.

Grammy had a soft spot in her heart for Meghan. Meghan had the same flaming red mane, and a subtle spark and genius that her grandmother saw from the beginning. She was gentle, and soft-spoken, but kept a diligent concentration on any project in front of her. Her concentration was astounding, Grammy thought, and would no doubt serve her in later years.

Her girls always lived in Virginia, far away from her grounds in Massachusetts. She had always wanted many children, but due to many medical complications, and a few miscarriages, her son, Sarah's father, was her only child. She had always wanted a girl, so Meghan and Sarah were gems.

Their visits were frequent when they came to see their father in the summers and winters, and the girls would come to her residential home, St. Michael's, which, in previous years, had been St. Michael's, the Catholic all-boys school, which her son attended, but was now a residential home for old folks. They renovated the place nicely and she was happy in her small living quarters.

To the last day, she never let anything go. She always wore her best outfits with her necklaces and bracelets, and she always smelled like Grammy — a distinguishable aroma of baby powder, perfume, and antiquated goodness. She loved to wear different shades of purple and blue, and shuffled the girls along to social events to the last day she could walk on two feet. The minute they walked into her sweet haven, she was on the phone with every relative within a one hundred-mile radius. Sarah dreaded it at the time, talking into that perfume-smelling phone with lipstick caked on the edges, but she understands now why she did it. She knew those girls needed to feel as if they belonged to a family. And she would die attempting, even until the last moment, doing so.

114

Visits involved trips to the pool, and the Fourth of July picnics with thousands of relatives and cousins. Grammy knew each one by name, whom they were married to, how many children they had, where they went to college, whom they were related to, and performed her little social duties. Sarah and Meghan's father disappeared for all of these events. He had endured enough during his own childhood, and certainly did not want to relive the memories he had spent years forgetting. He resented it, and spent the majority of his adulthood estranging himself from the relatives that his mother had tried so intensely to connect him with. It was not their fault. Yes, all families have their goofballs and their idiosyncrasies and strange behaviors, but that's what families are about, right? They make life interesting. And Grammy was a woman of persistence, and continued the practice of social graces with her grandchildren. And the social graces would later prove to be the saving graces for the family, as Grammy was the one sense of normalcy that the two girls would remember as they reached adulthood. She was the one true preserver of a generation gone by where social callings and gatherings were still revered.

Sarah and Meghan always felt awkward at these gatherings and house visits. They weren't accustomed to calling on relatives and cousins, to have a glass of lemonade on a summer afternoon, or to sit around a living room to talk. The relatives always brought out the finest dishes and patio sets for their grandmother. They always took the girls to the nicer areas of the house – to the living room – to engage in conversation. Sarah awkwardly looked around each room, each house, studying the wall decorations, the pictures, the knick-knacks, the memorabilia. There were always school photographs of Meghan and Sarah displayed throughout each home, no doubt supplied by Grammy. She was the one connection, as their father didn't perform such social customs, and certainly, neither did their mother, although the former knew the customs and the rituals quite well, as he had been born and bred on them. And Grammy, God rest her Soul, even took her grandchildren on social calls to their mother's side of the family! Imagine the courage, the strength and the humility it took for her to make calls, for the grandchildren's future, to their mother's aunt's small apartment. Sarah's mother never took her there, so the reason why Meghan and Sarah got to know their great-aunt from the Polish side of the family was because of the sheer fortuitousness and insight of their Irish grandmother. Think of the humility! Think of the wisdom! The two women didn't speak between the times that the grandchildren visited. Grammy made the calls for them. But the two girls didn't realize this at the time. It was just another home they were visiting – another person to talk to – another person who asked questions about school activities – another house that wore different photographs on the walls – a different house that seemed to roll out a red carpet at her grandmother's presence.

# Chapter Fifteen

*When I stand before thee at the day's end, thou shalt see my scars and know that I had my wounds and also my healing.*

**Rabindranath Tagore (1861-1941)**

So, Grammy died at a symbolic time. At this time, Sarah wanted nothing more but to forget the family she came from, and Grammy's death seemed to bring everyone together. All of the people whose houses they visited, all of the countless cousins at picnics, and even people she didn't know, from the community, from church, from her previous mysterious life that she never talked about but that seemed to command a respect and royal treatment, came together for her grandmother's death. But Sarah was in another world. She could not muster the energy to understand these mysterious implications. She was trying desperately to block out the events of her past life, which even included the good times, as memory is not selective in situations as grave as these.

A plane ticket arrived at Lucy's house, and Sarah flew to Massachusetts for her grandmother's funeral. She was still in a cast and crutches, and was very much aware of her awkwardness and lack of movement. When the memory and mind try desperately to forget unspeakable pains of the past, the brain can only concentrate its efforts on the emotions of the present moment, and Sarah felt as if her whole body was encased in the cast that, in reality, only occupied her leg. Nonetheless, it was the first funeral she attended, and was quite curious, mostly because of the open-casket wake. The wake was a beautiful two-hour period of peaceful and tranquil conversations with friends and family. They flitted in and out of the old New England home with gabled porticos that protruded from the second story, creating quaint little nooks on the inside of the upstairs rooms. Sarah peered for the last time at Grammy's snowy white hair, and thought fondly of all of those moments that etched themselves on her heart.

Like this one, for instance: Grammy never learned how to drive until her husband died, when she was in her late seventies, so she got her drivers license, a gigantic, black car, with a bench front seat, and the best damn air-conditioning system this side of France. It was an Oldsmobile, with the automatic shift gears on the steering wheel shaft. Meghan always sat by the window, and Sarah sat in the middle, in between the two. She loved sitting here as she was close to her grandmother's smell, and the comforting tinkling of the movements of her necklaces and bracelets with trinkets and beads, as she shifted the gears of the car. Plus, she was directly in front of the air-conditioning vents. Imagine going from a nineteen hundred and seventy-one Volvo, full of six children vying for attention, and even a mere glimpse of an air-conditioning vent that may or may not work, to a new Oldsmobile, driven by a clear-headed and patient woman who always listened when you spoke, and never solicited an inappropriate comment, with a front row seat to the air and the action! Sarah felt as if she had become queen for a day. But what intrigued Sarah the most, with the jingling sounds of jewelry, was the full view of Grammy's right arm as she reached for the gearshift or air controls. The skin that hung below her tricep was milky white, and softer than any blanket Sarah had ever touched. It looked as if it had never been exposed in the near eighty years of her life. And only when Sarah was feeling a bit daring, would she touch it. Who knows what Grammy was thinking, as her youngest grandchild touched the underside of her tricep of her right arm, but she admired the child's curiosity and wonder. Surely, she saw that Meghan had softness and a quiet intellect, but Sarah was the spitfire, the one to test boundaries, the one who would endure the most trials throughout her life because of it. The little subtle things in life, like her grandmother's milky white arm, and the jingling of the trinkets on her grandmothers charm bracelet that donned profiles of her grandchildren's heads, or the aroma of baby powder, perfume, and raisin-oatmeal cookies that her grandmother emitted, these things always went unnoticed by her older sister. Meghan looked out of the window and contemplated how she was going to change the world. She contemplated the implications of Grammy's generation and her constant use of the word, "Coloreds," to describe the black folks in the street. Sarah delighted wide-eyed at her grandmother's arm and the strong, cold air that seemed to blow directly into her nostrils.

But as they drove that hot summer day, Sarah noticed that Grammy was driving on the wrong side of the road, heading toward oncoming traffic. Meghan and Sarah had joked in private about Grammy's driving style, but their snickering was always about subtle discrepancies, which she quickly corrected. But this was a blatant infracture, and as they cruised down the road, cars swerved and blew their horns at the massive, black Oldsmobile cheerfully coasting down the wrong side of the road. Sarah began to chuckle and elbowed Meghan, as she stared wide-eyed at the events occurring in front of her eyes. Neither girl said anything to Grammy. It wasn't their place – she was driving, she was in control. Surely, Grammy heard the blaring horns and saw the swerving cars. Finally, after a few minutes, and after Sarah was nearly in a laughing, wide-eyed hysteric, Grammy smoothly and seriously maneuvered the massive piece of black machinery over to the correct lane and resumed the correct driving position without a word. Sarah whipped her head and looked at Meghan who was equally as baffled at what they had just experienced. No words were ever spoken about it. And to this day, Sarah wonders if Grammy did it to catch the two whippersnapper girls off-guard. Perhaps she knew that the two girls snickered about her driving. But surely, she would give them something to *really* snicker about.

# Chapter Sixteen

*A bibliophile of little means is likely to suffer often. Books don't slip from his hands but fly past him through the air, high as birds, high as prices.*

**Pablo Neruda (1904-1973)**

Grammy's death came quickly. She had begun to forget little things in the last year; bills were not being paid, and her son's daily visits revealed more things that indicated a deterioration of her mental capacity.

She was thrilled and thrived when Meghan came to Massachusetts to live her with father for the first half of her senior year, as she saw Meghan frequently throughout the week. In between Meghan's three jobs, she always found enough time to swing by St. Michael's in Northampton to see her grandmother, to keep her updated on her life, on school, on college pursuits.

Northampton was a northern cultural center for eccentric activity and intellectualism. The main thoroughfare, Pleasant Street, was lined with natural shops, vegetarian restaurants and book stores, and the sidewalks were speckled with the diversity of its citizens. Used book shops and coffee houses were frequented by musicians, artists, poets and writers, and the independent theater scheduled cultural performances and movie premiers of documentary films like "Theo and Me," the story of Vincent van Gogh and Gauguin's friendship. Smith College, with its massive stone gothic architecture, emanated its intellectual, antiquated presence, and was supplemented by the other four colleges within a twenty-mile radius: University of Massachusetts, Hampshire College, Amherst College and Mt. Holyoke College.

Smith College was nestled along Elm Street, which branched off of Pleasant Street and the main thoroughfare, which led to the smaller towns of Western Massachusetts, including Florence. The houses that speckled themselves along Elm Street were unique, massive structures with character and a rare New England charm. One house was completely round, one had dozens of alcoves and gazebos that seemed to turn the house into a cookie-cutter's masterpiece. One house was surrounded by tall green shrubbery that seemed to have grown itself right out of an English estate's courtyard. And since Sarah had primarily grown up around these houses during Christmas and summer holidays, she associated these massive home-like structures with colorful Christmas trees, and American flags and banners. Each time they drove through the town of Northampton, Sarah counted the Christmas trees she saw in the windows. The conversation in the car was mute muffles to Sarah--- she was in her own world of counting Christmas trees and imagining the lives of the families that existed within the warm glow of the houses.

Northampton was also famous for its numerous used book shops and Bart's homemade ice cream. One could not take a trip to Northampton without stopping at Bart's for a treat—and oftentimes, a specific trip to Northampton was made for Bart's----it was that good. And soon, Bart's opened another ice cream parlor in Amherst, a town a little closer to Sarah's father's house on the banks of the Connecticut River. And soon, all of UMass's thirty thousand students discovered the divinity of Bart's. It was no longer an O'Higgins secret.

A little further down Elm Street, about a half a mile from Smith College, was Cooley Dickinson Hospital, where Sarah was born. Across the street from the hospital was Child's Park with its serene walkways and white, bulbous concrete studs that marked the flower-lined paths. Grammy took her granddaughters here in the summer, as it was only a short distance from her house, and organized Fourth of July picnics at the other park in town—Look Park.

Grammy always lit a novena candle to the Virgin Mary when her granddaughters left, and kept the candle burning until their return. She never talked about this with them, but Sarah noticed whenever the two arrived, after Grammy greeted them with thousands of kisses and "OOOOOOs" and "AAAHHHHHs," she walked over to her desk and blew out the candle. Once Sarah realized this ritual after every journey, she delighted in blowing out the candle herself, as a symbolic gesture that she was indeed there. And each time the girls left, Grammy stood watch in the row of five windows that lined her living room-apartment on the third floor, and waved goodbye. She never once forgot to wave goodbye. And she stood religiously, in that window, even far after they were gone. When she was very young, Sarah imagined that Grammy stood there all day, all night, all season, until their next visit, leaving the window only to light the novena candle.

Every Sunday, Grammy took her two granddaughters to St. Mary's Catholic Church which was across the street from St. Michael's. And Sunday Mass was always a requirement and a production. Grammy knew the priest personally, as she attended daily Mass, and had attended the same church for the past forty years or so. And I am quite certain that when the Church solicited its parishioners for a three million dollar renovation project, Grammy contributed a large donation for its new facelift. Grammy introduced her granddaughters to all of the church personnel, many of the familiar faces of the church, and the priest always knew that when Helen's granddaughters were present, they carried the gifts, the bread and wine, which were later turned into the Body and Blood of Christ, to the front of the altar where the priest stood waiting for them. Grammy always sat in the second or third pew, and always held her rosary in her hands. It was just another type of jingling and tinkering that accompanied the necklaces and bracelets that adorned her body. Sarah fidgeted, without understanding most of the words, meanings and rituals, and watched the mannerisms of her grandmother, which always fascinated her. The rituals of the Mass were intrinsic for Sarah, she knew every prayer, every motion of the body, every progression of the Mass, as she had been raised on it every Sunday, but she never understood their meanings. It was just a part of her life – like eating and sleeping. Mass was part of survival, and would prove in later years to be her only respite as the darkness of her memories that she spent years and years repressing came flooding back. It was only later, when she discovered what all those signs, symbols and rituals stood for. And by then, they had already become an intrinsic part of her being. Understanding their manifestation in her was just a part of the humbling mystery.

Sarah went back to St. Michael's Church, across from the campus of Smith College, in later years to pay respects to her grandmother's favorite haven, to relive a few of her fondest childhood moments, and to see if the same priest was still there. Alas, he was not, but Sarah did speak with the new Pastor of the parish and told him all about her grandmother: how she attended Mass everyday, how she helped to pay for the renovations of that lovely church that they were now sitting, and the priest seemed aloof, he seemed distant, as if to half-hear what Sarah was saying. Then, he even had the gall to ask *her* for a donation for a new renovation that was underway! "This is strange," Sarah thought and proceeded to ask the Pastor for an annual report, or a financial statement to verify the capital campaign's goals and objectives. He grew indignant, and seemed offended that Sarah would ask for such a document. His anger increased, as he back-peddled and back-peddled himself further into a corner, and Sarah left the church, the church that her grandmother loved, nurtured and cherished, with a heavy heart about the turn that one of God's priceless homes had taken.

Grammy still had her hopes set on Smith College for Meghan, and plugged her opinion every chance she got, but Meghan seemed to have another plan. At any rate, Grammy bathed in the time she had with Meghan. It was unlike any time she had spent with either of the two girls, so she cherished it, and held it close to her heart.

After Meghan left to finish her senior year in Virginia, Grammy's health deteriorated rapidly. Meghan and Sarah traveled to Massachusetts that summer, weeks before Sarah was hit by a car and broke her leg, and their father had moved Grammy to a nursing home. The Alzheimer's had taken its toll and their father could no longer manage the medication, meals and other bizarre situations he found when he arrived at St. Michael's each day. He was operating on autopilot himself, as he was not ready to deal with his mother's deterioration and the switch of the caretaker roles. She had always been the caretaker for him. Never, in a million years, did he think that he would be forced to take care of and make decisions for his mother. He wasn't ready for the change and he wasn't ready to face the reality of the death he knew was coming soon. He hadn't yet spoken his peace with her, he hadn't yet talked about his childhood and all the harbored resentments he had toward her doting behavior, nor about the love and respect for her that lay buried beneath thoughts and words. His father had gone quickly and silently in his sleep. This was easier for him, as he could deal with the pain of his father's death quickly, just as it happened. But this was different. He was forced to watch his headstrong mother, the woman who commanded the utmost respect from every person she came in contact with, lose all sense of dignity, wit and sharpness, and he was forced to make decisions that he didn't want to make. So, Sally, his wife, did most of the work. She went through all of Grammy's things, her furniture, her jewelry, her antiques, all of the things she acquired through the years in her jaunts to Europe, gifts from friends of the Jerner family, other mysterious gifts like the Irish linen set from Roosevelt's Secretary of Treasury, and every single letter and correspondence with every acquaintance she had. Grammy kept everything. But Sarah's father couldn't bear to go through it, so Sally did most of the work: decided what to keep, what to throw away, what to give away, and what to save for Meghan and Sarah. Sarah received a few things after her death – silverware, an opal ring, and a glass-blown candlestick from Germany – but they were few. Most importantly, though, she received two of Grammy's rosaries that she had acquired in Europe – one with black onyx beads, and another with crystal beads. These rosaries, in later years, would serve as Sarah's only beacon of Hope and Strength in the dark-filled nights of pain.

So, when Meghan and Sarah arrived the summer before her death, their father tried to prepare them for what they would see when they visited the nursing home. But no words could describe or prepare them for what they saw.

As they rode in the car toward the nursing home, Sarah's father turned down the classical music from the public broadcasting station. Meghan was sitting in the front seat and Sarah was in the back seat watching the fields of cattle roll by.

"Girls, I just want to tell you that Grammy looks very different."

"Dad, we know," Sarah said from the backseat.

"She's lost a lot of weight," he continued.

"It'll be fine. She's still Grammy."

Sarah looked back out into the sea of summer New England green that rolled past the window, as the sweet breeze brushed against her hair and face. She caught Meghan looking at her from the passenger-side mirror. Their eyes met to acknowledge what was happening. Sarah looked away back to the greenness of the fields.

Sarah's father dropped them off at the front entrance and said he'd be back in a little while——he had to run some errands, he said, but he wanted to give his two daughters some alone time with his mother.

Meghan and Sarah walked into the small room. Her bed was closest to the door. Her roommate's bed was empty and neatly made.

"Grammy!" Sarah exclaimed when she saw her, as if nothing was wrong. She wrapped her arms around her grandmother's neck.

Grammy lay in that bed with no spark, and no life. She had lost nearly forty pounds, and her cheeks had sunken into her skull like sandbags. Meghan and Sarah maintained their energy and enthusiasm for their entire visit, and even on the long walk down the nursing home hallway that led to the activity room, the two girls jabbered and chattered gaily around the hobbled, shuffling figure.

Another little, old lady appeared, and grabbed Sarah's hand as both girls were walking their grandmother down the long hallway to the activity room.

"How sweet," Sarah thought, "This woman must have no relatives to visit her so she is trying to share Grammy's visitors." Sarah clutched her hand but then the old woman began to walk faster than Grammy and Meghan, and pulled Sarah into another room, talking gaily about her family.

After a while, Sarah patted the old woman on the hand, "I'm sorry," Sarah said, "but I should get back to my grandmother."

Sarah joined Meghan and Grammy in the hallway and Sarah reached for her grandmother's free arm and they clutched each other, recognizing their differences and mistakes, but showing their loyal love. When they reached the activity room, Grammy sat on the small couch in the sun, as its rays filtered through the curtain-less window.

Sarah played a few short songs on the antiquated, out-of-tune piano that lay abandoned in the corner of the nursing room's empty activity room, and the two girls walked Grammy back to her bed. The two girls were not prepared for this role reversal. On all of their previous visits with their grandmother, she steered the events, she offered cookies, or made phone calls, or scurried about for something she had in safe keeping for the girls, she walked from room to room, displaying greeting cards from relatives, photographs from social gatherings, a newspaper clipping or a prayer card. There was always something new and exciting in their grandmothers' hands. But here, Meghan and Sarah were left with the task of steering the conversation. They felt awkward, and unnatural. Sarah was somewhat comforted by the prolific display of their school photographs throughout the room, but she was still at a loss. That was the last time that Sarah saw her grandmother alive.

How does life prepare one for such a moment? When one is young, one doesn't realize the beautiful attributes that a human being brings life until they are no longer in it. Grammy drifted through life with grace--- she never imposed herself on anyone, and she always helped others from the sidelines, without asking for accolades or recognition. She was quiet and humble. But her presence always commanded respect----both from the people she knew and those she didn't know. She gave her granddaughters everything she had.

When Meghan and Sarah left the nursing home on that bright summer afternoon, they walked away from the stifling air of the suffocating institution. The stench and air of the building seemed to saturate their lungs, and although they upheld their enthusiasm and spirit within its walls, they now gasped for air as they walked side-by-side out into the sunshine.

Once they were not within eyesight of their grandmother, and only a few mere meters in front of the front doors on the flower-lined brick walkway, they turned to each other and embraced with reckless abandon. They clung to each other for dear life. Tears ran from both of their eyes, and their bodies convulsed as they embraced each other in a desperate attempt for comfort. No. Indeed, no words would prepare them for that. And no words could be spoken after they left----only pure emotion.

Their grandmother's death was a uniting point of much more than what it initially appeared to be. During the wake, a peaceful and ominous snow began to fall, deep into the afternoon, and by the time they left the old New England house where family and friends gathered for Grammy's sake, a good six inches blanketed the ground in a splendor, and placed a calming trance on the town. The world seemed to stop for a moment, as if to savor the last moments of a saint's life gone by. The burial was quick and brief, and her body joined her husband's beneath a simple granite grave with a simple and orderly ceremony. Sarah's father seemed to remember all of the social graces that he had been taught years ago by the woman who lay in the open casket before him, and it surprised Sarah, as it was the only time she ever saw it in action. The morning soon turned to evening, and everyone seemed to be relieved that the formalities were over.  Sarah's father drove her to the Hartford airport the next day, and that was the last time she would visit Massachusetts by plane.

She returned to Brownie's home in King's Gate, and she returned to school and the life ahead of her.

But she had no idea where her life was heading.  She knew she wanted to go to college, to be successful, to love, to be loved--- and it was nothing more complicated than that.  She didn't know much about the woman's life whose funeral she had just attended.  She just knew her smell, her milky-white skin, her large eyes that she tucked away behind her bifocals, the jingles of her bracelets and necklaces, and the love in her heart that was only felt years later-----much later, after she was gone.

# Chapter Seventeen

*Live all you can. It's a mistake not to. It doesn't so much matter what you do in particular, so long as you have your life. If you haven't had that, what have you had?*

**Henry James (1843-1916)**

By Christmas, Meghan had secured an apartment in one of the cheapest complexes in Williamsburg. It was situated off the main thoroughfare behind a string of restaurants and hotels. To tourists, the main thoroughfare consisted of the famous Captain George's Seafood Restaurant, the Ramada Inn, and the small outlet shops that included Ralph Lauren Polo, Fila, Linen and Things, American Tourister, Mikasa, and Ben and Jerry's Ice Cream. But only the locals knew about the cheap apartment complex tucked far behind Richmond Road.

She secured a two-bedroom, specifically for the purpose of housing her sixteen-year-old sister. Sarah moved to her new quarters, and her mother bought her an inexpensive car to carry her back and forth to school. The apartment was located in James City County, and Sarah did her best to hide her whereabouts, as she was technically, illegally attending Somerset High School, as she was a James City County resident, even though she was much closer to her high school. But for tax purposes, her mother was still claiming her as a dependent, so her residence, was, according to the government, in York County.

Sarah slipped from middle to upper-income family living to apartment living in a borderline-ghetto area fairly quickly. She didn't care much as she felt she was free, she was with her sister, and she was not constrained by any five-minute phone rules. Her free moments of homework and after school projects were soon replaced with other activities, and her grades suffered. She managed to finish her junior year without too many complications. She always, by some stroke of good fortune, maintained a high B average, and graduated nineteenth in her class with a grade point average of three point twelve. But this semester, and this year, affected her average dramatically. She maintained friendships with all of the same friends, but also began to hang out with a different sort of group – these were the folks who also lived in apartments, and didn't have a strong parental influence. These were the folks who prided themselves on their freedom, and partook in activities with reckless abandon, and without any contemplation of the consequences. The memories and experiences of years of anguish were easily buried in these surroundings for Sarah. She didn't have to think about her past. She could create layers and layers of new friendships and new lives, where the daily conversation centered around the newest Budweiser commercial or the latest drug bust in an apartment complex across the way.

Sarah saw crack deals behind gas stations. She sat in the middle of smoke-filled rooms as people passed all different sorts of colorful bongs around the room, coughing until their eyes rolled back in their head. She once went to one apartment where she noticed a large hole, about the size of a quarter, in the living room wall that led to a bedroom. She inquired about it and discovered that someone had accidentally shot a sawed-off shotgun from the bedroom on the other side of the wall. The bullet flew through the living room, and penetrated the opposite wall. The living room contained several people who had stopped by for their daily bong hit. The bullet missed a person sitting on the sofa by a few inches.

This new type of living was, in a strange and convoluted way, comforting to Sarah, because they didn't care who she was. She didn't have a role to fulfill with them, and most of them were so high anyway that they probably didn't notice her presence. She usually sat with these gatherings, on the sofa, somewhat involved with the group, or involved enough that they didn't cast a suspicious eye on the girl who always passed the bong without taking a hit. She sat and intently observed everyone's mannerisms: the way they talked to each other, the things that they talked about, what happened when a newcomer entered the room, what happened when someone knocked on the door, what they watched on television, what music they listened to, what kinds of people entered, what types of clothing they wore, if they felt comfortable or not in the room. She silently slid into the sofa, and silently observed. Most of the time, the music was blaring so loud through speakers that the sound could put an outdoor concert to shame, so conversation wasn't always needed or possible. Sarah could lose herself there, and blend with the music, as everyone else did, and run fearlessly and boldly away from her problems.

She learned a lot about speakers and cars during that time, along with all of the paraphernalia that go with such interests: Momo steering wheels, ground effects kits, hydraulics, the legal and illegal limits for tinted windows in the state of Virginia, how low a car can be lowered on its suspension springs without acquiring a ticket from the State Police, the proper way to wash and wax a car, the difference between biscuit tires and fifteen-inch-rims, the difference between ten-inch woofers and twelve-inch-woofers, how tweeters should be installed, the difference between Blaupunkt, Kenwood, Alpine and Sony stereo systems, how to change a tire, how to change the oil, how to gut-out a catalytic converter system to make a car sound mean (but never learned that the process kills the environment), how to impeccably clean a car with Armoral, how to install fluorescent lights underneath the carriage of a car, and when it was safe, and when it was not safe, to turn them on. She learned a lot about football, too.

She learned what two-for-two meant, she learned what it meant to "blitz," she got to know the team players' names, and noticed when they switched teams, or were injured.

She saw a very different kind of lifestyle, very quickly, and she quickly forgot about the white macadamia-nut cookies that Brownie made every week, or the little notes she left on the counter with her perfectly penned writing, or the cutest collection of Halloween decorations that were sprinkled throughout the house. There was none of that to be found there. There, existence became a banal form of survival. But she didn't know it at the time, she was just living.

About the same time, Brownie had been thinking a lot about her own marriage, and her own sense of harbored freedom that seemed to grow wings overnight. The dreamer in her was beginning to surface, and her strong sense and determination began to make decisions about her own life. A new condominium complex had just been built in York County – the first of its kind in the county – and Brownie felt that the time was right to break out on her own. She had felt that her independence had been stifled for long enough, and she was ready to be free.

In the beginning of her marriage she was instrumental in the shaping of the League of Women Voters in her small Ohio town, and highly involved in politics, both on a local and national level. She always kept herself highly informed of all the elections and any other political endeavors that ensued in the areas where she lived. She worked meticulously and diligently in the early 1970s, in Betty Freidan's prime, while pregnant with her first-born son, with the League and its impact on the area. She found a network of women, also pregnant or with children, with whom she could interchangeably talk politics or talk motherhood. But, without fail, her summers were always spent on Long Beach Island in New Jersey, a tradition she adored from her youth. And that tradition continued with her children, and still continues today.

Sarah grew to know Long Beach Island well, as she accompanied Lucy and her mother on two summer vacations. The original house, a small Cape-Codder, was situated on a corner lot on the sound. The house was owned by Auntie Ginger, Brownie's mother's sister. But it served as a gathering place for both families: Brownie's mother's side, and Auntie Ginger's side. Auntie Ginger had two sons, Bob and Ted. Bob became an investment banker in Philadelphia, married Martha Stewart's twin sister (well, almost!), Barbee, and had two children, Scott and Samantha. Sarah never met any of this side of the family, but felt as if she knew them well by all the stories. Ted, on the other hand, was a spitfire. He had a spark that nestled itself comfortably in his chest, and Sarah immediately nicknamed him, "Rebel Ted," just from the way he maneuvered his silver-bullet Volvo station wagon through the streets of Long Beach Island to their favorite Italian restaurant, Luciano's. He married Connie, had two lovely children, Little Teddy and Rosalind, and a beautiful black lab, Buddy, whom Sarah took an immediate liking to.

Sarah always had a special connection with dogs. She had always been around them in her youth, and perhaps the love stemmed from her grandmother who had been around the Jerner's family kennel as a young woman, or perhaps it came from her father who insisted on owning an Irish setter in his first marriage to Sarah's mother. He and Brannon, the full-bred Irish Setter, that was wounded in a hunting accident, and was no longer suitable for the strenuous hunts, were best friends. Sarah's father taught him all sorts of useful tricks, and often draped the large dog around his neck like a woman's shawl or afghan blanket. The dog loved it – didn't squirm a bit at such antics, and loved his new life as man's best friend. Sarah's father loved to pretend like *he* was Brannon, and approached the young girl on all-fours, with a cold wet nose, that sniffed and sniffed and sniffed on Sarah's bare neck, until it got closer and closer to her ear, and the young girl couldn't help but squeal with delight. She often tried to see how long she could withstand the sniffing human nose, which thought it was a dog, before she was overcome with the chills and sensation of the tickles. So, perhaps, this is why she was so fond of dogs – because they reminded her of the silly childhood games her father played with her. Sarah always joked that she thought she connected with dogs more than with people, as she always seemed to know what they were thinking. Or perhaps they had always been personified for her, even by her sister.

Her sister was always a serious child. She took the world very seriously, and never quite grasped the good humor that her father possessed. Sarah will never forget the day, about two years after their father left, that Meghan approached her one morning after she had stayed awake much later than their usual bedtime. Meghan was allowed to "stay-up" with Brannon, the trusted Irish setter, which their father had left behind, much to the dismay of the trusty dog. The next morning, Meghan approached Sarah with a serious and concerned look that commanded Sarah's immediate attention. Meghan explained to Sarah in a slow and methodical voice that Brannon had talked to her the previous night. Both of the girls, aged four and eight, sat in silent awe for a few moments. Sarah was jealous that the moment in which Brannon chose to speak was the moment when she was asleep. The two sisters joke about this story now, as the seriousness that surrounded the conversation was riveting.

So, the combination of the family's fascination with dogs created a nostalgic feeling in Sarah, who visited a foreign home on Long Beach Island, so she instantly took to Buddy, the happy-go-lucky black lab. Sarah soon discovered that a certain type of "language" she used produced an immediate response in the dog, which the family had never heard from the dog before, so Sarah was quickly welcomed into the home, on account of Buddy.

Ted worked in Philadelphia as well, but always made a point to spend the majority of his summer at the beach. This was a priority for him, and it was reflected in his tranquil demeanor. He was calm, always in control of his senses, cracked an occasional joke, but he had the spark in him. One could see it in the sparkle in his eye. And even though Sarah observed him now, as an adult, with a wife and two children, she could see the young boy in him; she could see the young boy that Brownie played with summer after summer on those same beaches and sound docks. He kept the child within, which is a difficult task, as any adult can attest to.

He lived life like an adventure, never took anything too seriously, and delighted in his children's' pursuits. Connie and his children spent the whole summer at the beach house, and Bob and his family, and Brownie and her family, came for two weeks or more throughout the summer. The investment banking industry kept Bob in the city most of the time, and Scott and Samantha were working summer jobs on their break home from college, so the house was never quite full.

A couple of years before Sarah traveled with Lucy and Brownie to Long Beach Island, the house was completely renovated. The old Cape-Codder received a face-lift and a new modern, bright and cheery house emerged, with clean crisp angles and windows to make use of the beautiful sunsets that graced the sound. The back French doors led straight to a dock, where generations of families learned to sail. Connie decorated the home with white wicker furniture, white-framed pastel beach prints, and clean, crisp linens that seemed to sing a fresh song of newness and rebirth every morning. They walked to the beach everyday, with their beach bags, their beach novels, snacks and plenty of sun tan lotion. And as they sat on the white sand, with the gentle breezes and the thunderous warmth of the crashing waves in the distance, Brownie's memories of childhood on that same beach came flooding back. She grew up on that beach, spent her summers there, met crushes and boyfriends there, and made memories there. And she watched it change, too. She saw people come and go, she saw the same summer stalwarts, who decided to renovate their homes, or sell them. She watched the monstrosity of a beach cottage emerge directly next to their corner lot, which inconveniently blocked some of their view of the left part of the sound. She watched its inhabitants come and go, and keep to themselves. They weren't *real* Long Beach Islanders. If they were, they would have come over for an ice-tea and a chat on the porch on one of the breezy evenings at sunset.

And Brownie sat on this same beach with her daughter, who she hoped would bring her own daughter to continue the legacy. Sarah felt so privileged to be a part of that gathering. Everyone took her in like a family member, and gave her a piece of tranquility that they have experienced summer after summer. They relished photograph albums of the years gone by, including the detailed construction of the house's renovation. Sarah saw pictures of the house, which the two cousins, who faced her now as adults, had run and romped through. They, as children, had run through the back door, letting the spring bounce on its hinges, and swing behind them as they ran to the opposite end of the house and out of the other door that led to the dock. They ran down the slight decline and jumped into the small schooners, making adventures, dreams and memories. Brownie could take her father's sailor stories and live them here, with trusted cousins. She loved these times, as she had only her dolls and other such animated creatures at home. Ted was a dreamer, and she connected most with dreamers.

Lucy and Sarah walked on the beach at night, sat in the sand, looking up at the stars, and talked about their futures, their wishes and their hopes. They talked about God and their views of spirituality and religion. They talked of love, and art, and predictions of what their futures held. And as Sarah looked up into the night's sky, she witnessed her first shooting star. It was pure magic, that moment. A moment she will never forget, and it was a moment, a friendship, and a lifetime, sealed by a shooting star. Sarah saw many shooting stars after that time, but her first was a magical moment, and it represented everything her best friend had been, and would be, for her.

# Chapter Eighteen

*I want it said of me by those who knew me best, that I always plucked a thistle and planted a flower where I thought a flower would grow.*

**Abraham Lincoln (1809-1865)**

Brownie moved herself and Lucy to the new condo complex in Williamsburg. Soon, thereafter, Sarah's mother gathered the strength and courage to leave Casp, and moved to the same condominium complex, where Sarah could now live, and legally attend the York County School. Sarah's mother was the third mother out of Lucy and Sarah's group of friends to leave their husbands and move to the condo complex, so the community was conveniently dubbed the "Divorced Wives Commons" instead of "Williamsburg Commons," which it was properly named.

Williamsburg Commons was erected on a plot of land along the railroad tracks and about a half a mile from the main train station. It was nestled behind a row of chain hotels, the Cracker Barrel, and other tourist restaurants that concealed the fact that anyone actually lived in the town. The elegant townhouses and condos went up quickly and introduced a new way of single-living in the York County district of Williamsburg.

Once again, Brownie came to the rescue in Sarah's life, whether she meant to or not. Lucy and Sarah now lived about fifty meters apart, and although Sarah technically lived with her mother, she spent most of her time with Lucy and Brownie in her condo.

Lord knows what happened to Sarah's mother in the last eight months in her old family home. As Sarah adjusted to her new life at Brownie's, her next life in apartment living, and endured the countless adventures and tales that accompanied each, Sarah's mother was fighting her own battles in a different environment. Sarah was lucky, in that, she was able to wade through the murky waters of repression and memory at a relatively early age when the layers of new life experiences hadn't completely suffocated their existences. But Sarah's mother had been living on auto-pilot since she left her mother's haven at the age of eighteen, building new life experiences with each circumstance, and any memories or events that may have been harmful from her youth and far forward, were now buried beneath many more years of experiences. Even though her mother was now on her own, away from Casp's idea of a family home, her existence was still surviving in a world she had grown accustomed to accept as life. She was suffering horribly, and it was painful for Sarah to watch. This was the mother who twisted butterfly carpet cleaners after her first husband left her, who preached about hope and resurrection, who completed her master's degree while working full-time and raised two children. This was the mother who stopped when she saw a fallen flower from a nearby tree on the sidewalk, and slipped it behind her ear. This was the mother who always came running to Sarah's bedside in the middle of the night if she was ever sick. This was the woman who followed her heart when she met the man she knew she wanted to marry, and boldly broke free of her mother's hold. This was the woman, who after a year or so of husbandless life, had different suitors calling on her at every weekend, each one bringing new and exciting gifts for the two girls. One even drove a motorcycle, which Sarah delighted to sit on and imagine she was driving as the wind whipped through her hair. This was the woman who boldly and fearlessly accepted another man's four children and agreed to raise them as her own. This was the woman who always, without fail, turned to the Church when she was having a problem. This was the woman who read Little Red Riding Hood, The Engine that Could, and other moral-like children's tales to Sarah and Meghan when they were young children. This was the woman who drove in one of the worst snowstorms Vermont had ever witnessed on Christmas Eve, just to ensure that her daughters could sleep in a comfortable bed, and wake up the next morning with family, as they discovered that Santa knew they had traveled to Vermont. And this was the woman who always kept the youthfulness of such magical things like Santa Claus and the Easter Bunny even into her teenage years. So, Sarah, could not, and would not, watch her mother at her lowest point, as she barely breathed to survive. Thus, Sarah spent her senior year at Brownie's, while her mother tried to heal herself.

But, never mind the atrocities that occurred to her when she was separated from her daughter, she was now plagued with the guilt that accompanied the knowledge that she had stayed in that house, and watched two of her daughters leave. Now, at least, she was back with Sarah, and felt she had at least one year to once again establish some sort of parental figure in this child's life. She wanted to provide Sarah with a role model. She wanted to atone for the experiences she had been through in the past years. She only wished that she could take back the time she had lost with the last and youngest daughter.

But it was too late in Sarah's eyes and heart. Sarah had already seen and endured too much. She wanted nothing more but to run from and forget the experiences of her past. The mother that now stood before her in a desperate attempt to establish rules and discipline was seen as an impostor after her exposure to another lifestyle, after her few months of freedom and apartment-living. Can you show a child what the world is really like, and then take her back under the wing of discipline and protection and pretend as if the knowledge isn't there?

Nevertheless, Sarah's mother provided a stable roof over her head, as she slowly recovered from the abuses she endured the previous eight months. Sarah spent her time at Brownie's where she provided a special haven for creativity, spontaneity and gaiety. The girls embarked on such adventures, created songs, chants and stories, watched movies and worked on homework, played Boggle and Trivial Pursuit, and progressed through their senior year of high school.

# Chapter Nineteen

*Occasionally in life there are those moments of unutterable fulfillment which cannot be completely explained by those symbols called words. Their meanings can only be articulated by the inaudible language of the heart.*

**Martin Luther King, Jr. (1929-1968)**

Sarah grew closer and closer to Brownie, as she always talked freely about her life, her childhood, her experiences, and her newfound acquaintances with old friends from her past. Sarah watched as Brownie whittled her time putting quaint little finishing touches on her new home. She watched as Brownie sent an old family heirloom armchair to be reupholstered. She watched her make balloon-fashioned curtains for all the windows in a large, pink-and-purple floral motif. Brownie brought all of her delectable decorations with her – the delicate Easter Bunny tree with the white base and the thousands of pastel eggs, the Halloween figurines and ceramic

witches that hung in the windows, the "Mama" cookie jar, that had
been her mother's and that used to squeal, "Mama" as a hungry child
opened the jar, but now stood silent from generations of use. The jar
was always full with homemade treats. Brownie sat in her
reupholstered chair for weeks and weeks, it seemed, carefully
stitching a bunny blanket for a newborn relative. She sat and stitched
and listened to the girls' tales of the night's events as they came home
every evening.

Lucy and Sarah passed the time by creating stories of all the
characters of the Commons. This was one of Sarah's favorite
pastimes when she was bored. She made up stories and lives about
the people around her. It first started with the neighbors that
surrounded Sarah's mother's condo. There was Snipper, the black-
haired butterball woman who trimmed her plants everyday with a pair
of scissors. Or Perv, the middle-aged, grey-haired man who slunk
around the neighborhood everyday with his shirt unbuttoned to his
navel to show off his chest full of grey hair. He was clearly going
through his midlife crisis. Perhaps his wife had left him months
earlier for a younger man, and he only wanted to feel adequate and
young again. And there was Blue Bitch and Brian Ross. These two
characters were married, and lived in the condominium across the
street from Brownie's. Blue Bitch continually parked her car on the
other side of the lot, on Brownie's side, sometimes occupying their
own spots, as Lucy had her Chevy Blazer here. The girls always
wondered about this, as she didn't mind the longer walk to her condo.
After a few days of observing this behavior, Sarah realized that she
only wanted to park her car in the shade, and didn't care much that
she was taking other people's parking spots. Perhaps she wanted to
preserve the paint job on her Oldsmobile; perhaps she didn't like
getting into a hot car. Her car was blue, hence the name, Blue Bitch,
as the girls had no other reference to the woman other than the strange
behavior she exhibited with her car. Perhaps she was Executive
Director of the Colonial Williamsburg Foundation, perhaps she was a
school bus driver, perhaps she was a direct descendent to the third
president of the United States. Sarah didn't think about these things,
she only observed behavior. And weeks later, Brownie recounted that
she had come home from work one day, and as she placed her key in
her front door, she had a strange feeling that she was being watched.
She looked up toward the window where Blue Bitch and Brian Ross's

condo was situated, and there, in the window, was their twelve-year-old daughter, standing only in a pair of underwear, with binoculars, staring down at Brownie as she entered her home. It sent chills through Brownie's body, and she scurried inside.

Condominium living is a different sort of ballgame. It is as if condo residents have a secret desire to observe other people's strange behaviors. If one ever feels the need to feel normal, or whatever that means in the world, one should live in a condominium complex. They'll be cured instantly!

Brownie's condo became a safe haven for Sarah, and she actually enjoyed occupying her time here more than any other place. Brownie was always in good spirits and listened to the girls' tales of the nights, offered her advice if asked, but most frequently, just listened and observed (between episodes of Melrose Place and the videos of Wonder Years episodes she had taped from years earlier). Sarah never held anything back from Brownie, which felt wonderfully freeing.

Sarah's senior year moved swiftly. Lucy was accepted into James Madison University. Sarah was accepted into Virginia Tech. They spent a wonderful summer together knowing that the next year would change both of their lives for good. The more experiences that Sarah acquired, the more layers began to form on top of the painful memories that she escaped so long ago. Their sting had been buffered and soothed by Brownie's presence, and they were soon repressed and buried underneath thousands of new memories, and hopes and dreams for the future. Her old life and experience of the world had been uprooted and reshaped by Brownie and Lucy's family, and Sarah now only wanted to go to a good college, to excel in her grades, to eventually get married, have children, and have a successful career, if possible. She wanted to have her summers at the beach, to involve herself in politics, to always be in good humor and thrive as a social butterfly. These were the wishes of an eighteen-year-old; the simple wishes of a youthful heart.

After graduation, Sarah, Lucy, and four other girlfriends had saved all year for the infamous "beach week," which capped every senior's graduation ceremony with a week full of parties in Kill Devil Hills, North Carolina. The girls had picked a beautiful house on the main thoroughfare along the beach, on mile post ten in Nags Head. The house was beautiful, spacious, but most importantly, contained a hot tub on one of the back decks. Brownie signed for the house, and the girls planned their week vacation with assigned dinners, and shared expenses for food and beer. They planned a party for the second night they were there, as most of the graduating seniors from high school in the Hampton Roads area were there as well. During the party, an undercover Alcohol Beverage Control agent entered the house, and all but one partygoer were underage drinkers. Everyone was sent home, the house's rental agency was notified, and the six girls were informed that if they did not have a parental chaperone by the next day, they would all be evicted without a refund. Brownie was called that night. She was scheduled to work the rest of the week, but she cancelled her work schedule, and drove the four hours down to Nags Head to spend the rest of the week with the girls, and to save them from the eviction. Brownie was a sight for sore eyes, as they had been looking forward to this week all year. Certainly, it was neither Long Beach Island, nor the face-lifted Cape-Codder on the Sound with the schooner at the dock, but it was a beach. And although the girls thought it was an inconvenience for Brownie, she was relieved to receive the call – she got to spend a nearly expense-free week at the beach!

Summer flew by and all the girls (and boys) who had grown so close throughout elementary, junior high and high school were preparing to go their separate ways. They often talked with each other about how special and unique their group of friends were, but they didn't realize the extent of that uniqueness until much later when they had enough time and experience in the world to sample other people, see other people's personalities and mannerisms. Most of the others, after an inability to find that closeness again, usually threw themselves into their jobs, or clung to a boyfriend, who eventually turned into a fiancé, or a husband, or attached themselves to another group of friends and pretended that they were experiencing the same closeness and uniqueness they had experienced in high school, but knew deep in their hearts they were missing a fundamental core.

What causes these pockets of time when a group of people can come together - their lives can coincide - in a beautiful, melodic harmony, where all of the factors – personalities, energies, spirits,

144

intentions, needs, wishes, and dreams – seem to come together in a concentric circle to form a whole, where everyone involved can just be – and live? What forms these pockets of time when all of the subtle nuances of life seem to blend, and move along toward a distant future? People generally don't notice time in these periods, they just move with the flow, fully engaged in the moment. And if one little piece, or person, is removed from the whole, perhaps another one extends him or herself to fill the gap or join hands with the other, perhaps the wheel continues spinning but the others feel the slight bump in the road when the wheel gets to the missing piece, the others feel it, and reach out to mend the gap. Where does that desire to reach out and help others come from? Is it intrinsic or do we learn it from our environments, our social classes and structures? The pockets of time when we can look back on a lifetime lived, or a lifetime just beginning are the times when we know a time is coming soon where the wheel will be formed again, to form another pocket of time when the hands will join together to form a whole, and the wheel will just flow, like it is supposed to flow, without time for reflection, because we won't have a concept of time – because we will be living.

# Chapter Twenty

*No one should drive a hard bargain with an artist.*

**Ludwig van Beethoven (1770-1827)**

But surely, Brownie was not the only shaping maternal figure in Sarah's life.

What about Sarah's mother, the woman who seemed to have a pure heart of gold, the one who trusted, and lived boldly and courageously in the gravest of circumstances? A human being is not born this way. She must have had a few blows underneath that soft heart to allow her to rise, time and time again. Where did she come from? Where did she stand?

She was born in 1947 in the small town of Millers Falls, Massachusetts. She was the third child in a line of five. Her father attended Boston College, was a Classics and Greek major, and happened to be visiting his cousin's farm, Darcy Farm in Millers Falls, when he caught the eye of a young lass with strawberry blonde hair. He graduated from Boston College in 1929, married her, the girl from Darcy Farm, and soon took a job with the United States State Senate Investigative Committee, and relocated to Long Island, New York. He traveled often, to the South, for his job as he was assigned to research the black lynchings that were hitting the papers in the South, specifically Mississippi and Alabama. Their life looked promising. They had two children, Mary and Tom, and the new family took to Long Island life well. He was a tall, dark handsome man, with dark eyes that seemed to sink deep in his head from thought. They were dreamy eyes, but they soon sparked to attention when he bounced a young child on his knee. He took a particular delight in his firstborn, Mary. He took her everywhere he could, and she lapped up every minute of the attention. She was a sure-fire Shirley Temple girl, with a charming smile, and a line of freckles across the nose that made any male, youthful or adult, like her father, swoon. She listened to all of his stories, and looking back now, Mary, out of all of the children, benefited most from his company and stories. Later in life, she went on to become a delegate for the House of Representatives in the State of Vermont, which is a sure-fire indicator that she was wide awake when her father talked quickly and swiftly in all of those car rides. She learned the talk of politics, and the way government workers thought and acted, at an early age. Tom was born, and shortly before 1947, their father mysteriously lost his job with the government. The investigations were called off, as some foul play must have occurred, and he found himself unemployed with a wife, two children and a dream for a prosperous future soon down the drain.

His cousin worked in the insurance business back home in Millers Falls and offered to give his cousin a job in the interim. He moved the family back to Millers Falls in 1947, and soon thereafter, Sarah's mother was born, fifteen years after the eldest, Mary was born. The next nine years were difficult, as her father never really quite recovered from the loss of his job. He spent more and more time, away from home and on the road. Two more children were born, Peter and Andrew, and Mary soon found a husband shortly after they arrived in Millers Falls. Her husband, an engineering graduate from Massachusetts Institute of Technology, took to Mary right away, and

Mary, feeling displaced from her new life away from the comforts of Long Island, was eager to start a new life away from the troubles that loomed in her father's house back in Millers Falls. Needless to say, Mary received a much different childhood from her younger sister, Sarah's mother, even though they both came from the same parents.

Mary and Louisa's mother came from a Polish family, and the Polish presence in the small town of Millers Falls was prominent. Every Saturday night, the Polish community gathered in the dance hall where traditional music was played, where many of her relatives formed the basis of the music with accordions and violins, and the town came alive with dancing, magic and music. She raised her children to go to church everyday, particularly the third born, Sarah's mother, Louisa, who seemed to be born with a silver spoon in her mouth. Even cousins teased her by calling her, "My Lady." She sent Louisa up the road to go with another family to church (she never had time to go herself), but for every Easter or Christmas, she always prepared the food and had everything ready on the table early in the morning when the one priest from town walked to each home to bless all of the food. The nine years from Louisa's birth passed as most childhoods do – she occupied herself in the backyard, making adventures in streams and the woods with her brothers. Her mother made all of her school clothes, sent her off to school each morning, and tucked her in each night. But in 1956, when Louisa was nine years old, her father died of a heart attack. The event came suddenly and unexpectedly, and her mother was left with four children, as the oldest boy, Tom was still at home, to support and raise. Her husband did not have a well-paying job, nor did it have benefits, so she was rendered penniless, without many skills herself. She managed to get a job as a nurse at a local hospital and worked the night shift. She came home in the morning to see her children off to school, and slept the rest of the day until it was time for her to report for the next shift. So, at nine years old, Louisa was not only left fatherless, but practically became motherless, as her mother only slept when she was in the house. And what about the two young boys? Louisa learned very quickly how to be a mother. She made their lunches, ensured they did their homework and kept a watchful eye on all of their activities. She blossomed in high school, as the boys grew older, and her responsibilities as a fill-in mother were lessened, and she could partake in a somewhat normal high school life. She became an active

148

member of the drama club, and was a cheerleader for the football team.

Although she was quiet, sweet, had an occasional boyfriend, she kept to herself and maintained a sense of order in a rather tumultuous household. Her older brother Tom, as we know it now, had a mild case of autism. But in that day, before what we know today about the disorder, autism was viewed as a severe mental retardation. And with that label, Tom was treated as such. When a human being is labeled by a debilitating disorder, and shuffled around to various mental hospitals, there isn't much room for improvement, or a proactive funneling of his energies into something worthwhile. He was not mentally impaired, but had a concentration deficit. He concentrated very acutely and very meticulously on certain things like collecting objects like stamps or keys, and learned every single detail about these hobbies, at a remarkable genius level, but lost interest in other things like people. In the right environment, he could communicate his knowledge well, but back in that day, mental disabilities in the family were something to keep quiet about. So, Tom was kept from the rest of the world. No one talked about him, and he performed certain activities around the house after his father died, like mowing the grass, or fixing the plumbing, but his life was dubbed useless by a very early age, as soon as a deficiency was detected. And a bright boy, who could have been ushered into the right environment, came to a standstill, and has stood there ever since.

The younger two boys, Peter and Andrew, were night and day. They never had a stable father figure, and were left to entertain themselves with boyish games, fishing jaunts, and a sister, who also served as a mother. Peter was always a sweet boy, and always invited his older sister to partake on their fishing and exploration excursions. He taught her how to skip rocks, and look for frogs in the warbling brooks and streams, and how to pick the best walking sticks in the thick of woods which is now a National Forest behind their childhood home. Both possessed the intensity of concentration, and lack thereof, as the older boy possessed, but the younger two were more fluent with their language and could communicate their interests well. Peter was a talker, still is, and if you asked him the right questions, he could thoroughly explain the scientific phenomena of sunlight on any object, animate or inanimate, in nature. He loses

149

himself in this kind of technical talk, and even today, as he talks about these scientific interests, he speaks rapidly and swiftly with the same energy he had as a young boy. He speaks about infrared and radar beams with various types of velocity to anyone, as if everyone should know these things.

He spent most of his life outdoors, as he wasn't allowed in the house when his mother was sleeping, so he naturally developed an intense knowledge of everything that nature represents. Some would argue that nature is the best teacher, as countless cultures before our time only had nature, and the subtle movements within it, to teach them the cycles of the world, which in essence, represent the cycles of human beings. Andrew, similarly, developed an intense interest in the Earth, in the minerals and rocks that form. He studied their patterns, their shapes, the way the natural resources of the Earth affect one another, and spent his time in the land digging and using his hands to occupy his time. He also nurtured a bit of a pyromaniac within him, and loved to watch the way fire affected the Earth. For someone who had an intense interest in the Earth, and the way that the other elements affect it, this intense interest was not necessarily a strange thing. He usually started a fire and was responsible about its potential spreading nature. He was a curious boy, as most boys are, and didn't have much supervision, so he occupied himself with his interests. But one day, one of his fires got a little out of hand, and burned half a field, which wasn't exactly his property. The police were called and Andrew was then dubbed as the strange boy who liked to play with fire. He never quite escaped the prison that society had built for him either. He was always told that his interests and intensity were strange, were not normal, so he believed it, and never quite broke out of this mold. He has, throughout his life, occupied himself with odd jobs in the Millers Falls area that utilize his hands – carpentry jobs, painting jobs, whatever he can find – but he never really made it, even though he has a brilliant mind. If you happen to get him talking about gems, minerals and rocks, he could probably put a mineralogy professor at Harvard to shame. He doesn't know it though; he thinks he is strange and abnormal.

Peter showed the most promise of the three boys. He had a boy-like charm that he carried with him to adulthood. Similarly, he became fascinated by the way sunlight affected certain objects, and

150

began playing with the sun and mirrors as a small boy. That interest grew with intensity, and he began devising makeshift telescopes and other such devices from pieces of scrap metal or discards he found at junkyards and on roads. He was quite crafty actually, as he didn't have any money, so he learned to build things, with his hands, using natural elements and pieces of trash and discards he found on his daily excursions. Years ensued and he used this interest to hone his precision by working for a fiber optics company. Today, he builds telescopes, and spends years building them, as he refuses to embark on any project if it is not seen through the last detail, meticulously and laboriously. He only builds them for friends, as it takes a lot of time and effort, and he builds them in his basement at home in his free time. But hands down, it is probably the best telescope that money can buy, as Peter doesn't take shortcuts in his work. He is diligent, and is not pleased with anything less than perfection. Since the days of playing with sunlight on mirrors, laser beams and radar have now taken the place of such games, and most of his work, his genius, is generally contributed to the government, in some contractual form or another.

# Chapter Twenty-One

*As death, when we come to consider it closely, is the true goal of our existence, I have formed during the last few years such close relations with this best and truest friend of mankind, that his image is not only no longer terrifying to me, but is indeed very soothing and consoling! And I thank my God for graciously granting me the opportunity of learning that death is the key which unlocks the door to our true happiness.*

**Wolfgang Amadeus Mozart (1756-1791)**

After Louisa graduated from high school, she attended Greenfield Community College and met Sarah's father at a party of a mutual friend whose boyfriend was Sarah's father's roommate at Boston University. He was instantly taken with the Irish-Polish lass, as she seemed to hold the same stability and strength that his own mother possessed. He needed someone to challenge him, to keep him in line, as his machismo sometimes got the best of him, and Louisa seemed like the right person. But he wasn't the typical male who traversed through the typical and socially accepted dances that were required in that time for asking a girl out. And Louisa certainly wasn't the type of girl who would date just anybody. She was born with a silver spoon in her mouth, and any boy she dated needed to show wit, intellect and a good deal of charm and spontaneity to win her lashes. Even though his mother had taught him otherwise, his Irish wit got the best of him and he decided to pen the following letter to the girl who lived in Millers Falls:

*Dear Louisa,*

*I belch in public. I push little old ladies who are carrying grocery bags out into the street. I sell Cracker Jack boxes to little kids and remove all of the trinkets inside.*

*But, I like you. Do you want to go out on a date?*

*Yours,*

*Patrick O'Higgins*

Louisa accepted, and they were married three years later.

# Chapter Twenty-Two

*The way to see by Faith is to shut the eye of Reason.*

**Benjamin Franklin (1706-1790)**

The group of friends back in Williamsburg prepared themselves to leave the protective web they had spent years creating as friends, and travel to their respective colleges. Their freshman year passed swiftly, and even though Sarah was attending Virginia Tech, a good four hours from their home in Williamsburg, she spent her weekends traveling to other college campuses to see her friends, or back to Williamsburg to see her boyfriend, Brownie, her mother, her sister and all the countless comforts of home. Meghan was finishing her last year at the College of William and Mary, and some friends were still in the area, as they commuted to Christopher Newport University in Newport News.

Sarah's first semester in the valley of Blacksburg was a trying experience. She went from a small high school in a small town where everyone knew each other, to the largest university in the state with twenty-six hundred undergraduates. She was a number, and as most of her classes consisted of the freshman core classes, she was normally in a theatre-like classroom with anywhere from two hundred to five hundred other students. Her biology class alone was the size of her entire high school. No one noticed her, and as she had never been in a situation where she must actively search for friends, she let the new feeling of anonymity envelop her. She usually made it through the week, going to a few classes here and there, but the classes were too big for anyone to notice her attendance, so she showed up on exam days, which normally occurred four times throughout the semester for each class. The rest of the time, she concentrated her time and effort on the next trip she would take on the weekend. She thoroughly explored the New River Valley, West Virginia and all the little towns up and down Interstate eighty-one. It is beautiful country out there, the heart and soul of Virginia, which she had never seen before. She certainly couldn't keep still in her own dorm room, which felt like a rattrap to her, so she took to the open road in her free time. She was one of the only freshmen with a car. In October of that freshman year, she acquired a small settlement as a result of the broken leg that had happened two years earlier, so she spent the money on a new car, among other things. The car was hers, and for all intents and purposes, was one of the first things she ever owned that no one had any control over except her, and it served as a symbol for her freedom. She put a nice stereo in it (with two twelve inch woofers) and this black bullet of a little car became her haven. She lost herself in the music, in all the scenery that passed before her eyes. She went to Smith Mountain Lake, traversed through the mountains of West Virginia, and made frequent trips to Radford University, which was just across the New River Valley. One of the friends from her group in Williamsburg, Emily, attended Radford. Emily had always been closer to Lucy, and Sarah had never grown close to her, as their personalities were extremely different. But at this point, in both of their lives, they needed that comfort of the group they had lost, so a new kind of friendship was born. Emily involved herself in the party scene at Radford (who couldn't?) and Sarah went along with her to some of these parties, but the whole scene seemed like a strange semblance of bodies and wretched filth to Sarah. How could people do this night after night? Sarah definitely had her fair share of partying, but this scene, this mass of foreign people who seemed to cling to people that they didn't know, and shout obscenities, and upchuck their night's consumption in house corners, this was not the same. She had enrolled in college, and was attending a university, because it was the thing to do. She was here. She attended classes sometimes, she went to a few of the parties that all the other thousands of students her age who came from good, or not-so-good homes, did and seemed to enjoy. But something didn't feel right. She felt as if she was living an existence that was not her own. She didn't quite know how to express this feeling in words at the time, all she knew was that she felt safe, comfortable and at peace, in her car, with all types of music you can think of, all types to blend with any of her moods, or form them, with the open road before her. She made plans with Emily frequently, and drove to Radford about twice a week, but she enjoyed the drive more than the destination when she got there. Emily was heading in a different direction. Emily loved her newfound freedom of parties she could walk to on a nightly basis, and she loved the group of people on her hall, who all seemed to shout at each other, rather than talk. She needed this. But Sarah wasn't convinced. And Sarah didn't need what the others needed.

Sarah barely received a 2.0 grade point average her first semester. She wanted to come home. Her jaunts on the open road became more and more frequent, and the mass-body classes became less and less appealing. For the second semester, she purposefully enrolled in two senior level literature courses, much to the dismay of her advisor, as she needed smaller classes, with a subject she was interested in to re-ignite the spark. But her habit of never attending class was already fully blossomed, and she stopped going to nearly all of her classes. She managed to barely pass three classes, and failed the two literature classes that she never attended. In all essence, she could have filed a petition to drop the two classes she wasn't attending, but the thought of going through the long process of standing in line at the Burgess's office, and filling out all the paperwork, seemed like a hassle to the girl who spent her time finding ways to leave the campus. The only time she walked across that drill field was to attend class, and if she made it through the whole class, the last thing she wanted to do when she left the building was to make another trip to another building to stand in line. The campus was dark to her. The walls of all the buildings were dark and gloomy. And we won't even begin to mention those mornings when she did manage to go to her eight o'clock English class in the dead of winter in New River Valley where the wind chill factor was, at some days, twenty-four degrees below zero. So, Virginia Tech, and everything surrounding the experience, was associated with pure torture in Sarah's mind. Her grade point average for the second semester was .09.

The next year, she transferred to Christopher Newport University, lived with her mother, who had moved to a much more spacious condominium in James City County in Williamsburg. She enjoyed this time with her mother, as she had regained much of her energy and spark, and the two girls, mother and daughter, learned much about each other during this time. This was the first time that her mother had purchased a piece of property by herself, without two little girls to support, and she seemed to thrive in her new surroundings.

Mother and daughter woke up at the same time every morning, and she walked into Sarah's room with the same song, "Rise and Shine and Give God His Glory, Glory," that she had remembered so well from her youth. They coordinated their shower times in the bathroom, as there was only one, and oftentimes found themselves on top of each other in the bathroom, with curling iron cords, and baby powder clouds going in every other direction. But they both whistled and sang, and somehow managed to leave the house at the right time every morning. Well, at least, Sarah did.

Sarah's mother had this endearing little habit that Meghan and Sarah always snickered about in previous years.

Louisa was not the most punctual human being. This used to drive Sarah crazy in her youth, as her mother was her sole source of transportation to any of her countless activities. Sarah was embarrassed that she arrived to cheerleading practices, or dances, or parties, fifteen, sometimes thirty minutes late. Sarah's mother wasn't to blame, as she had a car-full of children to coordinate. And if she drove Sarah anywhere, the little twins, Jacob and Fanny accompanied, as she couldn't leave them at home. And any mother knows that the process of loading kids into cars is not always quick. So, this punctuality deficiency was still going strong, even when she didn't have six children to coordinate. Somewhere around five 'til nine o'clock in the morning, five minutes before she was supposed to be at work, she rushed downstairs and began scurrying like a mad woman, all the while, yelling upstairs toward Sarah, "Sarah, can you bring down my glasses? I forgot them on the night stand?"

"Sarah, can you turn off the water in the sink upstairs? I forgot to turn it off." She always left a trickle of water running for the cat in the morning. The cat did not drink out of her water bowl, but only lapped up water from a bathroom sink.

"Sarah, can you make sure all the bedroom doors are closed upstairs before you come down?"

"Sarah, can you make sure the shower curtain is closed? I don't want it to collect mildew."

"Oh, shoot, Sarah? Can you throw down my watch? I forgot it on the bathroom sink."

These charades happened every morning, without fail. And Sarah performed all of her mother's requests. Some mornings it grated on her, but for the most part they were both able to get a good chuckle out of it, especially if it involved throwing any item down the landing. If Louisa had forgotten anything upstairs, she stood in the downstairs foyer, while Sarah stood on the upstairs landing, and the two girls tried to coordinate their hand-eye coordination, with the added obstacle of height. Soon, this little habit was reversed, as many of Sarah's clothes were downstairs in the laundry room area, or folded in a basket in the living room area. So, Sarah yelled, "Mom, can you throw up my green cardigan sweater that's in the basket by the stairs?"

Sarah could have easily walked down the twelve steps and retrieved the sweater herself, but she had grown to love this custom of playing throw and catch with her mother. And it became a morning ritual. Louisa arrived at the bottom of the steps with a green cardigan, but the WRONG green cardigan.

"No, the other one."

Louisa came back to the landing with the right sweater. Louisa was at a bit of a disadvantage, as throwing an item upward to the hands of someone who is leaning over a banister, is a bit more difficult than dropping an item into a person's hands down below. But Louisa threw the item, sometimes toward the opposite wall, sometimes behind her (no wonder Sarah's father didn't like to play tennis with her), and in between giggles and laughs, the item finally reached Sarah's hands. Through the two years that Sarah lived with her mother in this condominium, they perfected the art of throwing a number of different items. And each one always stopped what they were doing, no matter how rushed or late they were, to play the throw and catch game, under the premise that they needed the other's help, as they were too rushed to descend or ascend the steps themselves.

So, as Louisa rushed around downstairs, five minutes before she was supposed to be at work, all the while remembering and forgetting things she needed to do, she always seemed to feed the cats, water the plants, unload the dishwasher, leave Sarah a note, retrieve the paper from outside and pack her lunch in those five minutes. But the most amazing thing was that she always fried an egg for breakfast. Meghan and Sarah marveled at this, because she seemed to be in such a mad panic because she was late, every single morning. But, without fail, she always felt she had enough time to fry an egg. Remarkable.

# Chapter Twenty-Three

*I see little of more importance to the future of our country and of civilization than full recognition of the place of the artist. If art is to nourish the roots of our culture, society must set the artist free to follow his vision wherever it takes him.*

**John F. Kennedy (1917-1963)**

Sarah's best friend from the sixth grade, Belle, had had a similar freshman experience at George Mason University in Fairfax, and transferred to Christopher Newport University at the same time as Sarah, so the two friends coordinated most of their classes, as both were English majors. If the two friends were not close enough, this period of time, the next three years of their lives, was one of the best Sarah can remember. The two friends commuted to campus together, attended classes together, studied together, and generally pushed each other to the next level. If one was not feeling particularly motivated to go to class, the other served as a sounding board and a voice of reason in an unmotivated moment. There were times when they both decided to skip class, and they found themselves in one of their cars, driving around the back neighborhoods and streets of Newport News and Hampton, discussing literature, art or life's events. Belle lived deeply, just as Sarah did, so they reveled in each other's company and felt comfortable talking with each other about abstract issues, but could easily switch to the daily laments of parents, boyfriends or classmates.

Christopher Newport University was new at the time, the former Senator Paul Trible, became its President, and began to work to establish a name for the budding university. Greek Life began to flourish on campus, but lacked the presence that it had at Radford or other universities. Belle and Sarah received a taste of this type of living and behavior in a few of their classes where the prominent cliques of sororities and fraternities were present, and they watched at a distance, the squabbles and melodramatic scenes that ensued before and after each class. They discussed these observances afterwards, studied their affects, analyzed their implications, and served as reassurances to each other that *they* would never succumb to such behavior. Belle prided herself on being an intellectual snob, and Sarah seemed to soon take on that same air. Belle was smart, and always seemed to score about two points higher than Sarah, which always drove her crazy, as she has always harbored the competitive spirit in her. But Belle always received A's, which meant Sarah always received A's, scoring two points lower than her friend. They read each other's papers, making suggestions or asking questions. They scanned each other's notes, and prepared each other for tests and exams with note cards and study sheets. And they studied together in that same room in Belle's parents house that she had known from the 6th grade. This was the room where she surveyed Belle's perfume collection, listened to old vinyl records of the peace generation, made prank phone calls and made a new friend from the other high school, and now they were reading Chaucer's Canterbury Tales to each other for university classes, stopping for each foreign word to analyze its meaning. Belle loved these times as well, because Sarah was so curious. She asked so many questions, so many innocent questions about literature and the world, and she listened to Belle's responses, and always took them to heart.

As English majors, they often took four different literature classes in one semester, peppered with a History or Art course here and there. The English Department at Christopher Newport University was a tight-knit one, and was comforting to Sarah as it seemed to resemble the Literary Arts Magnet School at Somerset High School, which she had grown to love. She often received the same professors for several different classes each semester, and they grew to know each of their students. Each professor had a personality, and Belle and Sarah delighted in these observances and quirky personalities after class. English professors are a class of their own lot. They don't belong in any category, because they never fit any mold. They are a class of their own, and in my opinion, higher above any caste system we have created on Earth. Each one has a quirk, energy or spirit that simmers below the surface with wonder and strength. As each one stood in front of the classroom, Sarah allowed their words to float through and over and around her head, but she took in their whole presence, not only their words and their teachings of the great masters, but their backgrounds, their styles, what they brought to each classroom, and each one was different. Each one had their love, their specialty, their favorite author (or animal) and time period, and they worked together to form a beautiful whole.

Dr. Herbert Sillar, may he rest in peace, was a saint. He came from a prominent family in the South, was the son of a missionary doctor, and came from a long line of over achievers. His parents always expected him to go to the best Ivy League School and become a doctor. He even made it through the first year of medical school, but something burned in his chest, something magical and full of light that pushed him toward English Literature, much to his father's dismay. He graduated from the University of Richmond, Brown University and the University of Pennsylvania, with honors in each, and when faced with where he would teach English classes, the whole world of universities systems seemed to be open to him. He had a prominent Southern family name, had high honors and had authored several journal articles and books, and could have chosen any college or university. Any college professor hopes and dreams to teach students at one of the Ivy League schools, or at least one in the top twenty-five, as the intellect, interest and motivation are much higher in these institutions, both from faculty and students. The students are smarter, and seem to always push the professor to a high intellectual

162

plane. But Herb would hear nothing of the sort. He chose to teach at a local community college, one that had just opened, near his aging mother. He chose to give a spark of his enlightened life to students who lacked the flare of the Ivy League schools. Some of his students were single mothers. Some of his students came from work, and would return to work at the end of his class. Some of his students were adults who were returning to school after years and years of idleness. Some of his students were young kids who didn't know what they wanted to do and were just passing the time. And one of his students was Sarah.

Herb wasn't an interactive professor; he just filled all of his students with knowledge. He stood in front of the class, behind a podium, with a Norton Anthology textbook, and a piece of chalk, nothing else. He didn't bring a notebook. He didn't bring a briefcase. He didn't bring anything but literature and his quick wit. He always walked into the classroom, beaming, wide-eyed, and looked at the class as if he was seeing them for the first time. It was almost a look of surprise, as if he was saying, "Wow, you are all here." His classes were always full. No one even dared to skip Herb's classes, because you never knew what you were going to miss. Herb taught literature, but you also heard the stories of his life. And boy, that man, that saint, led an adventure.

For instance, about the same time that Steven Spielberg's Extra Terrestrial was produced, Herb thought about the uncanny resemblance that many of ET's characteristics and mannerisms had to Jesus Christ. Now, Herb was not analyzing this in a derogatory or blasphemous kind of way, as he was the son of a preacher, and had always fashioned his life to the strictest morals and ethics of a religious man. But as the commercialism ensued over this alien movie character, Herb, haphazardly and almost, jestingly, penned a little essay about the similarities between Jesus Christ and ET. One of the classes that Herb taught at the University was the Bible as Literature, so you can say that he was a bit of a professional on Jesus Christ, as well as the teachings of the Bible. Well, someone took an interest in this little essay, and the next thing he knew, the essay was printed in Time Magazine. Steven Spielberg got word of this strange little man who seemed to be criticizing his original character, and even suggesting that it was not entirely original, and filed a lawsuit against him. Herb was beside himself. He was just a man, who went to class every day in his wool sports jacket, with a smile in his face, a twinkle in his eye, and a pair of black shades if it was sunny. He walked with a spring in his step through the few halls of the small community college, and went home every night to his wife and two daughters, who were heading off to college themselves. He was just a man who worked, read literature and journal articles in his free time, and penned a couple of essays if the creative urge surfaced. And here he was being sued by Steven Spielberg.

Well, the media couldn't keep quiet about this, particularly Pat Robertson, who had his own television show at the time. And Herb soon found himself being interviewed by Pat Robertson on his show. The hype increased, and Herb's life suddenly grew exciting and interesting, all on a whim of a thought.

Finally, after both Herb and Spielberg grew tired of this bizarre little turn of events, Herb agreed that he would not write any more essays about Jesus Christ and ET, and Spielberg, in the end, dropped the charges.

And this was just one of the stories Sarah heard in between The Miller's Tale and The Reeve's Tale.

Sarah took three classes with him in all, as she was hooked on his teaching style from the first class. In an Early American Literature class, she listened to Herb's quick and animated style as he discussed Thomas Paine. Now, Thomas Paine was one of Herb's favorites, as he had written one of his college theses on the man, and took a particular liking to *The Age of Reason,* which they were reading at the time. As they proceeded through the text, and Herb brought all of his enlightened wisdom about the man and his philosophies on God and Nature, he lost himself again in another personal story, which captured Sarah's attention like nothing she had experienced before.

Herb felt the pulse of Thomas Paine. Tom was a rebel at heart, born in England in 1737, not wealthy, with a bit of a discontented spirit toward the British government, but he always nurtured his writing craft. By a stroke of good luck, he met Ben Franklin, in London, who suggested he come to America. He did, his pen found a

164

home, and his prolific, and somewhat controversial writing career, was born. He was a soldier in Washington's Army, among other things, and felt the pulse of the new country. Herb knew him, it seemed, and this knowledge and passion seemed to come to life in the classroom. He studied him, all his writings and his life, but was most intrigued by the end of his life. Tom died in America, on his farm in New Rochelle, New York. But, word has it that in 1819, a relative exhumed his body and took his remains to England, where they were properly buried on his home turf. But no one has been able to find his remains in England, so this information, still remains, hearsay. So, Tom Paine's whereabouts continue to be a mystery. Well, Herb couldn't sit right with this information. The man, this prolific writer who he adored, needed to be located. So, Herb located the location where Tom's farm had been in New Rochelle, and approached the little old lady who now owned the property. She was a fragile old woman, who lived alone, as her husband had died years earlier. She sat in her house day after day, fed her cat, watched her television, and waited for some unknown event to occur. Her life passed, day after day, with the same breezes, the same sounds from the field and the same cat that rubbed up against her legs when it was hungry. But, one day, she heard a strange car coming down the long gravel driveway. She heard it from afar, knew it was different, pulled back the thin sheer curtain that had hung from the window for the past sixteen years, and watched as a little brown car parked itself in front of her farmhouse. A little young man emerged, he was fit and trim, had a bit of a bounce in his step, but she didn't know him. He knocked on the door, and she soon found herself facing Herb Sillar.

Herb explained the situation, that her property was situated on the land which had once been Thomas Paine's, and since no one could find his body, Herb believed his remains to be buried beneath her soil. He asked for permission to start the digging process. She thought long and hard about it, but decided in the end, that she liked her tranquil life, and she didn't want a bunch of unknown men, diggers and literary saints, digging around her property. So, she told the young man that she didn't have many more years to live. She knew her life was numbered, so she told him he could dig as much as he wanted when she was dead and gone. Herb left the house, pleased enough with that answer, and at the time of Herb's lecture to Sarah, he was anxiously awaiting the death of an old woman in New

Rochelle, New York. And I hope that Herb made that dig before his own passing.

After stories like this, who wouldn't listen to The Age of Reason, and Rights of Man, the prolific writings of the man whose body is still floating in oblivion?

Or what about this one? Sarah often heard about Herb's wife, who had recently divorced Herb after both of their daughters were gone from the home. But, earlier in the marriage, his wife insisted that the two travel to an old Pennsylvania town, where an old schoolgirl friend was getting married. Herb didn't know the girl, nor did he have much interest in traveling with his wife to attend a marriage ceremony that held little interest for him. He had things to do, like contemplate Thomas Paine's whereabouts. But, in the end, like every good husband, you understand that there are certain things you must do in a marriage to ensure a tranquil level of emotionality in the house. So, he went. They stayed in a hotel in the old town, and like a good investigative literary scholar, Herb immediately talked with the town folk to find out the best antique places, the historical museums, and any other item of interest. He had noticed an old house in close proximity to the hotel that seemed to be in disrepair, as the shutters were falling off their hinges, and the paint was peeling off the wood like paper. He inquired about the house, in his nonchalant and whimsical way, and discovered that it was scheduled to be demolished the next day, and a new house erected in its place. This was before the time of concerted preservation that our country has now entered, so Herb saw an opportunity.

That night, as his wife was getting ready to go to bed, and chattered about her old friend, and the outfit she would wear at the wedding the following day, she noticed that her husband was fully dressed with a flashlight in hand. He put on his coat and started to say, "I'll be right back, honey," but instead heard, "Where on Earth are you going at this hour?"

Herb explained the situation, and told her that the town was demolishing the gem of a house that was situated at the end of the road, and he wanted to make sure that nothing inappropriate would be demolished, along with the house's foundations. His wife was horrified!

"Do you mean you're going to trespass on someone else's property?"

"Oh, honey," Herb pacified her resistance, "it's nothing really. The house will be gone tomorrow. No one will know."

So, Herb went off into the night, in a strange town, with a flashlight, toward the old house from the Civil War era, which would lose its life in a few short hours. He entered the house and found a treasure chest of old books. He looked in closets, where several Civil war uniforms were left hanging. Most of the house was abandoned, but a few discarded pieces of furniture were scattered about the house. But Herb spent his time near the treasure chest of books, as he was a collector of first editions, and most of the books that stood before his eyes, were first editions. The smell of the old pages and leather-bound backs alone were enough to quicken his heart's pace. He began stuffing books in his coat and pants until he could no longer comfortably walk and carry anymore. He walked out of the house and back to the hotel room where his wife slept. The house was demolished the next day. It was gone when he came home from the wedding. But the literary saint saved a legacy.

# Chapter Twenty-Four

*There is no use trying, said Alice; one can't believe impossible things.
I dare say you haven't had much practice, said the Queen. When I
was your age, I always did it for half an hour a day. Why, sometimes
I've believed as many as six impossible things before breakfast.*

**Lewis Carroll (1832-1898)**

And Herb was just one of the characters of the team that helped to
build on the literary foundation that Sarah had begun to build. All of
the professors seemed to fill a certain part of a well-rounded
education that every person should receive.

Another professor was Dr. Todd Collard who filled a different sort
of knowledge about literature. He was a soft-spoken man, tall, with
long curly blonde hair. He had the air of a foreigner as he was new to
the school when he taught Sarah, and she was used to two of the other
professors who were older, had been with the University since its

inception and who had established strong roots in the Virginia area. Todd, on the other hand, had arrived in Virginia from California, a few years earlier, after graduating with a doctor of philosophy from University of California, Irvine. He wore T-shirts and tan jeans to class, and the contents of his tee-shirts always piqued Sarah's interest, as it offered a glimpse into his life outside of the classroom. Her favorite, and one she actually inquired about since she did not recognize the man on his shirt, was Miles Davis. And this was Sarah's first introduction to a master of jazz and soul. Todd was a laid-back sort, who took nearly eight years to finish his doctor of philosophy and dissertation, which is not necessarily a bad thing, as he used a lot of his time to travel. His personality stood in direct opposition to the traditional Southern older males she had been used to thus far. But he stood steady, in a sea of foreigners, and later stood steady enough to become Chair of the entire English Department.

His passion in literature seemed to rest itself in the countries far outside of the traditional realm of literature, and it was through Todd that Sarah learned Latin American Literature, magical realism, Japanese Literature, African Literature, Indian Literature, Brazilian Literature, and completed her senior thesis with him in Israeli and Palestinian Literature. As literature reflects the pulse of the world in each culture, these lessons opened Sarah to a world of politics, struggles, generational riffs, new customs and cultures, but most importantly, the vast differences of class and culture we have all created on our own sides of the world. Todd didn't stand at the front of the classroom, but sat in a chair, and in the smaller classes, the students formed their desks in a circle around him, to better participate in discussions about the stories. His specialty was Latin America, particularly Chile, as he had spent some time in the country studying its literature and history. Pablo Neruda had always been one of Sarah's favorite poets, as he was introduced to her in Literary Arts Magnet School, and was furthered built by her father's love of the same poet. Sarah and her father sent each other books in support of their shared love of his craft. But Todd supplemented all of these literary figures and characters with the historical facts of the time, as much of the literature, including Isabel Allende's *The House of the Sprits*, outlines history with fictional characters.

And the Christopher Newport University English Department, at the time, had a rotating senior thesis schedule, where each of the professors switched each semester teaching the group of graduating seniors about theme-based literature. In Sarah's final semester, she happened to have Todd as a professor, and thus learned about the differences between Israeli and Palestinian literature, and the politics and feelings behind each one. They studied newspaper articles, studied the words of Arafat and Netanyahu, and then saw a direct correlation of these conflicts reflected in the great literary masters representing each country. Sarah learned of the kibbutz, and the generational conflicts that ensued because of this different type of class living, and analyzed its social implications throughout literature.

This was a different type of teaching. It was interactive and mind-opening. Each class served as a beautiful haven for Sarah. And Belle seemed to be beside her the whole time, taking in her own perceptions of the classes, and her writings reflected as such. They still read each other's papers and ideas and pushed each other along to the very end, their graduation. Sarah graduated with a grade point average of 3.49.....quite a long way from the .09 at Virginia Tech.

During her whole tenure at Christopher Newport University, Sarah worked part-time at the local hospital in Williamsburg. It was the only other institution, along with the library, that saw the town's citizens from all three districts, and even cared for the tourists, if God forbid, they needed care on their vacations. It was the first hospital ever established in the town, and grew from a small building to a large institutional entity with state-of-the-art medical equipment of the day. Its doctors, nurses and caretakers were the mothers and fathers of the community who cared for its citizens in moments of birth to moments of death and everything in between. It hosted bake sales and yard sales and sponsored community events with the Colonial Williamsburg Foundation and the College of William and Mary. It breathed life into the community while caring for its citizens and visitors.

Sarah got the job at the hospital from her boyfriend's mother who was Director of the Admissions department. She learned as much as she could about the medical community, while meeting its citizens and the heartbeat that sustained the town. She registered patients for outpatient and inpatient procedures, and learned the whole insurance process, surgical processes, inpatient processes, and all the little nuances that accompany a working hospital. Williamsburg Regional Hospital was one of the few hospitals left that had kept its autonomy and non-profit status, without affiliating itself with a big-name health care company. Everyone in the town liked this fact as it retained its old world, friendly charm. The Chief Executive Officer had been in that position for more than fifteen years, and had established a name and a presence in the community. He was a charming, Southern man who knew the pulse of the town, and ran the hospital as such, as it was important to make his patients, who were his family and friends, comfortable. The place contained a family atmosphere, and it seemed to exist as a bubble in a vast ocean of health care changes. Sarah's boss was a sweetheart and always communicated to her that her school was first and scheduled her work hours accordingly, as Sarah sometimes had the tendency to put work above school. But her boss, her boyfriend's mother, allowed her to read, to work on papers and other school projects while working, which helped Sarah more than she ever realized. In between registering patients and studying, she heard the occasional story from a patient. One older gentleman stopped by the front desk to inquire which room his wife was situated. Both appeared to be in their eighties. As the older gentleman waited, he talked about the first time he had met his wife, at a dance. She was engaged to someone else, but when he saw her, he knew that she was the one. He wooed her that night, and she broke off the engagement with the other chap. They married, and he went off to war and returned. They brought three beautiful children into the world. And as he stood and waited to hear the location of his wife, he seemed to be sifting through the beautiful memories he had made with her. Sarah listened, as she did with many of the hospital's visitors who told stories and anecdotes of their lives.

As Sarah began to become more interested in the pulse of a business organization, she became interested in the prospect of hospital administration, and grew more and more interested in the politics of the organization and its relationship with the community. The hospital was a cornerstone in the community, in all respects, as most of Williamsburg's residents worked there, and the organization contributed money to all sorts of worthwhile causes, formed volleyball and softball teams, and supported all of the community's events, along with the Colonial Williamsburg Foundation. So, Sarah was intrigued with the way this massive machine worked with the politics of the town. She supplemented her English classes at Christopher Newport University with business classes, and formed a minor in Business Administration to add a practical edge to her English degree. And as her interest in the hospital grew, as she spent most of her waking moments there and heard all the inside scoop from her boyfriend's mother, she initiated an internship with the public relations department of the hospital. Christopher Newport University supported internships with various businesses within the English department, but most of the businesses were located in Newport News. The public relations manager at the hospital agreed, and Sarah soon found herself as an apprentice to a young, smart woman who coordinated all of the hospital's outreach and communication efforts.

# Chapter Twenty-Five

*God could not be everywhere, and therefore he made mothers.*

**Rudyard Kipling (1865-1936)**

Stacy, Sarah's new public relations mentor, was a young woman, about twenty-nine at the time, with two young children at home. She graduated from Virginia Commonwealth University with a degree in Journalism with an emphasis in public relations. She had a young face, and a bright heart, and wore the smartest business suits to work everyday. This was Sarah's first mentor in the business world, and she picked a good one, as Stacy held impeccable standards for herself and for the organization, but had a big enough heart to shine through in all of her work. She worked part-time as she had two little ones at home, so Sarah could work in her office during the time that she was away. Stacy gave her writing assignments within the hospital, and Sarah found herself interviewing doctors, cardiologists, board members, volunteers, and all sorts of people to find out information for the stories she was assigned to write, and she thrived talking with all of these folks, as people loved to open up to her. Some doctors just talked shop, others touched on their lives. Volunteers who had lived in Williamsburg all of their lives, talked about how they had watched the hospital grow within the community. Department directors and nurses talked about their passion for their jobs. Board members talked about their involvement in the hospital but from a different organizational standpoint, as most came from the Colonial Williamsburg Foundation or other businesses in the area. Stacy taught her everything: how to arrange a layout, how to use graphic design software, how to write with a business edge, how to write press releases and feature articles. She took her under her wing, and lifted her up little by little.

During this year, the hospital went through many changes. The Chief Executive Officer, who had been a stalwart with the community, was told by the board of directors that it was time to affiliate with another big named health care system. They couldn't resist the financial package that the other hospitals were offering, as the hospital seemed to be growing by leaps and bounds. They had just embarked on an expansion project that was costing millions of dollars as was, and a projected ten years down the line only revealed more and more growth, as the town of Williamsburg itself was busting at the seams. The Chief Executive Officer, the stalwart Southern boy, refused. He had seen that hospital establish its friendly and family-like atmosphere, and damned if he was going to sit back and watch as the young boys with their slick business suits came in to take over his old-charm hospital. So, he was asked to resign. He did so, under the premise that it was his time to retire, and he wanted to travel. Soon, a new young buck came in, whom the board guaranteed would usher the affiliation with another big-time health care company without a hitch. He came from another state, didn't know the pulse of the Williamsburg network too much, and didn't know quite what he was getting into. He knew he would usher a change, but he didn't quite know what that change meant for the community.

So, the renovations continued, the new president came in, the new wing and surgical units were built, a grand opening was held, and Hospara swiftly penetrated the scene and took forty-nine percent of

174

the hospital's ownership. This last part was done as the board wanted to reassure the town that they still had ownership. But years later, the fifty-one/forty-nine split was soon forgotten, and the hospital was soon swiftly in Hospara's river, heading downstream with the current of the health care industry.

Sarah's internship ended, which saddened both Sarah and Stacy. Sarah graduated, and Stacy continued to contract writing assignments with Sarah, but it wasn't the same, at least for Sarah. The assignments now took on a different meaning, as she was no longer learning, but now a professional that made contracts for writing assignments. It was a privilege for Sarah. But it was a dynamic she was not accustomed to.

In her last year of college, Sarah felt it was time to move out of her mother's condominium, as it was now her decision, and she felt as if she was back in control of making decisions in her own life. A friend from her group of close stalwarts from elementary, junior high and high school, Karen, had returned after graduation from James Madison University, and was looking to move to an apartment in Newport News. Sarah thought this was an excellent opportunity, so the two girls moved into one of the newest and best apartment complexes in Newport News, Mill Creek. Mill Creek was a planned community, one of the first in the area, with all types of living arrangements including large and small houses, apartments and condominiums, and the area was laden with golf courses, pools, clubhouses and guest houses. It was located right next to the airport and the interstate, was a convenient location for travelers, and was closer to Christopher Newport University. Sarah still drove the 30-minute commute everyday to Williamsburg for the hospital, her mother and other friends. Sarah's life seemed to be coming together at this point. She was bubbling with energy and excitement, she had a new boyfriend, who treated her well and made her laugh, she was nearing graduation when the world seemed to be opening its doors to her, and she was always in good spirits. The memories of her past life were long forgotten, and buried beneath layers and layers of happy pursuits and promises of a bright future. This was one of the best times of her life, as she broke out on her own, in her own terms, and thrived both in her work, and school setting.

Karen had moved to Williamsburg from Tennessee when the girls were in the third grade. She came with the most delectable Southern accent, and long blonde hair with a few curls on the end. She was a beautiful little girl, and knew it. She wore different color ribbons in her hair every day, coordinated her outfits just so, and used her language to charm all the teachers and the boys. Sarah and Karen didn't become close until junior high when they were cheerleaders together. They had known each other, been in the same Brownie and Girl Scout troops, been on the same swim team, but cheerleading brought them closer together.

In the fifth grade, Sarah developed a bit of a crush on a boy in her class. He was the dark, brooding, intellectual type, or at least, as much as one can be in the fifth grade but his hair was a sandy blonde. He was intellectual, buried himself in literature and didn't seem to get involved with all the melodrama of their group of friends. His older sister was Meghan's best friend, so it seemed to be fate that the two would begin to date, or whatever dating consists of at that age. The two star-crossed lovers exchanged teddy bears. Ducey, the teddy bear that was made by one of Sarah's mother's De Colores friends when Sarah was two, was given to Brian, and Brian gave his Paddington Bear, sans the blue coat and yellow hat, to Sarah. It was a symbolic gesture, and seemed like the thing to do for the person one loves, at such an age.

Brian and Sarah continued this relationship until the ninth grade when things began to get a little out of hand and unstable in Sarah's life. He wrote her letters when she took trips to her father's house in the summers and winters, and wrote with a penmanship that only comes from reading good classic literature. He used words that Sarah had never heard before, and spoke with an intellectualism that was far beyond his years. Brian, too, lived in King's Gate, along with Karen and Emily.

# Chapter Twenty-Six

*The Past -- the dark unfathomed retrospect! The teeming gulf --the
sleepers and the shadows! The past! The infinite greatness of the past!
For what is the present after all but a growth out of the past?*

**Walt Whitman (1819-1892)**

King's Gate was one of the most prominent neighborhoods in
Williamsburg at this time. Queen's Point was the only gated
community in Williamsburg at the time, but it was located in James
City County, and a little more removed from the din of their world.
King's Gate was not gated, and it didn't need to be. It would have
lost its essence had it been gated. It was in the heart of the woods,
and all of the street names came from the world of Robin Hood and
Sherwood Forrest, as the darkness and the mystery that the woods
possessed seemed to encase and blanket all of the families, the
struggles, the melodramas, and growth that occurred there. Those
woods had eyes.

The neighborhood consisted of the West Side and the East Side, with the center directed around the lake, and about four hundred and fifty homes. The West Side consisted of a long road that swept around the western side of the lake, with a few streets that branched off into other smaller streets, and every street and cul-de-sac, was protected by this canopy of trees. The sun was always shining above, and a few beams would seep their way between the branches of the trees, but for the most part, the neighborhood existed within an enigma. Fewer houses were on the West side, and were much larger in size. One of the prominent doctors of the town lived on the West side with his five daughters and one son, who attended the Catholic private school in the town. And a prominent architect, Harlton Saggett, lived on the West side. Sarah would later study his architectural work in her Literary Arts Magnet School, as he not only designed his house, but also designed the Muscarelle Museum at the College of William and Mary, where Sarah held an internship during her senior year of high school. One of his brilliant drawings of a ship, which largely resembled a photograph, if one stood far enough back from it, donned one of the front halls in the hospital where Sarah worked everyday, years later. The West Side was a little further removed from the din of activity on the East Side.

The beginning of the neighborhood, as one turns left onto the shaded Lakeside Drive, is directly parallel to the infamous Colonial Parkway, which runs from the Fort at Jamestown, to the Battlefields of Yorktown. It's a symbolic road, lined with dogwoods in the spring, which Sarah's mother loved to drive down on spring Sundays. It holds a magic like no other. There are no lines on the road, and it is paved in a cobblestone like surface, as it is grainy, and sand-like in color, but possesses an old-world feel. Lakeside Drive, leading into King's Gate, runs parallel to the Colonial Parkway. At first, only a few sparse houses can be seen, as the first house on the left, was the house in which Brownie and her husband first lived when they moved from Ohio. But as one penetrates the forest, a vast display of houses can be seen to the left, with various roads branching outwards and inwards, and every which way. The houses are hidden, between small thickets of woods, between other houses, and no house is the same, nor resembles the other in any way. Deeper inward was Brownie's house, the one that Sarah lived in for those few short months, and one house over was Chad's house, a trusted high school friend, who had

an energy and spirit that gave his father more gray hairs than he ever
wanted.  More inward was Emily's house, which sat on a corner lot in
the heart of the Eastern side.  Emily's house was an anchor in the
neighborhood, as Emily's mother was one of the best social butterflies
this side of England.  She organized parties, kept up with the town
and neighborhood gossip, maintained her presence at the pool and on
the tennis court, played doubles every morning with another
neighborhood couple, and somehow managed to keep all of the
families in constant communication.  Her husband left her when
Emily was in junior high, and she also had two other sons to think
about.  She had never worked, maybe in a few part-time jobs in
boutiques, but nothing to support the huge house she then lived in, not
to mention the three kids.  But saving that anchor was of utmost
important to her, and rightfully so, as it served as an anchor, not only
for all the neighborhood families, but for her children as well.  She
eventually remarried, and her new husband moved to the anchor
house in King's Gate.  Further inward was Belle's house, which was
situated right on the lake, with a large wooded expanse between the
lake and the back deck of Belle's house.  Right across the street was a
little dock, where the family kept their canoe, and Belle and Sarah
often took canoe trips around the lake.

Further east was Karen's house, which would have liked to have
been the anchor of King's Gate, and it stood out like a Colonial
monstrosity.  It was a beautiful house, and always had the most
impeccable yard and landscape shapes (much to the credit of Emily's
brother), but there was something ominously out of place about it.
Anyone heading to the clubhouse, or to the pool, or the tennis courts,
or to the West side, was faced with this monstrosity as they cruised
down the road.  One couldn't escape it.  It loomed there, as if with a
big sign, "Look at me!"  Karen's mother installed lights that shone on
the front of it, to illuminate its facade at night, and always donned the
front door with a Colonial wreath full of fresh fruit or autumn-colored
flowers.  The inside was always impeccably decorated, and a bit
disorderly in areas, which was always a bit refreshing.  Complete
perfection is always a bit unsettling. But something was always a bit
off.  Maybe it was the note on the door that Karen's mother always
displayed which read, "Don't knock. I'm sleeping."  Or maybe it was
the fact that every time Sarah entered the house, another room was
being renovated, wallpaper changed, furniture changed, what have

you. Karen's father was an emergency room doctor for the big-named health care company that came and swooped up Williamsburg Regional Hospital. He was quiet, methodical, and was a knowing eye that always kept a short distance. He was one of those figures who was never there, but always knew. When he was there, you felt as if you had known him your whole life. He once stitched Sarah's finger on the spot as her finger was pierced by the spoke of a bicycle at one of Karen's parties. He was a beacon of true light in a house of artificial lights that seemed to dominate its presence. Karen's mother didn't work either, but spent her days renovating the house, which was always laden with impeccable wallpaper and furniture, and was peppered with papers and magazines---the things that keep women going.

Further inward, more toward Belle's house, on the same side of the same lake, was Brian's house. And this is where Sarah came to spend her time with her first love, her schoolgirl crush. Brian liked to sit outdoors, near the lake, on Sunday afternoons in the fall. He was raised well, by one of the strongest women Sarah knew. One wouldn't notice by her size because she stands at about four feet and ten inches, and speaks with the softest voice. Sometimes, Sarah couldn't even hear her voice when she picked up the phone to say hello when Sarah called their house. She worked with taxes, in the Internal Revenue Service, and taught her only son how to cook, how to do his laundry, and all of the countless other tasks that are important for young boys, but many mothers forget about. Brian cooked dinner for the family once a week, and at that age, this was impressive. Sarah never tasted the meals, and that is a different matter entirely, but think of the lessons that type of practice teaches.

Brian and Sarah talked about their plans for the future, where they wanted to go to college and how many children they wanted to have. He talked of his older sister, whom he immensely admired. Brian was also quite knowledgeable in the five-minute phone rule, as he was often a recipient of a dial tone throughout the conversations. But these types of experiences were enough to fuel Sarah with enough energy to get through the next hours of daily life that were her world at the time. She tried mainly to retreat to her bedroom, where she didn't have to hear the events of her own house, which always seemed to exist on a banal level. She had a future to look forward to.

So, Karen and Sarah grew close in cheerleading in junior high. Karen and Sarah's relationship had always revolved around cheerleading, as they were around each other for practices and camps. Sarah liked Karen because she was always jovial, always had the ability to laugh and share a good joke.

Sarah moved in with Karen in the apartment in Mill Creek. It was a beautiful apartment, brand new, and very spacious. Karen, or rather, Karen's mother, bought all of the furniture, stereo equipment, etc. Sarah contributed most of the artwork and wall hangings, and it soon turned into a lovely little start to a new beginning. Sarah's mother bought her a new bed for her graduation, and Sarah began her first bookcase collection with three simple shelves of the books she had acquired in her youth and throughout college. The duvet, curtains, sheets and pillows were all coordinated, and Sarah loved decorating her new home to her tastes. She held a bit of Brownie's spirit and impeccable decorating tastes with her, and added her own touches to the mix.

Sarah was in such good spirits during this time, and much of it was attributed to her new boyfriend, Matt. After her five-year relationship with a boyfriend who showed her the finer things in life, like crack deals, fifteen-inch rims, and the like, she was relieved to be free and heading toward her future. As an elective in one of her last semesters in college, she took a Classic Music History class, to learn the progression of music through the years, to recognize composers and symphonies. She had learned to recognize the great masters, but only through solo piano pieces, like short sonatas or Polonaises, but not from the scores of music they created for symphonies, ballets, operas and other compositional productions. And here, in this class was Matt. She knew Matt because he had gone to her high school, lived in her same neighborhood, but he was a friend of her younger brother, the middle stepsibling. And since she never really wanted to fraternize with anyone who was in anyway close to the situation in her home, she did not speak to Matt much. Matt was quiet, kept to himself, and didn't quite look favorably on the group of people that Sarah was friends with. So, the indifference was mutual, on all sides.

But, for some strange reason, and by some stroke of Fate (yes, God does have a sense of humor), a friendship developed in this class, they began studying together, and the next thing Sarah knew, they were inseparable. Matt was a dreamer, a poet, a brooding type that spent moments in a dark room, strumming the same chords on the guitar for hours. He found solace in music, and spoke with unbounded energy at times, and then some days, slipped into a thoughtful stupor. He had the brightest blue eyes that always shone when he saw Sarah, and his boy-like and utter innocence and gaiety was like a salve on Sarah's heart. His parents were going through a bitter divorce at the time, and both Sarah and Matt seemed to throw themselves into each other. It was passionate and blissful. He loved without abandon, without end, and enraptured Sarah's heart. But Sarah, knew, deep down inside that their lives would never coincide. Although he was a dreamer, he was a stagnant dreamer, who would one day settle down in a family life, and at that point, Sarah did not see herself heading in this direction. She had her eyes on the world, and she knew that Matt did not share the same vision. They separated, with much friction and pain, on both sides, but both eventually made it. They had spent nearly every day together, passionately and intensely, and a separation was difficult to bear.

Soon thereafter, an event occurred which would change Sarah's life forever.

# Chapter Twenty-Seven

*The Brain is wider than the sky.*

**Emily Dickinson (1830-1886)**

Sarah had begun to hear from employers, and had traveled to Boston for a few job interviews, but nothing seemed to feel right. She continued sending resumes out, and continued working at the hospital full-time. One Thursday, in November, one month before her graduation, she received a phone call from her boss that an employee had called in sick to work for the night, and asked if she would come in to cover a four-hour shift on the front desk. Sarah agreed, and soon found herself flying down Interstate sixty-four to the hospital. She walked behind the front desk, unloaded her internship and resume books, and noticed a young man standing in front of her. She had not even clocked in yet.

"Where is the woman who was here a few minutes ago?" the young man asked.

There are moments in your life when you look into someone's eyes and feel as if you have known the person your whole life, even though the physical features are not recognizable. And as this young man stood before her, and asked this simple question, she felt something tingle through her body when she looked at him. Everything in her life, her past, her present, her future, her resumes, her mother, her stepsiblings, her grandmother, her father, her literature, were lost somewhere in those eyes. Everything was there, and she stood there, looking into an ocean of vastness and of mirror-like quality. She didn't quite recognize the vastness of history that stood before her, for at that time, she was just living her life, with the events of her past long forgotten. She knew they were there, but was quite happy creating a new life for herself, and hoped that the more and more layers she formed on top of the pain would eventually annihilate the former, and she could go on living happily, in denial. Where did he come from? What was this feeling traveling through her body? A million thoughts engulfed her mind at that moment.

"I don't know. I just walked in the door," she managed to say.

He explained that he had arrived minutes earlier, and was registered by an older woman who was sitting in the desk she was now occupying. Sarah understood him to be speaking of her boss, but since she was nowhere to be found at the time, the young boy continued talking. He explained that he had come in for an X-ray, but had locked his keys in his car.

"I do this about once a week," he added with a charming smile.

He explained that the woman behind the desk had called security. But at this point, all he needed was a butter knife, as he had grown quite accustomed to unlocking the door from the outside himself. Sarah knew that their break room housed all sorts of forks, and knives, and salt and pepper shakers, and packets and packets of soy sauce and ketchup and duck sauce and any other possible condiment or utensil one could need while eating. So, Sarah told him to sit tight and she would return in a minute. She walked to the back room, and began rummaging through all of the drawers in search of a butter knife. After several minutes, she realized that their break room, at that particular moment, housed every single item, except a knife. So, she walked back out to the front desk with the next best thing, a spoon! He smiled, took the spoon and walked to his car. He returned, minutes later, successful. But another hospital visitor was talking with Sarah at the front desk. Sarah watched from her periphery as the young man nodded a polite "Thanks," and took his book and registration material he had left on the counter, and walked out of her life.

Sarah sat there stunned for a moment. What had just happened? Any other person would have seen this as such another experience that occurs at the front desk of a hospital. Things happen, people lock their keys in their car, and people have nice-looking eyes. What's the big deal? But, something was different here. Sarah couldn't explain it at the time, but she felt as if she had just collided with a star.

An hour later, she received a phone call from the young man who had walked out of her life the hour earlier. He asked her out on a date, she accepted, and she soon found herself falling helplessly in that beautiful, wonderful, heart-wrenching, painful, body-wrenching, delectable, and spiritual pit called love. She had boyfriends before, lived passionately and deeply with them, and each contributed in some way in her life. But this was something she had never experienced before. This was not something that she had read about, or something that she had learnt in a classroom, or from a literary saint. This was not something learnt by a friend or a mentor or a parent. This was celestial, ethereal, un-Earth-like and piercing. She was flailing in uncharted territory, as was he.

William was a student at the College of William and Mary Law at the time. He graduated from University of North Carolina with a degree in economics, spent a few years in Chapel Hill renovating a dilapidated house he bought, sold it for a profit, and then traveled to Central America for a time. He didn't have any intention of coming home either. He had gone through the motions of school, college and the like, just as Sarah did, but when graduation came and went, and he was expected to get a job, something didn't feel right. He worked with various construction companies in Chapel Hill, learnt the industry in building and contracting, and helped renovate many of the old historic buildings in downtown Chapel Hill. He liked to work with his hands, to build things, to concentrate his efforts diligently and intensely with a project in front of him. He liked to see his hands at work, and see the finished product. He had always been like that. It started with little things when he was a little boy, and grew as he grew, and he was soon building houses. But even a few years after graduation, he wasn't sure what he wanted to do. He had a past as well that he didn't quite want to remember, but it was a different sort of past.

William could trace his roots back to the first colonist that landed on the banks of Jamestown in 1607. His family had always been large plantation owners, and his family, and extended family owned half of Garden City County, that delectable tract of land that lies on the banks of the James River between Williamsburg and Richmond. William was a direct descendent of the fifteenth president of the United States. He came from a long line of lawyers and judges. He had freedom, democracy and the essence of America in his blood. It ran through his veins and thrived in the tips of his toes. He had a head of steel and the tenacity of a bull. He was a different sort of lot all together. We can speak of literary saints, mothers, fathers, friends' parents, bosses, sisters, professors, or any of the other characters that grace our lives with a sense of placement. We know where they belong. They carry a presence and a meaning and a purpose. They have a role and a duty. But William resided in a class unlike any other Sarah had ever known. She had seen the upper echelons of society; she had seen the banal levels of society and everything in between. But this, this man, and everything he represented, was not a class, but an essence, a presence that had a destiny. His presence, his actions, his morals and ethics and the little daily rituals of his life conveyed his destiny. And Sarah had grown accustomed to meeting all sorts of different kinds of people in her life. She recognized the dreamers, the thinkers, the dead-enders, the helpers, the ones who always seemed to place an obstacle in the path, the blenders, the walkers, but William – William was not a kind that she had ever seen before. It was not something that could be totally summed up in a class description. He was William, he was America, he was the land, and he was the heavens and everything in between.

# Chapter Twenty-Eight

*Happiness is a butterfly, which, when pursued, is always just beyond your grasp, but which, if you will sit down quietly, may alight upon you.*

**Nathaniel Hawthorne (1804-1864)**

William traveled to Central America, as he had finished the house in Chapel Hill, and still wasn't sure where he was heading. He had always nourished a travel spirit within him that came from his mother. His mother always harbored the adventurous spirit in her, that's why William's father married her, but she didn't get the chance to explore it much, as she soon found herself married with two children. William was the youngest. His older sister, Elizabeth, was four years his elder. The family grew up in Portsmouth, as William's father was a math professor at Tidewater Community College. Much like the literary saint Herb Sillar, William's father could have taught at any university, as his family name and knowledge would have served him well. But, the gentle and humble spirit that he was, he wanted to teach the commuters, the working class, the students who paid for their own classes when they scraped together enough change after paying the phone bill and the rent. He wanted to bring a touch of his gentle spirit to their lives, as they had no other opportunity for exposure to it. They lived in Portsmouth to be closer to his job, but traveled to Garden City County on the weekends, where his father lived in one of the plantation houses. His father was an Assistant Attorney General and a judge for the State of Virginia, but was retired and spent his time documenting the history of the county. William spent his weekends here, and enjoyed playing with friends and cousins in the surrounding plantations that dotted the banks of the James. He grew up on its fields, in its woods, on its water. And if King's Gate harbored a quasi-Sherwood Forest environment, these wooded lots, these trees, this whole area was the real thing. And his great-great-grandfather, the fifteenth President of the United States, named it as such when he retired from the Presidency: Sherwood Grove.

And that it was. Driving from Williamsburg, as you cross the Chickahominy River, one of the tributaries of the great James, one enters into a dark canopy of stately trees. It didn't matter if the sun was at full throttle; one was immediately emerged in the shadiness and protection of those watchful trees with hearts and eyes. They held the secrets of the past, long before the first settler arrived, with the Pamunkey, Mattaponi and Chickahominy tribes. They had created a culture of governing their lives by the subtleties of the land, air, sky and water, and even today, Garden City County still holds that essence. Sherwood Grove was like a web, with a great powerful spider at the helm. It watched as people came and went, and caught those who were worthy to grace its land. The drive was long, from Williamsburg to the plantations, and was a straight shoot, with a few turns and bends to keep the driver alert. Its land was rich with natural resources, farms and people with hearts and souls of pure gold. They all felt the soil, the history and the past in their souls, and one could hear as much in the tones of their voices, the cadence in their speech, their easiness and lack of time.

And William liked to travel, as he could be anyone he wanted to be when he traveled. He didn't have a past, he wasn't linked to the history of the country, and he could travel with and maneuver within the lowest of class societies in other cultures with relative ease. No one knew who he was, and no one asked in those types of situations. He could lose himself in the surroundings, in the music, in the outward and unfettered displays of affection and movement. This type of passionate living and dancing without abandon was new to him, and the people in these cultures, reveled in his curiosity of such a surrounding. So, they took him in like a friend, like a son, and he found himself in others homes, feeling and sensing the pulse of Latin American culture. He was free of all the expectations, and his past which followed him around like a ball and chain. And his unknown destiny that he ran unknowingly and helplessly from.

But too much freedom can cause a person to think without boundaries, which is not necessarily a good thing for a wandering traveler. So, William decided that it was time to fulfill his duty, and at least, part of his destiny, and enrolled in the College of William and Mary's Law School.

He wasn't like the rest of the students. He kept to himself, maintained one of the highest averages in the class, but he didn't quite seem to fit in well with the others. They clung to each other, as if for dear life. They studied together, went to law parties together, and hung out in the same law study lounges together. It wasn't as if he snubbed them; whenever he saw them he was cordial, like a good Southern gentleman, and perhaps even sat with them sometimes. When he felt like being social, he would grace a party or two. But he did his best to keep his distance from the crowd. He saw them in class, in the law buildings, in the only two bars that grace the corner of the campus. That was enough. When class was finished, he drove the thirty minutes to his plantation home in Garden City County.

He didn't live in the large plantation house where he had spent his childhood weekends, and where his own father was raised. He lived here for a few months when he returned from Chapel Hill, but he was living with his sister, who had graduated from the University of North Carolina years earlier, and was now working at the Rockefeller Foundation, in tours, costumery, and period dancing. And while he loved his sister dearly, he wasn't exactly happy about sharing a living space with her. His grandfather, years earlier in the 1960s, had moved a small two-bedroom house to his property to house anyone who happened to land in the county, and on his property, for work. It was a small house, with two small bedrooms, and was in disrepair. It stood on the western side of the larger brick home, and as the years went by, the old house was forgotten, and seemed to decay beneath a blanket of brush. Well, William, fresh from renovating a house of his own in Chapel Hill, had the grand idea to renovate the old worker's house, which had been left neglected, and change the house into his own home. His parents agreed, plans were drawn, and William and his father began the project. They completely gutted the inside, repainted the floors and the rooms, installed new kitchen counters, and appliances, and William built a beautiful wrap around, screened porch on the East and North sides of the house to make full use of the afternoon summer breezes that swept off the corn fields. The new house was beautiful, white on the outside, and a combination of hunter green and white on the inside. William's mother decorated the inside with old black and white photographs from her youth, her own paintings that she had painted years earlier, and his sister planted a beautiful herb and flower garden around its perimeter. William displayed the textiles and masks he had acquired in his travels to Central America, Indonesia and Europe, and even planted a small vegetable garden on a small plot of grassy land on the Western grounds, where he grew the most delectable cantaloupes. He was most happy working with his hands, saving houses, things and animals, as he always seemed to bring home the stray dogs in the county. And he was happy with his creation. His bedroom faced the western side of the house, with perfect views of the setting sun, and he hung a crystal in the window above his bed to refract the suns rays every evening.

He had always kept to himself, even in high school at Tidewater Academy. He didn't hang out with any particular group, because their dramas seemed so petty to him. He played football for the school, was even quarterback for the team, but he wasn't the typical quarterback who loved the attention that the school often lavished on the star player. He liked the game. He liked the strategy. He liked the way the coaches thought, and the way they planned each play. And William was the one to get all the orders, and who carried them out on the field. He would later serve as manager for University of North Carolina's football team.

But William was in law school now, fulfilling some type of destiny he wasn't quite aware of yet. He was playing football that day, on a makeshift Law School team, when someone's body slammed into the back of his body. He fell to the ground, in utter agony, thinking that his lumbar spine had split down the middle. But he was never one to lay in injury long, as he had a massive scar on his left knee to show for it. He blew his knee years earlier that had put an end to a future in football, not that he planned on being a pro. So, he quickly got up, and walked off the field, knowing that he would not be playing the rest of the game.

William had this endearing little habit of refusing to go to a hospital even when he was badly hurt. This would show up again months later when William and Sarah embarked on a snowboarding trip in the snowy banks of Snowshoe, West Virginia, when he broke his wrist in seven places, and did not go to the hospital until he got back to Williamsburg. It is not an adamant refusal, per se, it is more like a "wait-and-see" phenomenon. Or perhaps he didn't believe he was hurt. Or perhaps he liked to see how long it took for him to finally make the decision to go. All he knew was that three days later, a large bruise appeared on his lower spine, and he was having trouble sitting down, so he decided to go to the hospital to get an X-ray. The college doctor prescribed the test, and he pocketed the script with the intention of going, sometime, in the future.

He wasn't too convinced that he necessarily needed this test, but his insurance was paying for it, and he would appease his worried mother's heart. So, as he drove by the hospital on his way back to Garden City County one day, he looked over at the sign, and decided, "What the hell. I'll get the X-Ray." He brought a book he was reading, which was recommended to him by a professor at University of North Carolina, and ducked in for the long haul. The wait was short, surprisingly, and he soon found himself walking back out to his car to go home. As he walked to his 1982 Toyota Landcruiser with the gun racks in the back, he felt in his jeans pocket for the keys. "Well," he thought, "Not surprising," as he had locked his keys in his car a week earlier. He had learnt very early in life that things

191

happen, and to get upset over these things was a waste of energy. So, he walked back into the hospital and informed the woman, who had registered him only twenty minutes before, that he had locked his keys in his car, and did she have a knife or a coat-hanger?

This was not the first time someone had locked their keys in their car at the hospital, and she knew that the appropriate procedure was to call security. She made the call and disappeared behind the desk. William walked to his car, and then walked back into the hospital, looking around for these ominous security guards, who never seemed to appear. When he walked again to the front desk, he found himself faced with a young blonde girl. "She looks like my old girlfriend," he thought. He explained to her the situation, and she disappeared behind the wall of registration cubicles. She produced a spoon; he unlocked his car, and walked back to the front desk. When he returned, the young girl was speaking with another patient. He thanked her, noticed the name on her nametag, and drove to Garden City County. During the drive, he couldn't get this girl out of his mind. "The minute I get home," he thought, "I'll call her and ask her out."

And this was how Sarah's world met William's.

♥

# Chapter Twenty-Nine

*How could I have been anyone other than me?*

**Dave Matthews (1967-    )**

Throughout all of the dramas and the struggles, the loves and the losses, the searches and the quests, the town of Williamsburg served as a uniting whole for Sarah's world. It was not a town, it was not a village, it seemed to have an essence and a spirit that slept soundly at times, but stood guard at others, and nestled itself snugly into their lives.

And it is a growing attachment. It doesn't happen all at once, as soon as one moves to its shaded streets and candlelit walkways. How quaint, one thinks, at first, but this is just the tip of the iceberg. After many years, one finds that it has a pulse of its own, a soul and spirit that sweeps throughout the atmosphere. And it was here where Sarah was raised.

Sarah's favorite festival was Grand Illumination. Many colonial towns have Grand Illumination, the historic lighting of the town before Christmas, but Williamsburg's Grand Illumination had a spirit like no other she had seen. She had gone to Grand Illumination with her family in the early years, and remembers the large baskets of brush that stood high above the sandstone streets, and their ceremonial lighting with brush torches that seemed to have come straight from the Colonial Era. She remembers the carolers, and the people in traditional Colonial costumes greeting visitors and families as if they were old friends. Grand Illumination, and the days leading to Christmas Day, were more special for Sarah than the actual day. It was the progression of anticipation leading to a culmination point. It was a festive gathering of like-minded folk who came out of their houses to come together as a whole to participate in the town's celebration of not only the roots of their Americanism, but the roots of Christianity. They saw their friends and families from school, from King's Gate, and the other families from James City County whom they had met through church. The night was always cold and dark, but the fire torches, and baskets of flaming brush high above Duke of Gloucester Street and the small road that led to the Governor's Palace were enough to add a peaceful glow on the faces of all the passersby that streamed through. And Grand Illumination was not a Grand Illumination without a steaming cup of hot apple cider to go with the music and the atmosphere. And the event was always topped with the grandest display of fireworks. Later in Sarah's life, she would witness the fireworks in many other towns, including Fourth of July in Washington, DC, and the firework displays never compared with those at Grand Illumination in Williamsburg at that time.

As Sarah grew older, her role of Grand Illumination observer, soon turned into participator, as her junior high and high school chorus performed here, with a long list of Christmas carols. Sarah first involved herself in chorus in the seventh grade. She knew the choral instructor, Mr. Angel, from her sister Meghan, who was choral accompanist for the high school chorus. While Mr. Angel was a brilliant accompanist, he liked the help of these two sisters as accompanists, as it freed him to lead his chorus from behind the piano, and it also provided a valuable learning experience for the two girls, but especially the younger, Sarah. He saw it in her, that she was not a follower. She couldn't stand, day after day, like the others, in a choral formation, and receive direction from a choral director. She needed to do her own thing. And Mr. Angel had the skills to lead the group of singers, and lead the piano player to his right, day after day. Angel knew music theory, jazz, classical, and could listen to a tune once, and create elaborate personal renditions of the same song he had just heard. He could play all the songs that Sarah was playing by looking at the sheet music once, but Sarah had to practice, and practice, and practice. And Angel pushed her, like no other teacher did. He was often angry with her, if a note was wrong, or if she forgot to look in his direction, or if she wasn't progressing as he had expected. But it was tough love, and she respected him, so she always rose to his expectations, which pushed her to the next level. But, without fail, after a performance, Angel lavished her with praise and thanks, which were moments that Sarah cherished. All those angry looks and wrong notes seemed to disappear after a performance. He was pleased and that was all she ever wanted.

Mr. Angel taught chorus at both the junior high school and the high school. He started at King's Gate Middle School in the mornings, where he taught Sarah, and then drove to the high school in the afternoon, where he taught her sister and the other high school students. Up until her involvement with chorus, Sarah had only learnt the classics, a few other songs that her piano teacher supplemented, and she learnt to play all of the pieces her sister was working on, too. Her desire to learn music was insatiable. And Mr. Angel provided all types. They sang sacred songs, arranged from Mozart masses or modern composers, many of which were sung in Latin, they sang secular pieces for school performances whose words conveyed longing, or hope, or farewell partings, or love, and they performed singing plays and patriotic performances for the school. And if Sarah wasn't behind the piano, she was in the alto section, or in one of the lead roles of the play. But most importantly, Mr. Angel taught Sarah soul. Mr. Angel was black, a regular churchgoer, and a lover of good gospel music. So, many of the choral performances included several gospel pieces, and Sarah found herself, many times, playing accompaniment for them. Now, Angel could get behind the piano in a heartbeat, hum the first note, and accompany a chorus without any music in front of him, and he would release all of his African soul into his fingers, which would resonate throughout the choral room or the stage. But to Sarah, this was a bit of a challenge. She didn't have the

African roots in her genes, but she would still try. So, she perfected her movements, tried diligently to play the pieces with soul, and helped to bring those gospel pieces to fruition. Certainly, they were not what Angel could have done, but Sarah learned soul. She learned the integral songs, like the Black National Anthem, and other songs that are important to African Heritage and the Longing for home. And even today, if Sarah hears the Black National Anthem, she finds herself singing along, much to the surprise of many black folks around her.

So, Mr. Angel involved himself in the community, and scheduled Christmas carol performances everywhere throughout the town of Williamsburg, and Grand Illumination was just one of their stops. As they didn't have a piano, in that cold night air, all of the performances were a cappella, with four-part harmony, led by the prodigious Angel. And these were moments that Sarah would never forget. The pure emotion that all of the performers, particularly the soloists, placed into their hearts and voices, could be heard ringing silently and solemnly throughout the night air of that one night a year when the town of Williamsburg came together to celebrate the lighting of old. Black and white came together at that moment, and seemed to blend in perfect harmony. It was one of those pockets of time that one cannot explain. It just flowed with utter precision and wholeness.

Angel's choruses also performed at the Grand Lodge, one of the top hotels in the Colonial Williamsburg Foundation. The Lodge had always been an anchor in the entire living museum, not only because of its hospitality toward visitors, but also because of its support of the town's events. The lobby, and adjoining conference and sitting rooms were thoroughly decorated with the paintings and decorations of a colonial time. Fireplaces of old sprinkle the sitting areas, and wingback chairs and leather-bound, overstuffed sitting chairs grace the dark colored Orientals and floor coverings. The minute one arrives in these rooms, one wants a Jane Austen and a hot cider to snuggle in for the evening. But at Christmas, the Lodge outdoes itself with various types of Christmas trees, toy trains, wreaths, reindeer, knickknacks, bowls and jars of Christmas treats and cookies, hot cider and cinnamon sticks. It was a dream world for a girl who lived in the classic books of old. Here, were the places she had read about. She was living in a novel.

And here, Sarah played the piano every Christmas, and even once, sang "What Child Is This?" as a solo. They also sang and played at the Fort Magruder Inn, which was equally spectacularly decorated, with a single Christmas tree as a center point, which easily stood twenty-five feet tall. All of these places and experiences were pure magic for Sarah. These moments released her from everything she was experiencing at home, and she threw her eyes and her heart into these moments, only to feel the magic they produced.

There were other little things too about the town of Williamsburg that helped to form all the necessary parts to make the wheel spin. They all, each organization, each business, each Brownie troop, each church, each Bed and Breakfast, each softball team, each school, blended together to form the working whole. They looked out for each other, supported each other during the down times, celebrated with one another during the upswings, and created, all the while, new programs, new organizations to fill a need of the families, new plays or productions or festivals that made full use of all of Williamsburg's children's talents and abilities. Each new program and production was formed by the idea of a parent, or child, then other families got involved, newsletters were printed, fundraisers were organized, and the next thing they knew, they had built a tradition.

# Chapter Thirty

*He who binds to himself a joy doth the winged life destroy. But he who kisses the joy as it flies lives in Eternity's sunrise.*

**William Blake (1757-1827)**

Take, for instance, St. Bede's Church. Sarah remembers first coming here from St. Mary's in Hampton. After Sarah's mother met the stepfather, she moved her two girls to the stepfather's home, as he lived in Hampton, close to his place of employment, the National Aeronautics and Space Administration. He was an aerospace engineer. His children were enrolled in St. Mary, Star of the Sea Catholic School, so Sarah and Meghan found themselves enrolled here as well. Sarah was in second grade at the time, and was delighted with all the new changes - - a new house, a new city, new brothers, a new backyard with a cemetery and an apple orchard, a new school with nuns and prayers and religion classes, but what sparked Sarah's eye the most were the uniforms. She loved these gray and navy blue plaid skirts with the white Oxford shirts and knee-high socks. She felt official, and new. She even began signing her name on school papers with her stepfather's last name. She was ready to put her old world behind.

About this same time, Sarah's doctor noticed in an annual check-up that her spine was a bit crooked. She was sent to a specialist, who diagnosed her with scoliosis and sent her to another specialist in Richmond. Since Sarah was still young, and had not grown to her full height, the orthopedist was certain that through braces, the young girl's spine could be molded and shaped and "tricked" into growing straight. A plaster mold was cast, of her entire torso, and she was sent home, with the instructions that the plastic mold, with Velcro straps, would be ready in a few weeks.

Sarah went home, told her sister, with whom Sarah shared a room and a big queen size bed, and her sister, Meghan began her mourning. She cried, and looked forlorn into her young sister's eyes and said, "You're going to be a cripple."

The two girls hugged and clung to each other for dear life, knowing that they only had a few short days together before Sarah became permanently immobile, and a cripple. The brace arrived, and Sarah was forced to wear the molded cast twenty-three hours a day. It started below her armpits, and above her breasts, which had not begun to form yet, and ended far below her hips, which had begun to show their first signs of shapeliness. She liked looking at the brace when it was not on her body- because it was her, it was her shape. She wore T-shirts under the brace, and on hot summer days, she sprinkled her skin with cornstarch to prevent any sticking or rashes. It was pure torture for her, but she always kept her smile and her enthusiasm. She just accepted this as life. When she took the blasted thing off for one hour a day, to take a bath, she felt as if she had been released from prison, whatever prison represents for one of that age. Her skin could breathe, she could move her body, and did so, every which way, like a cat. She had always been flexible and liked to stretch her body, so this stricture was pure torture.

Every several months, her mother and her took the long trip to Richmond, to the Children's Hospital, which she would later learn its historical roots to the city as a Public Relations Director for another health care organization in Richmond. And each trip entailed a series of X-rays of her spine, and each time, although not in the beginning, she covered her reproductive organs with a metal covering. She was so young at the time, and didn't quite understand the importance of such an act, but followed the radiology technician's instructions. She certainly was not thinking of her reproductive future at that time. And each time she outgrew a brace, which happened quickly at that age, she was strapped to another metal contraption that used cords and cotton straps attached to her arms and legs and hip bones that stretched her body, and straightened her spine. Two large orthopedic men stood on either side and wrapped wet, warm (sometimes hot) plaster gauze around her semi-naked body (she wore a cotton-gauzed tube protection), and smoothed it with their bare hands over the contours of her breasts, her hips, her stomach and back. Then the two, on either sides of her body, pushed the wet, warm plaster toward one another on the lower part of her back, until the plaster dried solid. Then, one would use a small, hand-held electric round hand saw, and cut her white plaster mold into a straight line directly down the center of her body, to remove her from her shell. A thick, narrow strip of cotton had been placed beneath her molded casting, just in case the saw got a little too close to her skin. Sometimes, she felt the hot, burning sensation in her stomach, which meant that the metal saw had got too close, but other than that, no mishaps occurred. She looked at that saw occasionally, but most of the time, just looked upward, as she didn't want her imagination to fly away with her. She squeezed her little body out of the new-formed crack, and she felt beautifully free again, in a little cotton-gauze stocking tube, which she was now dressed in. She didn't care much, as she stood before doctors and helpers. Everyone, including her, seemed to always breathe a sigh of relief after the success, as the whole process took several hours. It was a grand adventure for her, and everyone in the hospital treated her like a queen. She loved to go there, actually, because she was a star. But most importantly, she was alone with her mother. Sarah didn't feel like she was competing for her mother's attention, and always, without fail, her mother took her out to lunch. This was always a special treat for Sarah, as she could share something, alone with her mother. Never mind the torture that ensued on those doctor visits.

These doctor visits and new braces continued until the 6<sup>th</sup> grade – four years. The mandatory times for wearing the brace lessened as she grew, and in the last year, she was only wearing the brace at night. And often times, the brace was mysteriously removed in the night, sitting quietly on the floor next to her bed (or under the bed!) in the morning. 'Tis amazing what the unconscious mind (and body!) can do.

So, this new Catholic school was another grand adventure for Sarah. She wore her uniform, with the brace underneath each day, said the Pledge of Allegiance each morning, which was always followed by the Our Father, a Hail Mary and a Glory Be.

So, the following year, when they moved to a more "rural" area, to escape the commercialism of Hampton, the woods of Williamsburg seemed like a good option. They looked at a couple of farm houses, but finally settled on a two-story cedar house, newly built three years earlier, that sat nestled in a tangle of wood, off the beaten path of the Williamsburg route. It was still in York County, which was a priority for Sarah's mother, as they had the best schools in the state, but it was near the Toano line, heading toward Richmond.

The house appealed to Sarah's stepfather because it was a project begging for a carpenter's hands. The house was quite large – five bedrooms – but had double glass doors on the back that led to a drop-off. The original builder had planned to build a deck or sunroom, but ran out of patience, or energy. So, the stepfather built a sun room, as his brother owned a window business in Florida and shipped all the necessary glass to Virginia, as glass is one of the most expensive materials when building. And he eventually built a monstrous deck that led off from the sunroom.

But, the most important aspect of this house was the backyard. Immediately behind the house was a steep drop-off that led to a small stream, and swamp, and further back was a big lake. Sarah had never seen such untouched nature before, so she found herself tromping through those trees, those swamps, and pristine greenery, inventing adventures and stories. The two dogs always accompanied her, to ensure she didn't get lost, or fall in a rabbit hole somewhere. Sheba, the mother, and her son, Snuffy, whom they had kept from Sheba's last litter of ten, were pleasant companions. They always agreed with the plans Sarah devised, and if she changed her mind, mid-stream, they went along with the changes without much complaint. They never got tired, and went home when Sarah went home. Snuffy and Sheba were a pair – a Mutt and Jeff in the dog world. Snuffy would not have survived had he been without his mother.

But these woods were heaven, particularly when the neighborhood, Earlham Estates, received a snowfall. Sarah, and her childhood friend, Sara, took their sleighs and metal saucers down those hills and flew on adventures. They found a perfect hill, which was further back and east of the house, technically on their neighbor's property, which was the mother of all sledding hills. It had a smaller hill at the bottom of the large hill, which served as a ski jump of sorts that propelled them into the air at the bottom of the run. This was exciting and daring for these young girls, as they not only dodged trees on the way down, but also flew into the air at the bottom from Nature's own ski jump. The girls never told anyone about their secret hill, and in later years when all of Sarah's school friends congregated on the snowy days in the neighborhood of Abingdon Cross, where Patty lived, as it had the most hills, Sarah kept her secret quiet, as she didn't want her magical kingdom of adventures to be discovered. When the girls came up the hill, dragging their snow contraptions by a string behind them, with rosy cheeks and weary legs, the next door-neighbor, Ray, always inquired about the success of their adventures.

Ray was old, retired, and spent his days of retirement standing in the yard observing the many adventures of the house to his right. He was quiet, drove a truck with a few dog cages in the back, and housed a shed of beagles and hunting dogs which he took hunting every Saturday morning. Sarah never saw the dogs, but heard their howls, from somewhere behind his house. He was a silent listener and observer of the happenings of the house with six children beside his. There was always an adventure there, and when Snuffy and Sheba roamed over to his side of the property, he, without fail, lavished them with treats and biscuits. Ray kept a key to their house, just in case any one of the kids locked themselves out, and Shirley, his wife, always seemed to come to the rescue when they were missing an egg, or a teaspoon of baking powder for a recipe. No need in driving the long drive to the grocery store. They would return the borrowed supply in the next trip into town.  They were, after all, in the rural area of Williamsburg.

So, "down the hill" was Sarah's wonderland.  And it was here, down this snowy hill, where Sarah was on the twentieth day of January in 1986, when the Challenger exploded.

# Chapter Thirty-One

*Intuition and concepts constitute....the elements of all our knowledge,*
*so that neither concepts without an intuition in some way*
*corresponding to them, nor intuition without concepts, can yield*
*knowledge.*

**Immanuel Kant (1724-1804)**

School was cancelled that day, from a few inches of snow, and
Sarah had taken an early start on her adventures. When her cheeks
were rosy and her mittens full of snow, she stomped in the warmth of
the house only to find the grave video clippings, and Reagan's
address, on the television screen. Somehow, her magical adventures
didn't quite fly that day. The world was in mourning, including a girl,
who, most of the time lived in a book, or a piano song, or an
adventure. But in circumstances, like these, even the loftiest of
dreams must come down and reflect on the implications.

Sarah formed these adventures in the early years of her mother's marriage, when things were good and happy. Her mother reveled in her role of a stay-at-home mother, and organized neighborhood parties, and helped organize neighborhood dances and contests for the girls. And most importantly, Sarah's mother now lived down the street from one of her oldest and dearest friends from De Colores. Margie had seen Louisa go through her first divorce, and had even helped to introduce Louisa to her second husband, so she was thrilled when Louisa and her new family moved to the neighborhood. And Margie's daughter, Sara, was Sarah's age, and had been friends practically from birth.

Sara was adopted. After Margie and her husband had a number of complications with childbirth, they acquired several foster children, and one adopted daughter, Sara, who was Japanese-American. Sara possessed the same spirit and sense of adventure that Sarah had, so they became fast friends. Each day, one or the other rode their bicycles to the other's house, as they were only about a half-mile apart. They called each other on the weekend and summer mornings, and only said, "Wanna play?" Who knows what those words entailed, but they were soon constructing adventures, and stories, treasure hunts and forts, plays and gymnastic stages.

Sara was a dancer. She had taken ballet from a very early age, and progressed as a dancer rapidly. Every year, the Chamber Ballet produced a production of The Nutcracker for the town, which was always performed in William and Mary's Phi Beta Kappa Hall. This building was monumental to not only the college, but to the town, and to history, as William and Mary was the first school in the country to establish the Phi Beta Kappa Fraternity, of which many of our great forefathers were founders. The group was founded on the fifth day of December in 1776, in one of the rooms of the Raleigh Tavern on Duke of Gloucester Street in Colonial Williamsburg. Chapters were later established at Yale and Harvard, about four years later, but the College of William and Mary was the first to see such a high-honored society for scholars in liberal arts. The society was secret, and was represented by a special key that only certain members possessed. The key was displayed, and admission into the secret meetings was granted. Its members met to write, socialize and debate. So, this building served as a cornerstone for all town and college productions, and served not only as a symbol for the current time, but for the roots in which the town was founded.

Sara performed in various roles in each Nutcracker year after year, and there was no question, year after year, that Sarah and her mother went to each performance to watch Sara dance. And Sarah delighted in the year that Sara played Clara. The Nutcracker, by the Chamber Ballet, became another Williamsburg tradition, as all the young girls, and a few young boys, from the town, came together in a magical dance to perform one of Tchaikovsky's best. And Sara always shone. Sarah liked to watch her prepare for each performance, and practice, and was fascinated by her thousands of point shoes that she seemed to go through quite rapidly. And she was equally impressed with the bloody blisters, calluses, and other ugly maladies that her feet donned from her hard work. They were war wounds. Sara seemed to be proud of them, and so was Sarah.

The girls later took gymnastic classes together at the same location, and while the two were basically on the same level in ability, their two performances were like night and day. Sara was a gymnast from a ballerina's background, and Sarah was a gymnast from a cheerleader's background. And the two were completely different.

As time waned, their friendship soon dissipated, as Sara attended the private, Catholic school, Walsingham Academy in Williamsburg. And as Sarah's life became more and more marred by family struggles and barbaric practices, Sara and Sarah's lives seemed to separate for good. They connected years later as adults, as the two both worked in Richmond, but their lives had gone in two completely different directions, and their connection was based on a false premise that they could connect again as childhood buddies. Sara had been shaped by her school, by her friends, by the people she had surrounded herself with, and she looked down upon others who came from different backgrounds. She made comments about "public school" kids, as if they were in a class below her, and did not appreciate her own good fortune.

# Chapter Thirty-Two

*How does the Meadow flower its bloom unfold?  Because the lovely
little flower is free down to its root, and in that freedom, bold.*

**William Wordsworth (1770-1850)**

Adulthood does strange things to people, and Sara and Sarah's
"wanna play?" didn't quite transfer into adult terms.  Their "wanna
play?" soon turned into "wanna go get a drink?" where one drink
often turned into several.  And while they kept their smiles,
enthusiasm and spirit, their progress as human beings seemed to be
thwarted in that vast sea of bars and nightclubs.  A chasm was formed
between the two, long ago, by their environments and the way they
were shaped as individuals, and these delineations came through loud
and clear in the language, in the subtle comments and snubs on a class
that resided below her.  Sarah partook in these charades for a
time. They talked about their respective jobs, their struggles, and their
hopes for the future, and Sarah hoped that the period served as a

benefit to Sara in some way. Maybe it helped her to decide what she wanted out of life. Maybe it helped her to take more initiative at her job. Maybe it helped her to settle down and get married. But after a while, Sarah knew that their reconnection was not good for her. She was living on a childhood dream at a time when those repressed and toxic memories came flooding back. And she needed that happy familiar face from childhood for comfort. But words like that are never spoken among friends, especially when Sarah couldn't quite grasp her behavior and feelings herself. So, the two childhood friends split again as adults.

Friendships and relationships in whatever form they take throughout our lives are like little balloons bobbing in the air. Each one flies happily and blissfully along, bobbing on a breeze, ducking in and out of trees. And sometimes we see an old friend, and we bob and drift with them for a while. We reconnect, reacquaint ourselves with the others' lives, and then we drift off again to grow. Sometimes growth takes months, or it takes years. And then, we come back to reacquaint ourselves again, and to find comfort in that familiar face, in that familiar soul, who knows our story, who knows our dreams and wishes. And then, perhaps, there are friends that stick by in daily life, in each of the day's interactions. But these are not the ones from the beginning. These are not the ones who know one's past, present and future. These are not the ones who know one's soul, and connect with one's spirit. It is important to know that those moments of separation are not a period to long for the other, or to harbor resentment toward the other, but to lovingly know that the other must detach her/him self to grow. Friendships are beautiful things, but sometimes, they may stand as a barrier to individual growth. And when this happens, it is important to separate, not only for the good of both individuals, but also for the good of the friendship. Because the friendship doesn't end, per se, but only needs room to breathe and grow.

# Chapter Thirty-Three

*To me, fair friend, you can never be old. For as you were when first your eye I eyed. Such seems your beauty still.*

**William Shakespeare (1564-1616)**

So, back to Williamsburg. St. Bede's was quite a change from St. Mary's, Star of the Sea, for Sarah. But there was one thing in particularly that was most notably strange for her when she first arrived in the Parish Center.

Back in that day, St. Bede's was situated in an old colonial brick building, which stood right next to the College of William and Mary's stadium, and right across the street from the two college bars, The Green Leafe and The College Delly. The church was nestled among colonial houses that served as either family homes (college professors or Colonial Williamsburg Foundation executives) or bed and breakfasts. All these homes, including the Church at Christmas, had candles in the windows and a fruit-laden Colonial wreath on the front door at Christmastime. But shortly before Sarah's family arrived in Williamsburg, St. Bede's had acquired an old gymnasium, that the College had used as an intramural basketball court, which was located directly behind the church and directly across from the Rectory, an old three-story colonial home, where all the priests lived. They changed the old gym into a Parish Center, as the Church's congregation was growing by leaps and bounds and they needed more space. They began holding several masses here, and while they lavished the old building with an altar and chairs, the same old basketball court lay underneath their feet, which didn't quite reconcile itself in Sarah's mind. They were in God's house, but God's house had a free-throw line and a three-point line.

An impromptu folk mass was started here, with Sara's mother, Margie, on the piano, and many other family mothers and fathers on guitars, and even one father on a large bass. Here, a new kind of Mass was born.

All of the families of Williamsburg, from both counties, came with their children, as it offered a relaxed and comfortable atmosphere for people who knew each other well. Soon, the gymnasium floor was covered with carpet, the religious classrooms in the basement were renovated, lights were installed, and new altar furniture was purchased. Sarah's mother, along with several other mothers organized a Children's Liturgy for three types of age groups. And it was the delight of the Church to see all the little children- big and small—grouped together at the altar to be blessed by the priest, and led to their respective rooms to learn about the readings and the gospel in simple terms.

Sarah's mother loved to organize these events. Each Sunday, the children created little mementoes from the readings to help them remember what it was about. Sometimes they received butterflies for the resurrection, other times they received mustard seeds for the mustard seed parable (Matthew 13:31), other times they received pieces of construction paper which they pasted together to form a candle, other times they created a bush with various craft materials that Sarah's mother provided to convey the meaning of the "Don't hide your light behind a bushel," or perhaps they acted various skits to better personify the meanings of the parables. Sometimes they came back into the church, singing, "This Little Light of Mine, I'm Gonna Let It Shine." Each Sunday, Sarah's mother created something new for the hundreds of children of the Parrish. And to this day, Sarah's mother kept all of her records and plans from that time period, as it meant so much to her.

And as Louisa walked with the children to the classrooms, and back to the church, Margie played calming processional music on the piano. It was a beautiful moment in each Mass, to see all the children, walking independently and confidently back to where their parents were seated throughout the church. They were filled with hope, with resurrection, with love, with strength, by Sarah's mother.

As Sarah reached adulthood, she felt slighted that her mother was spread thin, that her mother had spent all of her time with other children, not only with the other stepsiblings, but with thousands of other children, in libraries, in schools, in church, whom Sarah didn't even know. Sarah felt that she had to vie for her mother's attention at every stroke and gill. But in the end, the world is a better place because of it. Now, Sarah only wishes that more children could have received a taste of the love that this woman possessed. And she continues, even in the darkest of hours, to provide light to the world. We can only hope that we as adults nourish our children to be mothers, in their own adulthood, like Sarah's mother. For that, is the only hope, of our world and future generations.

# Chapter Thirty-Four

*The miracles of the church seem to me to rest not so much upon faces or voices or healing power coming suddenly near to us from afar off, but upon our perceptions being made finer, so that for a moment our eyes can see and our ears can hear what is there about us always.*

**Willa Cather** (1873-1947)

But back to St. Bede's. The children were also led by an altar server, as he or she carried the crucifix to the back of the church where the children left. It was as if the children had become the center of the Mass, and Sarah's mother was truly putting Jesus' words to practice, as He said that no one will enter the kingdom of Heaven lest he have the heart of a child.

Sarah and Sara were both altar servers for the Parish Mass, which sometimes, was not always a good thing, as their giggles sometimes got the best of them. They sat in the front row, to the right of the priest in their white robes with the white-roped, tassel-ended belts that held the whole white contraption together. And they somehow managed to perform all the rituals without completely destroying a Mass. They carried the Crucifix, and held the prayer book for the priest; they carried the gifts and helped the priest place the gifts on the altar; and they washed his hands with holy water, and led the children to their own special Liturgy. But during the times when they sat, during the readings and the homily, Sarah's imagination flew, and they soon found themselves creating personified puppets with the tassel-ends of their white ropes, and were soon engaged in a playful stage on their laps, much to the dismay of their families, who sat on the other side of the church shooting darts with their eyes. Somehow, they made it, without being condemned to hell by the priest, and they served as just a mere piece of the whole which formed St. Bede's.

But, hands down, the most beautiful part of the whole Mass was the "Our Father." The whole church joined hands and only a few guitars provided accompaniment, and this beautiful prayer, the most beautiful prayer in the entire Catholic Church, was set to the Rolling Stones song, "As Tears Go By." The Stones original is slow, melodic and beautiful in its original form. But to hear the tune set to such a beautiful prayer was still magic. The church kept the tradition until a few years ago when all the old-school stalwarts seemed to dissipate, and a new fast-tracked choral director was hired. Back in those days, there was no hired choral director. People just came together, and filled in when a part was needed. Some Sundays, there was a young girl or boy on the violin, other days a flute, other days a drum, some days a banjo. People from the community just came forward, and blended what they could to contribute to that beautiful Mass every week.

It was always a festive occasion at the end of each Mass. The head guitarist, a large dramatic man who played a period man at the Colonial Williamsburg Foundation, always shouted as he strummed the last chord, "Have a Good Day!" to the whole congregation in a gay and booming voice. He was affectionately known in Sarah's household as the "Have-A-Good-Day-Man," and even when they discovered his real name, the first name was kept. He had earned his title.

The Parish Center soon developed a College Mass for the College of William and Mary folk, but Sarah started going here on her own in high school, when her family, or whatever was left of her family, began to go their separate ways. She always went to Mass with one of her best friends from the group at school, Shelley.

Shelley was a bit different from the others. She didn't live in King's Gate, like the rest of the clan, but in the neighborhood of the Owens Brockway factory workers, Harrison Hills. Her father was a plant worker for Anheiser Busch and her mother was a hairdresser. Her parents met in high school, married when they were 18, and are just as much in love today as they were at 18. They had three beautiful children, with Shelley in the middle, with many years in between the older brother and the younger brother – so the siblings were spread apart in years, but not by heart. They were the closest and most loving family Sarah had ever seen. And in all of the family households that somehow formed the great whole of Williamsburg, it is ironic to note that Shelley's household with the two parents who married for love and worked honestly and diligently in blue-collar jobs, are the ones who are still together. Not that they didn't have their share of problems. They certainly did, for several years before Shelley was born, but their strength and perseverance came through their devotion to the Church and their strength in God.

They were plain folk, hard workers – but always taught their children right and wrong, said, "I Love You" to each other at every parting, maintained an orderly and middle-sized home, and always supported each other's endeavors. Nothing was elaborate in their home, but it was always clean, and Shelley was always given her fair share of chores. She performed them without much flack, and kept a good humor all the while.

Shelley was not the same as the others, as she struggled to maintain a B or a C average. She was fairly decent in math, but she was never over the top in any other subject. But she always worked, spent hours on projects and homework, and never lost momentum in junior high or high school.

Sarah became close to Shelley in cheerleading in junior high. Shelley was small, petite and had no sense of fear. She ran in a

214

moments notice and popped a round-off, back-handspring, back tuck, or flipped a front tuck on a dare. She was spirited, full of energy, and Sarah loved it. And Shelley prided herself on making Sarah laugh. That sole desire became her quest over the years, as, looking back now, some of the things she did were downright absurd and silly, at best. But they were girls, and they were having fun.

They partook in all sorts of activities with their bodies. They balanced each other in the air on the soles of their feet. They flipped each other over their heads, and created all sorts of new ways to practice body gymnastics using the other. As Shelley was a bit smaller than Sarah, Sarah often spotted Shelley in standing back tucks and other daring gymnastics in the junior high school yard or in Shelley's back yard. Shelley placed her full trust in Sarah, and Sarah never failed her. She flew through the air, knowing that her friend would catch her. If they happened to accompany her mother on grocery store outings, Shelley picked an aisle, and began to pick things off the shelf and throw them over her head and backwards toward Sarah who was a few steps behind her. Sarah caught them, placed them back on the shelf, with just enough time to catch the next item that came flying in her direction. All of the items were unbreakable, just in case Sarah had a minor case of the slippery fingers, but for the most part, the two girls practiced their blind hand-eye coordination and trust. Shelley fell backwards, knowing that her friend would catch her, and created new body pyramids together on the sidelines of basketball and football games. Shelley always trusted that her friend would hold her, and catch her when she threw her into the air.

They created cheers, and tried to see how high they could create human pyramids with their squad of twelve girls. They were full of energy, and there was no stopping the two of them when they were together. They often wrestled too – and the two girls threw each other across rooms, or tackled each other to the ground – always ending in a full-throttle giggle. Their times together, in junior high, always involved much physical activity.

And in the eighth grade, their friendship grew stronger. At this time, Mr. Angel decided to work full time in the high school, thus leaving the choral instruction to a makeshift math teacher who didn't know a thing about singing or music. So, Sarah continued her accompanist role, but played teacher most of the time, as she knew the songs, and could direct the pace of the songs from the rhythm of the music she played. She knew most of the classmates from the previous year, so the group worked together to help the teacher flounder through a position he was given by the county because they didn't have the budget to fund a new music teacher. Shelley sat with Sarah at the piano and turned her pages. She knew the teacher well, as he also coupled as her softball coach. Sarah even taught her a few songs, and she picked up the piano quickly.

Shelley was also the only one from the group who attended Sarah's same church, so they attended religious classes together on Sunday evenings. It was customary in the Catholic Church back then to attend ten years of religious education, and then, in the 11$^{th}$ year, one could be confirmed. It was an honor, a privilege, and a rite of passage. But in Sarah's tenth year, she had had enough of these classes, which didn't mean much to her at the time, as she was going through a bastion of difficulties, so she dropped out. Shelley went on the following year to be confirmed, and Sarah was there for the ceremony.

Years later, Sarah struggled with her Faith, and at one point, even questioned the validity of God, as all of the memories from her past life and repressions came flooding back. She hated the Catholic Church, and despised everything it represented. How could God allow all those things to happen to her? But when one resides in a pit of blackness, questioning the very existence of light, one must reach for the light to shine it into the darkness, and extinguish its presence. Darkness is not the opposite of light; it is the absence of light. And darkness is such an ever-consuming phenomena that seems to be inescapable once you are in it, but it is so easy to reach for that light. And once you have it in your hand, it is the most powerful weapon on Earth. So, after years and years of going to church, and being raised by the Children's Liturgy guru, Sarah still fell. But it was because of this foundation that she had the knowledge and the tools to reach again for the light that she had always held, but never quite understood. And because she made the choice to reach for it, all the knowledge, and path toward peace were revealed, slowly, and surely, and all in God's time. Sarah is still not confirmed, but in retrospect, she is happy she did not embark on that rite at such a tender age when the knowledge and the meaning of the practice were ambiguous. Now, when she is confirmed, it will have meaning, and purpose, and it will be her own decision.

When Sarah was plummeted in the darkness, she had just ended her three year relationship with William, she was working, barely as a Public Relations Director for a nonprofit organization, and she was overcome with all sorts of bizarre thoughts and memories that seemed to engulf her, but they first manifested themselves in physical symptoms. She didn't really know what all these things were – the panic attacks, the dreams, the acne, the feeling of wanting to run, and continue running to some unknown destination. She had buried all those memories long ago, and had done a fine job of creating new lives – but they were all there, lurking beneath the surface. She hadn't been to church in years, felt content in believing there was no God, or rather, could not believe it. What God would allow her to feel the way she was feeling? She was desperate, alone, afraid, but blissfully smiling and carrying on as normal in a desperate attempt to feel in control.

And a beautiful sunny, summer Sunday in Richmond changed her life forever. And it was all because of her youngest stepsibling- the youngest stepbrother who, to her, represented the family that she hated, the family she was running from, the family that brought her the most horrible memories. But here, the son of her stepfather who relentlessly hit her, lovingly and affectionately brought her back to the light.

# Chapter Thirty-Five

*There are more ideas on earth than intellectuals imagine. And these ideas are more active, stronger, more resistant, more passionate than "politicians" think. We have to be there at the birth of ideas, the bursting outward of their force: not in books expressing them, but in events manifesting this force, in struggles carried on around ideas, for or against them. Ideas do not rule the world. But it is because the world has ideas... that it is not passively ruled by those who are its leaders or those who would like to teach it, once and for all, what it must think.*

**Michel Foucault** (1926-1984)

Jacob was always different from the others, not only in his physical appearance, but also in his personality. He was blonde, with blue-green eyes and fair skin. His two older brothers, and twin sister, Fanny, were dark-haired, brown-eyed with olive skin. He was an anomaly, to them, but to his credit, he possessed the most of his mother's genes, which makes him, all the wiser. Sarah is not sure if his sensitive personality was genetic, or if it was formed by the years of abuse from his brothers and sister who always teased him that he wasn't really related to them - that he was switched at birth. While this may have been all in good fun in their eyes, it simply is not right to tell a little boy this, as it causes a complex. Jacob was always a quiet little boy, stood a step behind the others, but he was imaginative, and observant. He kept a close watch on all the activities of the house. So, the two girls, Meghan and Sarah, took to Jacob more than the others, but particularly Meghan. Meghan encouraged him to create stories, create character names, and nurtured his creative spirit. He was curious with the way things smelled or they way they felt, and always seemed to get himself in trouble by touching things. One situation led to another and he soon found himself with the nickname, "Hands."

Like this one, for instance: Louisa went to the mall, with the two little ones, Jacob and Fanny en tow. Jacob was fascinated with manikins and touched every one he possibly saw. One day, he shook the hand of a manikin woman and the entire arm came off. Instead of dropping the arm, or attempting to refasten the arm, he continued to walk, but with the arm in his hand. He whispered, in a panic, as he did not want his mother to hear, "Fanny, look!"

"Jacob!?! What have you done!?!" Fanny was used to these exchanges, as Jacob always seemed to get him in trouble, and then, inevitably, pulled Fanny into it.

"I don't know what to do with it!" he said. Louisa heard the whispered commotion, pacified the scene, the arm was reattached, and the two were left scampering again behind their rushed mother.

And Jacob had a wandering curiosity. For instance, on one of the family vacations in the 1971 Volvo, the makeshift family stopped in a local park for a picnic lunch. They ate, and everyone helped to clean up and load the contents into the already packed car, including the six children. Somewhere in the mayhem, Jacob had wandered off and was not noticed by the rest of the family, as he was so quiet anyway. So, the family packed in the car, and Sarah's stepfather began to drive down the road. About two minutes into the drive Sarah's mother yelled, "Where's Jacob?" The stepfather spun a U-Turn faster than a jerky-speed roller coaster, and sped, tires spinning, back into the park they had just left. They found Jacob. He was sitting on a blanket contently listening to the mayhem and chattering of a black family, that was having a picnic as well. The stepfather scooped him up, thanked the family, and they gave a nod, as if this kind of thing happens every day. They were just happy for the young little blonde visitor.

So, Jacob was different. He was calming, sensitive and smart, with a spark of a curiosity that led him on his own adventures. Jacob and Sarah were relatively close when she still lived at the house, but when she left, she lost a lot of contact with him. It was too painful for her to go back there, and all of the stepsiblings, to her, represented everything unstable, everything evil and banal. She did not want to remember, and her life swiftly drifted to another world where they were forgotten. She heard about their school and their activities from her mother, but they had become acquaintances to her. They were not family.

But Jacob and Sarah's lives coincided much later when they both lived in Richmond. She was working, and Jacob was attending Virginia Commonwealth University. Sarah was spending her Sunday afternoon at a local Mexican restaurant that had an outside deck which overlooked the main street in Carytown. She swore by their margaritas, so Jacob joined her. As she talked about her latest laments, Jacob finally interjected, "Sarah, I just remembered that I am supposed to read for the five o'clock College Mass at the Cathedral. Wanna come?"

Sarah looked at her watch. It was ten 'til five o'clock. She thought it was a bit odd because Jacob was wearing a tee-shirt that read, "Rollin' in my six-four" and jeans. Plus, she hadn't been to Mass in a good two to three years, and she had a margarita, or two, in her. Jacob persisted, and she soon found herself in the Richmond's Cathedral, one of the most beautiful buildings in the city. It was built a little before the turn of the century, as the original church had been burnt in the Civil War. And the minute she walked in, and stood beside her stepbrother, she felt ashamed, and instantly humbled. Many of the prayers, the motions, the sincerity, seemed to have left her heart, and she struggled to remember all of the familiarities from her youth. She was humbled most by her little stepbrother's sincerity and interest in all of the words. He sang all of the songs, which all were much different from the ones she had learnt at St. Bede's. His hand motions, and the expression in his eyes as he exchanged peace greetings with all of his friends and family around him - - his church family he had formed in the year since he moved to Richmond – were moving.

Sarah had been lost and floating out in the world somewhere until this moment. She listened as her brother read from the Bible. This was the little brother whose diapers she had helped change. This was the little brother who endured the same dinner traumas. This was the same little brother who stood outside of her bedroom door as she stood with a cast and a urine-soaked bottom because he was curious to find out what happened. This was the same little brother whom had always looked up to her for guidance, and here he was, showing her God. It was truly, a moving and humbling moment.

And from that day forward, slowly and steadily, Sarah became a member of Sacred Heart's Richmond Parish, and renewed herself with God - - because of the little stepbrother who came from the family that Sarah wanted desperately to forget.

It wasn't their fault. They weren't the ones to beat Sarah on those two occasions. But they came to represent their father, and her mother's unhappiness, in Sarah's mind, so she ran from them. But they always seemed to reappear, forcing her to remember.

# Chapter Thirty-Six

*The dignity of the artist lies in his duty of keeping awake the sense of wonder in the world. In this long vigil he often has to vary his methods of stimulation; but in this long vigil he is also himself striving against a continual tendency to sleep.*

**G.K. Chesterton** (1874-1936)

And there were other things too that kept the town smoothly working as a whole: the Homecoming and Christmas parades which proceeded down the main artery of Colonial Williamsburg, Duke of Gloucester Street; or the Festival of the Arts, where local artists and performers displayed their work, on stages or on easels. Williamsburgers always found a way to bring the town together, to find places for all of the town's wide variety of talent and of love – for their fellow neighbor and for the good of the town. It thrived, and swirled, and breathed its peace into the streets of old, building on the camaraderie and strength that formed our great nation's roots. It is almost as if the great forefathers of old had ensured that its inhabitants maintain that sense of duty, character, humility and strength in the face of all odds.  It was important, not only as a town, but as a nation.

♫

# Chapter Thirty-Seven

*If you follow your bliss, doors will open for you that wouldn't have opened for anyone else.*

**Joseph Campbell** (1904-1987)

Sarah and Williams's relationship began slowly and playfully. Sarah told her mother that she had a date with some guy named William Gardner. And her mother immediately asked, "Is that a Gardner from Garden City County?"

"How did she know that?" Sarah thought.

Her mother mentioned that they owned half the county and had historical roots in the area, but Sarah let that information drift in one ear and out the other. She didn't want to be much bothered with pretensions, or expectations, she just liked the guy. He had a playful sense of humor that drove her wild, and he seemed to listen to her when she spoke, and act as if she was saying something profound or new. She wasn't used to this kind of treatment, and they were her ideas – she had had them for her whole life, but for some reason, she felt comfortable with talking about herself around him. Their first date went successfully and he then invited her to Garden City County. He was cooking.

"Fine," she thought, "I'll bring a bottle of wine." She purposefully chose a bottle of white wine from the Colonial Williamsburg label, but didn't know much about wine tastes, and their appropriate blending with certain types of foods.

She followed his directions to a tee, made a left onto the long straight driveway, with the large brick plantation house in front of her, made a right at the white fence, followed the white fence to the left, and there tucked behind a magnolia and a dogwood, was the little white house. It was immensely dark there. She had never experienced darkness like that, out in the country. His little house had no lights, only a few flickers of candles could be seen from the inside, and William stood outside with a flashlight to greet her. The stars were innumerable, and bright, at such an hour. And although it was late in November, she was not cold in the outside air, as her heart was thumping, and she had no time to think about her body's temperature.

He led her inside, and the candle glow from the few that peppered the living room created a soft glow on her face, on the photographs and artwork, and on his own face that searched hers for approval. The smell from the kitchen was mouth-watering, and Miles Davis moaned from the stereo. It was pure magic. She looked at all of the wall hangings, as she wanted to avoid his eyes at that particular moment. He had made everything perfect. She knew she was caught, but she didn't want to show him.

She was most intrigued by a set of three black and white photographs that lined the Eastern wall of the small living room, because they were photographs of black folk, from a time long ago – an old milk truck, and the black milkman, and a little black boy holding a chain-linked fence. As Sarah slowly walked from the living room to the kitchen, and peered outside to the back porch, he followed at her heels, inspecting her movements, and answered any questions she asked about the artwork or the wall hangings. They weren't questions really, but comments, which he always supplemented with more information.

She felt like she knew this house her whole life, as if it were built for her. In all of the homes she had been, this one felt like home, and she had only just arrived.

He had just finished lining the upper corners of the kitchen walls with an ivy-laced wall border that matched the hunter-green countertops. He asked her opinion, as if they had built the house together.

Dinner was ready, and he served the meal on a small kitchen table, built for two. This table would, a year later, seat five on the day that William left for South America, a symbolic day for many reasons. Sarah sat at this table with William's mother, father, and sister, as it was the last lunch before their son and brother would embark on one of his journeys. They sat together at the small table, in the small house that William had saved and renovated, as the kitchen in the large plantation home was near completion in its own renovation efforts. William spearheaded that project too. But it was a symbolic lunch because Sarah was there, for an important and emotional family event. William's mother was convinced he was going to die, and her displeasure in his decision was communicated by her movements, by the placement of her feet as she walked from the stove to the table to serve all of the soup bowls. But more than that, she was irritated by Sarah's presence. She didn't know this girl, hardly, and she didn't seem to quite belong. She was a foreigner. Sarah had never been treated this way before. Parents had always been friendly and cordial, and more than accepting of her presence, but Williams's mother was indignant. Sarah tried to talk to her, to get close to her, and even began to help her wash the dishes after lunch. Sarah mentioned something about their respective worried states for William's safety, and she replied, "He's going to die." ---which was enough for Sarah to realize that conversation with this woman was not in the cards at that time.

But that was a year later, and a much different mood from the one from Sarah and William's first cooked meal, with candlelit chicken alfredo with broccoli, and white wine from the Colonial Williamsburg label. The night was magic, and they moved to the living room, listened to music, and became comfortable in each other's presence, surveying each others' hands, facial features and skin tones. Sarah felt as if she was seeing his physical body for the first time, but knew his soul. They looked into each other's eyes for hours, speaking to each other's souls without words. They sat far away from each other at first, a habit that always seemed to stay with Sarah, even years after knowing each other, and after slowly touching each others' hands for a time, feeling the grooves of the others palms and fingertips, they slid closer to each other once a sense of comfort was established. It always took Sarah some time to get used to his body and his presence if she went for a few days or longer without seeing him, which happened often throughout the course of their relationship. And William was a kind soul to respect that sense of discomfort and to bear with Sarah's shyness until she felt comfortable enough to come near him. This was so new for her, and so frightening. She proceeded with utter caution and precision, as she was now in unchartered waters.

She continued to apply for jobs, but limited her big city search to the Washington, DC area, as she didn't want to be too far from William. It seemed absurd, in all actuality, that she even continued with the job search else where, after she had met such a man, a man who held her history in his eyes, but she had her mind set on this task, and he didn't ask her to stay, so she went forward with her plans. They spent the next few months together, learning each other, playing Scrabble and other card games, listening to music. He took her to classes and parties at the Law School, and parties around the county. He took her on walks around his property, and across the street to the pipeline. He showed her the James River behind his house, and took her on canoe rides. He pointed out the dilapidated houses he wanted to renovate, and showed her the Garden City County sunsets. And little by little, Garden City County became a part of her soul and part of her essence.

She lived in Newport News at the time, and commuted frequently to Garden City County. They often met in Williamsburg, at the meeting place for both of their friends, The Green Leafe. Or William drove to Newport News to experience Sarah's world with her friends in her new apartment. She didn't think much of his background, as he never talked about it. He didn't talk about social classes, and appeared to know the pulse of every class, as he adopted well in every setting – among law school tools, among her own friends, among adults, among his own family. She never thought that they were different in any way. In her heart, from where she was living during this time, they weren't different. They were two people with souls who seemed to come together at that particular moment in their lives to feel alive together, to feel loved and playful. They learned from each other, they taught each other things and meanings. They both questioned the world and their placement in it, but came down to Earth to be with each other, to experience one another – with music, with friends, with cooking and with activities. They were very active together with outdoor activities like hiking and biking. They both liked to try new things and they even learnt snowboarding and kayaking together. Their lives seemed to coincide at that perfect moment in time when everything seemed to click, when the wheel spins perfectly and wholly, without a bump or a hitch, but with unified strength and goodness. But it didn't last long.

Sarah accepted a job in DC and moved to the Ballston area of Arlington, which was right on the Metro line, and very near to the bike trail and access to the Key Bridge over to Georgetown. She was excited about her new move, as she loved exploring new places and cities. She had only been to Washington, DC with her Literary Arts Magnet School and with her Brownie Troop, and she was excited with the prospect that now she would be living in it. She wanted to involve herself in all sorts of activities there in the community – hiking, biking, running, but she also wanted to learn the museum network and attend cultural events.

William was a little hurt by her enthusiasm, and even gave her an "out" of the relationship, as he began to question the validity of their union if she was thrilled about moving away from him. But she assured him that she was not moving there to explore the young singles scene that was so prominent at that time. It seemed like Washington, DC was the place to be for all college graduates. So, the two decided to maintain a long-distance weekend relationship, as

William was still attending Law School at the College of William and Mary Law.

William drove to DC for weekends, and Sarah drove to Garden City County. They kept in close contact by emails and letters, and maintained a healthy balance of exploring a large city life on some weekends, and retreating to the haven of Garden City County, and the country for others. They made other little trips too, to Nags Head, to Ocracoke Island on the Outer Banks, to Assateague and Chincoteague on the Eastern Shore, to Snow Shoe in West Virginia, and to plenty of University of North Carolina football games in Chapel Hill. They did everything together, but still maintained their separate lives during the week.

# Chapter Thirty-Eight

*When you have once seen the glow of happiness on the face of a beloved person, you know that a man can have no vocation but to awaken that light on the faces surrounding him; and you are torn by the thought of the unhappiness and night you cast, by the mere fact of living, in the hearts you encounter.*

**Albert Camus** (1913-1960)

But little things began to surface. As William had spent his whole life running from his past and his family legacy, he now began to feel proud of it, as he saw in Sarah, someone he could settle down with. And while Sarah knew of his historical background, peripherally, she hadn't studied his lineage, nor particularly took any interest in doing so. Sarah's mother, the reference librarian, had made copies of the Gardner biographies and Gardner family trees, and subtly placed them in Sarah's things whenever Sarah came for a visit. But Sarah resented this. She didn't want her feelings of love to be tainted by some historical legacy that she was "supposed" to desire. She didn't want it, and indignantly trashed all of the copies her mother made. If this was love, she did not want to be influenced by ancestry.

So, she accepted him, for as he presented himself to her, and if he chose not to speak about his heritage, then it didn't exist for her. She accepted him to be the ideas and the beliefs he chose to talk about, not the past he came from. But now, he was ready to accept and own some of these legacies and he began to reveal as such with subtle actions.

For instance, Sarah had noticed that the marina near Mt. Vernon in Alexandria had sailboats that could be rented for the day. She had never been sailing before, just on motorboats on the Long Beach Island sound, so she mentioned her desire one weekend when William was visiting. He agreed and they rode their bikes on the bike trail that bordered the Virginia side of the Potomac to the Mt. Vernon dock. The cityscape from this ride was breathtaking on a sunny Saturday, as one has a full view of all of the national and historic monuments. They arrived at the dock and were told that they would only take the boat if they had a sailing license. Sarah thought this was strange. She had thought they would just be able to rent a boat and take it out on the water. How hard can sailing be? She knew that people took sailing lessons, but people also take skiing lessons, and there are people who can ski very well and naturally without the lessons, or license. So, with this information, Sarah was let down. But the dock manager added, "If you can pass this test, you can take a boat." So, William nonchalantly mentioned that he knew a little bit about sailing, and felt confident in taking the test. Sarah sat beside him as he answered each question briskly and with determined precision. As he worked, her eyes wandered to the lovely photographs of the Potomac through the years, and the next thing she knew William was finished, the exam was checked, and he missed not a one. Sarah thought this a bit odd, but she was soon on a sailboat, with the United States Capitol before her, switching sides of the boat as William maneuvered the sail. Nothing takes Sarah's breath away like the sight of the Unites States Capitol. There is no other building in the world that resonates such power and reverence, and to see it from a river's currents is a magical and powerful experience. The sail flapped majestically in the sunny afternoon wind and Sarah breathed in the smell of the majestic and symbolic river, the river that Washington chose to build his plantation home beside, the river that served as a gateway, in many respects to our country of old. The knowledge of William's quick wit on sailing techniques and precision was soon forgotten beneath her dreamy state of bliss – and a touch of the social class delineation began to form, unconsciously, beneath the surface.

Another incident happened in Garden City County, on a Sunday afternoon when they decided to play tennis. Lucy, Emily, Mindy and Shelley all played tennis in high school, and Sarah had played a few times in gym classes or with one of the four girls for as long as their patience lasted, but she was not good. Neither was William, he persisted, so he planned an outing to the county-run tennis courts just a stone's throw from the plantation grounds. Sarah borrowed a tennis racket from William's sister, Elizabeth, and prepared to get in one of their cars, but instead, William led her to the Western side of the large brick house where many old cars, mainly Volkswagens, were stored, one of which was a cherry-red, nineteen sixty-eight convertible Karmen Ghia. It was his, William said, and they drove, with the top down, the sun shining toward the tennis courts. When they arrived, most of the parks inhabitants were the black folk from the county, and all of the cars had tinted windows, twelve-inch woofers, ground effect kits and all sorts of supplementary car accessories to make the car stand out. All heads turned as the cherry-red Karmin Ghia drove to the courts, and Sarah felt as if she was on display. At this point, she felt torn, but this feeling was subtle, it rumbled beneath the surface, as she began to touch on the edges of her memory of her own past life of sub-inch woofers and tinted windows. They played a quasi-match, but something died in Sarah that day. She's not quite sure what died, but she felt sad to lose it. She felt unbelievably remorseful, and somewhat guilty, that she was now in the position that she found herself. One can easily slip into that role, and feel better than another person, and know that one has risen above in some way. But can one do that with a clear conscience? With a heart of gold? She didn't feel worthy. Nothing in her life had prepared her for that moment. Feelings and emotions were running rampant throughout her body and mind. She heard the sounds of their music, as music was everything to them, just as it had been to her, all of her life, but she also saw her love in front of her on the tennis court with a volley shot heading her way.  He stood with his shirt off, with a sheen covering of perspiration on his chest.  His expression was relaxed, and loving. She hesitated for a moment, but soon turned away from the music. She turned away from their actions and feelings of longing and escape.  Her ears soon tuned out the music, and she lost herself in the game.  They exhausted themselves on the court, drove home in the flaming red Karmen Ghia, and she forgot those pangs of guilt until much later.

# Chapter Thirty-Nine

*To know what is impenetrable to us really exists, manifesting itself as the highest wisdom and the most radiant beauty... this knowledge, this feeling is at the center of true religiousness.*

**Albert Einstein** (1879-1955)

William finished his second year of law school, applied for the master's degree of business administration program, to start the following year, and began a massive renovation project on the kitchen of the large brick house, and added a large screened porch on the north side, added a downstairs bathroom, an upstairs bedroom and an office. He worked day after day, and Sarah's trips to Garden City County became more frequent, as William was occupied with carpentry work. William was intensely focused on the project in front of him, and Sarah liked to see him so engaged and happy. She had seen him lose his focus and concentration with other aspects of his life, and knew the feeling herself, so she could only be most pleased when he was fully engaged in work. She spent most of the weekends making lunches or dinner, visiting her own mother, and she even helped with the tiling of the roof, and the painting of the upstairs bedroom, office and small closet space. William joked with her, "This is your room." But, time would reveal that he really wasn't joking.

Halfway through the summer and through the renovation project, he had begun to feel the travel itch again. It had been a while since he had been out of the country. He had two years left of school – one year of law school and one of business school. It seemed like a good time to do it, as he would not get the chance once he graduated and got a job, or so he thought at the time. So, he decided he wanted to purchase a motorcycle, and head down through Central and South America. The Panama Canal was still owned by the United States at that time, but would change hands in the next year. Who knew what the changes would ensue for future travel, so he made his decision to go.

He told Sarah about his decision on one of their weekend trips to Chapel Hill. She was so hurt. He would surely find a new girlfriend and new pursuits in his travels. He would forget about her. But she kept her mouth shut of her own selfishness and supported his decision, as she knew it was a big one, and a brave one. And then he added, "And I want you to come with me." He had planned to leave in October and come back the following August before the school year began. Eight months was a long time to be on the road. But she couldn't possibly do it. She had a car, which was paid for, a job, and a living situation which she easily could have got out of. All of the elements seemed perfect, in William's eyes, for her to go. And in all actuality, they were. But she didn't come from his same background. A car and a job meant stability, and you just didn't throw it all away to embark on some unknown odyssey. She shuddered at the thought. She immediately thought of her financial situation, which was an issue, especially since she had begun to max all of her credit cards from all the weekend trips, jaunts and apartment accessories in DC. William and Sarah usually split all of the expenses down the middle, but even those half expenses began to add up. William suggested she sell her car and drop everything. But what about after they returned? He hadn't asked her to marry him, and he skirted the issue every time it was brought up by saying he would eventually get married one day, and the "he" never included "her" so she assumed that he had no plans to have her in his future. She was just a buddy, a pal, just like those stray dogs that he always seemed to find and bring home. She was agreeable, was healthy, liked to be active, was interested in his life, and didn't nag him about anything. She was fun to have around, fun to pass the time. But that was it.

He mentioned that he knew she didn't have a safety net and would provide that for her when they returned; i.e., a place to live. But she wasn't about to sell everything she owned, including her car which had grown to mean freedom for her, and embark on a grand adventure, only to come home and have to start all over again, with the knowledge that he may or may not be a part of her future. He just wanted a traveling buddy, a pal to pass the time.

She did not communicate all of this to him, but simply said that she could not. William went ahead with the plans, found a Kawasaki KLR 650 for sale in Vermont, and Sarah made the drive with him up to Vermont to retrieve his new purchase. The Vermont town was near the Massachusetts border, so they stayed with her father for a couple of days. It was the first time Sarah's father had met William, and they became fast friends, as the two's personalities were very similar. Sarah and William returned to Garden City County, and preparations were made for the grand journey.

Both went ahead with their plans, thinking and hoping that the other would change their minds, but they both were stubborn, and both had pride of steel. Sarah did not want to beg him to stay, because she did not want him to feel guilty about leaving her behind if he decided to still go. And if he decided to stay, she did not want him to resent her and hold her accountable for thwarting a trip of a lifetime. So she supported him until the last day. She bought him all sorts of things for his trip – safety kits and repair kits for his tent, and first aid kits in case anything happened. She helped him waterproof his leather boots and jacket and kept a smile on her face the entire time. He finished most of the renovation, and left in late November. Before leaving, he purchased Sarah a plane ticket to Costa Rica for the winter holidays. She was thrilled that she would see him again in a month.

# Chapter Forty

*Experience is not what happens to a man; it is what a man does with what happens to him.*

**Aldous Huxley** (1894-1963)

Meanwhile, Sarah started working as a Public Relations Director for a nonprofit organization in Washington, DC and threw herself into her new job, as the learning curve was high.  She moved into an old Tudor house in the historic streets of Arlington, with three other girls, two University of Virginia graduates and one Dickinson graduate.  So, even though she felt as if she could not uproot her job and her living situation, she changed jobs and living arrangements in the month of William's departure.  This was a stab in the back to him, because the way he saw it, how could she make all of these changes in her life that demonstrated an impermanence in the areas that she said were holding her back from traveling?  And he had a point.  But Sarah just wasn't ready at that point in her life.  William had traveled before. He was a diplomat by nature, by genetics. This was a world that Sarah was not ready for. Traveling requires diplomacy, it requires a wisdom that only comes from parents who are travelers, it requires the ability to make split second decisions, it requires foresight and intricate planning, and most importantly, it requires an immense amount of faith. And Sarah possessed none of these things at the time. She was wet behind the ears in such worldly pursuits, and she knew that William would do all the planning, and all the communicating and decisions, but where would that leave her? It would create a dependent individual, solely on his skills and on his abilities. And her skills and abilities would soon wither and decay beneath his strengths. She needed the experience of the world to acquire all the skills for a traveling odyssey. But all of these reasons just stewed beneath the surface. They were there, but could not be put into describable words. So, Sarah's actions just looked like, to William, a direct contradiction to the reasons she provided. She didn't know why she couldn't go. How can you express that you need something when you don't know exactly what it is you need, as you are not aware of its presence, of its necessity?

So, Sarah's new roommates were different from her, but the house was nice, the neighborhood was quiet and safe, and the four girls paid relatively low rent. Sarah tried her best to adjust to her new life without William, but it was difficult. She had grown accustomed to sharing everything with him. About this same time, her credit cards began to catch up with her, her car began to have mechanical problems, and she only seemed to have enough money to pay her rent and the minimum payments on the credit cards, not to mention insurance and student loans. And her credit card balances just grew and grew. She tried to keep these weighted pressures out of her mind when she flew to San Jose for Christmas, but they were there. Nevertheless, the two connected again, reacquainted themselves with each other, and spent ten days touring the Nicoya Peninsula beaches and the rainforest in the mainland on motorcycle. Sarah had purchased a helmet in the States and brought the helmet down with her. It was a magical experience, and opened Sarah's eyes, for the first time, to a world beyond her reach. She felt her mind expanding by leaps and bounds, and began to realize just how much of the world she didn't know and how many beautiful mysterious wonders it held. But, still, in the back of her mind were her job, which she would return to, and her mounting bills and creditors. William knew nothing of this world, and Sarah was reluctant to share it with him, as she knew it marked an air of irresponsibility on her part. So, she returned to the States with a tear-streaked face, as she clung to her motorcycle helmet for dear life. William gave her a few books to read, and she soon found herself immersed in the Washington, DC working world again.

But this time, she needed to make more money and she needed it quickly. Her boyfriend was in South America- in a far away land — and she needed to pay off her credit cards. Her sister Meghan had always worked two or three jobs, so why couldn't she? So, she worked as a public relations director by day, and a waitress at a local Chili's by night, and she soon found herself in the throws of that banal life that she had lived so long ago. She had never waitressed before, but her sister seemed to like it in Williamsburg, so why not? But it was different here. The people were dirty. They talked with foul mouths and language, and worked without morals or integrity. Some waiters and waitresses purposefully wrote down credit card numbers from their customers' cards. Some servers let food drop on the floor and then placed it back on the plate. And when the manager trained her, he stuck his fingers in the food that was going to be brought out to a table. Massive amounts of food were thrown in the garbage can after every table was cleared, and tables were served, cleaned and shipped out of the restaurant. These were not people, but cattle that consumed massive amount of food, treated their server like a night-queen stripper, and got up from every table with a belch and a groan, as they rubbed their bellies that protruded far over the waistline. Families yelled at her, including children who barked orders at her. Other servers yelled at her. Managers yelled at her. And God help her when she worked the cocktail area. Hundreds of workers from the Tyson's Corner area poured in its doors during happy hour, and consumed massive amounts of beer and mixed drinks. And when they had begun to reach their maximum capacity, they either became increasingly indignant and angry with the friend that they had laughed with an hour before, or took an intense interest in the waitress in front of them. She was slipped phone numbers by old men, who came to eat dinner alone, she was slipped phone numbers by old men, whose wives sat directly across from them. She was raped by their eyes. On one of her first shifts, a man asked her opinion on what he should order. Sarah was a vegetarian, and there was only one vegetarian item on the menu, so she innocently suggested that one, and explained that she was a vegetarian. Well, this particular man took personal offence to such information and screamed at her, "Why? Why? And just why do you people feel the need to be vegetarian? Huh? Tell me!!" He went on and on, screaming at her, but never seemed to shut up enough to listen to her explanation. Well, after that experience, when people asked her what they should order, her new response was, "Yes, the triple-beef burger is delicious. Or better yet, order the combination plate with a chicken breast, a rack full of juicy ribs, smothered in a mouth-watering sheet of bacon. That's the best item on the menu." She learned to pacify each of the situations, and each one was different. She told herself that it was just for a little while, and each time she looked for that tip amount written at the bottom of each credit card stub. Her tips were always the highest out of most of the servers, because she learned how to play the role. She learned how to up-sale liquors, which was quite easy to do with a group of guys who wanted to impress their friends that they were not drinking the run-of-the mill vodka, but were drinking the top-shelf vodka. And by the time the bill arrived, they didn't notice that their top shelf vodka was seven dollars more, a drink. She ran back and forth, back and forth, from the minute she left her public relations job, until midnight, most nights. And when they closed the doors at eleven o'clock in the evening, Sarah was required to clean her station with a fine-tooth comb, along with cleaning all of the other food-encrusted appliances on the line. It was a banal world. But Sarah learned to live in it. She learned to pacify each situation, and if something happened with a customer that may have turned into something undesirable, she learned how to turn the situation around. It was only for a little while, she assured herself, until she paid off her credit cards. But her credit card balances grew, and she slowly, unknowingly, became a kind of person whom she had never wanted to become.

Sarah kept in touch with William on email, and heard from him every few days. She tried to hide from him, as best she could, her current state of desperation, but he could sense it. He wondered why she was working like a dog, but he couldn't worry too much about it, and didn't want to, as he was experiencing a different kind of journey. He wrote Sarah a few letters, which expressed all of these ideas, his questions, and the looming ideas about their future, but Sarah had reached a banal level of living that she just couldn't comprehend the implications of his letters. She sensed his longing and his desire to share his discoveries with her, but she could only think of the daily phone calls she now received from creditors, and when the next night would come when she could receive more than three hours of sleep. She wasn't sleeping at all, acne had begun to cover her face, her eating habits were a disaster, and she tried to cover the black circles under her eyes with layers of make-up, which made her look even more ghastly. She managed to make it to work everyday, but she began to resemble a walking zombie, thinking of nothing but her financial hole and how she would pay her next rent check. William knew it was eating her heart out, and he even told her to quit, but that was easy for him to say, she thought, and her responsibilities to the vulture creditors were far greater, so she continued to compromise her health to make her minimum payments on her credit cards.

# Chapter Forty-One

*The aim of every artist is to arrest motion, which is life, by artificial means and hold it fixed so that a hundred years later, when a stranger looks at it, it moves again since it is life. Since man is mortal, the only immortality possible for him is to leave something behind him that is immortal since it will always move.*

**William Faulkner** (1897-1962)

William, meanwhile, had met a group of like-minded, free-spirited travelers in Merida, Venezuela. They all seemed to meet at a point in their respective travels where they needed to rest for a few weeks, so the group of five rented an apartment together. One girl was from Japan, another from France, another from Switzerland, and another guy from Germany. They rented a lovely flat that overlooked the main plaza that was impeccably maintained. The center donned a majestic statue of Simón Bolivar, the liberator of the country, and many of the countries in South America, and it was peppered with tall palm trees, and with all sorts of colorful flowers and landscape designs. The Cathedral and several other municipal historic buildings flanked the plaza, and the area always hummed with the gaiety and energy of young students.

Merida was a liberal town, a good stopping point, as it was home to the best University in South America, La Universidad de Los Andes. The town was situated on a raised plateau in the middle of the lush green Andes, with Pico Bolivar as the highest peak on its Northern face. The peak was quite heavenly, actually, and ominously guarded the town with such power and grace. The town had an academic and bohemian feel, but maintained a high level of eco-awareness, as there were excursion, climbing and hiking activities abound. There were also a number of indigenous villages around which contributed to the historic feeling of the area.

So, William had been embarking in his own world of discovery – both of self-discovery and world discovery. Perhaps Sarah was the one for him, he thought. He was never one to think about settling down to get married, but as he traveled, bravely and alone, he began to think that he could see himself sharing his life with Sarah.

As he stayed in Merida, Venezuela for several weeks, he studied Spanish and talked with the locals. But one day, he received an email message from Sarah that indicated she was flying to Caracas for a four-day weekend to see him. It was Easter weekend at the end of March. He hadn't planned to go as far north as Caracas, but he didn't mind much, as he hadn't seen her in nearly three months. They coordinated their plans on email, and as he made the long drive to Caracas, he thought about the plans he had made for them to visit a Caribbean beach town for her short stay. He wanted to get as far away as he could from the city so she could enjoy the lushness of the Andes, and see the Caribbean. He had heard that the Eastern road from Caracas led to the Caribbean over a wide mountain chain, and through the rain forest. The road was windy, narrow and steep, and would be difficult for him, but he didn't mind much as he wanted Sarah to have a wonderful time. This was the girl he wanted to marry. And he was thrilled that she was flying down to see him.

He met her at the airport and was all teeth when he saw her. His eyes sparkled and conveyed a love she had never seen before, and it nearly broke her heart, because she could not return it. He stood there, admiring her for a while, but he saw it. The spark was gone. She was trying desperately, and valiantly to respond in kind, to show her love that was buried somewhere underneath her past, her present, her future, her creditors, her bills, her stepfather, her shamefulness, her doom, but the light of her love was too weak underneath of these pressures. Her heart had been eaten away from that sad beast that consumes the desperate souls.

The rest of the weekend was pleasant. They walked on the beaches, through the deserted narrow street with colorful houses, and sat on the stone wall, with the Caribbean waves crashing beneath their feet, just talking. They listened to Caribbean-African drumbeats, and watched the impromptu dancers on the boardwalk. They hiked through the lush tropical forest that bordered the town and led deep up into the cloud-covered mountains. He walked on rocks through the main stream that ran down from the mountain and bordered the small beachside town. But William saw it. She went through the motions; she walked and moved with listlessness. Soon, the four days passed, and she went back to the United States. William mounted his bike and made a beeline for Ecuador, with thoughts of a future marriage lost in Venezuela.

# Chapter Forty-Two

*Thank Heaven! the crisis --The danger, is past, and the lingering illness, is over at last --, and the fever called "Living" is conquered at last.*

**Edgar Allan Poe** (1809-1849)

A few months passed with the same circumstances. Sarah's situation worsened, and William lived freely, becoming more and more enamored with Latin American women, who seemed to hold an innocent grace and freeness to him. They were confident, open, beautifully fresh and alive, and didn't have all the masked layers that American women had. They spoke with a freeness and childlike cadence, but seemed to manage multiple responsibilities and family with an ease that they didn't seem to question. It was life. He had always been enamored with the language, and to hear a beautiful, dark-haired beauty speak it, was heaven.

Sarah had planned to fly to Peru, to meet William, there, and had managed to juggle her minimum credit card payments, rent, insurance and student loans to scrape together five hundred dollars for a plane ticket. She found a cheap travel agency and was on her way to buy the nonrefundable ticket, but something told her to stop by her office before going to the travel agency. She stopped by the office, checked her messages, and there, on her voice mail, was William's voice. He had got in a bad motorcycle accident on the Peruvian-Ecuadorian border, was hurt, and flew back to the United States to get medical treatment. He was back in Garden City County, and looked forward to hearing from her soon.

What a relief and a shock at the same time! She couldn't think. How badly was he hurt? When did it happen? What made him decide to abandon the trip? She was full of so many questions, and emotions. His voice sounded okay, but she couldn't seem to work for the rest of the day.

She finally connected with him that evening by phone. He got in an accident, and he and the bike had slid down an embankment. He broke his left hip, left wrist and sprained his left ankle. He went to a hospital in Ecuador, but didn't feel comfortable with the treatment. So, he purchased a plane ticket, and flew to Washington, DC where his parents picked him up and drove him to Garden City County. He was fine, except a little tired and sore, and was anxious to see her.

She was happy that he was safe, and still seemed to be in good spirits. But why had he not contacted her when he was in DC? He called his parents to drive him home, which felt like a slap in the face to Sarah. She felt as if she had been removed from the equation all together. Yes, she couldn't wait to see him, but she was scared, at the same time. She knew she had changed and could not give him what he was looking for. The girl whom he had met at the hospital, so long ago, was long gone, or so she thought at the time. That girl was buried, far beneath memories and banal experiences. She was buried beneath creditors and repressed emotions that had just begun to surface in physical ways. It took all her energy to make it through the day, and even then, she just wanted to sleep. She longed for the feeling she felt on those weekend trips, canoe trips, biking excursions, walks, or just the time lying together in the hammock, reading classic literature to each other. She knew she needed to be near him, as he was a calming salve to her heart.

She drove to Garden City County the next day, and she entered his house with mixed emotions. This was the house she had grown to love, this was the house that felt like home, but she hadn't been here in so long, and her world, her inner state was in no condition to appreciate its warmth. It didn't feel like hers anymore, and she felt like a foreigner. She looked different too. Her eyes were puffy and she had gained a few pounds. Acne covered her face. She was ashamed to show herself to him, because she knew what she looked like, she felt it inside.

He was gracious, as he always was, and didn't mind the changes that much. She just needed some rest and relaxation, in the country, he thought. DC life had certainly destroyed her in my absence, he thought.

# Chapter Forty-Three

*It often happens that I wake up at night and begin to think about a
serious problem and decide I must tell the Pope about it. Then I wake
up completely and remember that I am the Pope.*

**Pope John Paul XXIII** (1881- 1963)

So, life resumed as normal. They commuted back and forth to see
each other. William started the master's of business administration
program at the College of William and Mary. And Sarah began
searching for jobs in Richmond, as she knew that she needed to be
near William. She found a good job in a similar public relations role,
and planned to live with her mother in the interim, while searching for
a suitable apartment in Richmond. William did not want Sarah to live
with her mother, so offered his home in the interim. He had never
lived with a girlfriend before, as he had his own idiosyncrasies that
were difficult enough for him to deal with – and he certainly couldn't
expect someone else to deal with them. He was nervous about the

situation. What if he discovered that Sarah had an endearing habit he simply could not deal with? What if she changed into a domineering figure like his last girlfriend? The last thing he wanted was to feel strange about coming home to his own house. He was nervous – what if she decided to leave it, after he decided he liked it? There were so many what-ifs flying through his head. He didn't know how to approach the situation. So, he decided to play it safe and call it a "roommate" situation, even though they were dating, and had been dating for two years. But it was more than dating, they had supported each other, been best friends for one another, been soul mates to each other for the past two years.

Sarah moved her things in, and William cleaned out drawer space for her, and moved all of his things from the bedroom closet so she could have some space. They arranged their things in a workable order in the house, and her bookcase, which had now grown by leaps and bounds, was placed in the living room, nestling itself among leafy plants and artifacts from Central America. Her spirits improved, her financial situation improved, and she was beginning to see the light she had lost sight of so long ago. Christmas came, and Sarah spent her time beautifying their house with wreaths, candles, candy treats, table linens and stockings. They went to the front yard and chose a beautifully full and ridiculous-looking cedar tree, mounted it in the living room and spent a wonderful evening decorating it. It was the first Christmas tree William had had in his home, and it was perfectly imperfect. William and Sarah were good for each other. They laughed at one another as they decorated the tree, as William hung all of the decorations near the trunk of the tree. Sarah chided, "Don't hang them near the trunk! You won't be able to see them!" and William responded, "Well, you're hanging all of them on the ends of the branches and it pulls the branch downward!" They were a good balance for each other, as they seemed to stand on opposite points of the spectrum in all circumstances. She thought of all the little things that he didn't think of, beautified the surroundings, and remembered things like soap and shampoo and cereal. She made his lunches, and most importantly, they woke up to each other every morning. He liked having her there. She brought the smell and the feeling of a woman to the house.

Once, he invited a law school buddy to the house one Sunday afternoon to shoot skeet. Sarah had shot the rifle before, with William and his father, but didn't get much pleasure out of the sport. She liked holding the gun, but didn't like other people at her side watching her. She was always much more aware of their presence rather than the flying target. And probably because they were so surprised at how she handled the rifle. She held it as if it was a kitchen appliance, like she had known it her whole life, and shot without much preparation, and didn't flinch at all when the gun barrel kicked back against the front of her right shoulder. It hurt her, she must admit, but it's just a rifle, aimed at a flying object in the sky. She had her wits about her, and knew where to shoot. Her aim was not great, but she didn't have the practice. Perhaps a few more rounds would have sealed the hobby.

So, one day, Tommy, a law school friend, hailed from Gloucester County to shoot skeet in Garden City County. Sarah kept to the inside of the house to let boys be boys. But after an hour or so, William asked her to come outside and have a go. She wasn't particularly pleased about the request, as she didn't really know Tommy and was a little self-conscious, but took the gun, and fired toward the first release. The bullet whizzed passed the target, missing it by a few feet. She tried again, getting a little closer this time, but still missed the target. Her self-consciousness grew, as she didn't seem to be making the target. Then William added, "You're not even trying." That stung Sarah to the core, as she was trying a little, and she felt as if she was being watched, which did not necessarily contribute to her concentration habits. With that comment, she was embarrassed in front of William's friend. She gave the gun back to William and quipped, "Did you call me out here for this?" And she walked back to the house. She could feel Tommy's eyes on her – he was in a state of shock, half from disbelief and half from amazement. When the boys finished their fun, and came inside, Sarah had just finished baking a cherry pie, and served a piece to Tommy. He couldn't seem to muster any words to Sarah for the rest of the afternoon. Sarah thought she had done something wrong. Perhaps she should have stayed outside with them longer. Perhaps she offended him. Perhaps he was surprised at her comment to William. Or perhaps he had never seen a woman shoot a rifle.

# Chapter Forty-Four

*Faith has to do with things that are not seen, and hope with things that are not in hand.*

**St. Thomas Aquinas** (1225-1274)

William's family's property was a trove of all types of delectable fruits, and Sarah baked all sorts of pear and cherry pies with the land's treasures. They made fried green tomatoes for breakfast, with the Southern stable, cheese grits. William always joked that he wanted to own a grits monopoly, as he couldn't seem to ever get enough of them. They made different types of tomato sauces with the tomatoes from the garden. They made homemade breads and cookies. They made breakfasts on weekend mornings – alternating between eggs, toast and grits, and all sorts of pancakes – blueberry, banana, and apple. Breakfasts were important in that home, and became Sarah's favorite meal. It was the start of a new day and once breakfast was finished, it was a parting measure for their respective days. Sarah did her thing, William did his. Perhaps they connected throughout the day, or perhaps they only connected again for dinner. But things were happy and quite joyful.

One day, William's father informed him that he was driving to New Jersey to pick up a piece of furniture which their mother had bought at an auction, and needed William's assistance. William wasn't thrilled about going, but it was a few days before Christmas, and he hadn't done any Christmas shopping, and neither had his father, so the two boys agreed to combine a Christmas shopping spree into the trip. William left and Sarah stayed on the farm. A few weeks earlier, Sarah's ex-boyfriend, the connoisseur of car-stereos and supped-up cars, had contacted her by email, as he now lived in California, and mentioned he would be flying to Richmond for the holidays. Sarah knew that his parents and family were not always supportive of his efforts, and since she knew the feeling, she told her ex-boyfriend that if he needed a ride from the airport in Richmond to Williamsburg, she would provide, as she was working in Richmond at the time. He replied that he would let her know if he needed one. So, on the day that William went to New Jersey, Sarah received a call from the ex-boyfriend that he was sitting in Richmond airport and needed a ride. "Just like him to give me plenty of notice," she thought, but she picked him up anyway, as he sounded as if he didn't have any other option. The ride was awkward, at best. He was nervous and talked a lot. Sarah just listened, and was glad to know he was doing well in California. She came into his home to pay her respects to his little brother, and the other family members who happened to be there. She kept everything happy and cordial, hugged her ex-boyfriend goodbye, and with a sigh of relief, drove to Garden City County.

William returned the next day, happy to see Sarah, and immediately came to her to lavish her with kisses and affection. But when he came close to her, and nuzzled his nose in her neck, he drew back suddenly, looked at her strangely, and said, "You smell different." It was almost as if he rejected her from her smell. She hadn't changed her perfume, or body lotion, or soap, she thought. He didn't push the issue, warmed up to her again, slowly, and the new smell was long forgotten.

A few days later, Sarah and her mother were on a plane to Rochester, New York to spend Christmas with her older sister, Meghan, who had since whizzed through her master's degree at Ohio State University, her doctor of philosophy from the University of Florida, and was now teaching race relations at the State University of New York, Brockport. Sarah liked being around her sister and her mother again, as it had been a while since the three connected. Plus, she was beginning to feel as if her wings had been clipped. She had ceased using any amount of imagination, the wellspring that fed her youth, and she felt as if she was losing her passion for living. She had landed into a domestic role quite rapidly and easily, but with all of its pleasures, her own passions for literature, music and the great imagination had begun to wane. She liked her new life. She loved to be in love and to feel love everyday. She liked having a best friend that she lived with and slept with. She liked baking and cleaning and living from day to day in peace. But she hadn't touched a piano in years, and the last time she tried, she couldn't remember anything she had learnt. She picked up a notebook now and again to write creatively, but her imagination was dry. She hadn't written a poem in years, and she had even stopped singing, which was something she always did in the mornings. And she couldn't remember simple things. She was too young to develop Alzheimer's disease, but family began to notice that she mentioned things two and three times, she couldn't remember the things that she was always so good at like birthdays and times for softball games. She talked on the phone to her friends and family, but nothing they said seemed quite to penetrate her brain. She asked questions about what they had just said, but it didn't seem to have any relative coherence. Her self-consciousness seemed to be more enhanced, and while she continued the playfulness and good spirit that her and William always maintained, she seemed to be lost in memories and thoughts. William once emerged from his study room after an afternoon and evening of studying, and found Sarah on the sofa, under a blanket, listening to old soul music. She looked catatonic and far away. William approached her, knelt down to her face, and lovingly asked her a few questions to see what she was doing, and she just serenely smiled, and assured him she was okay, but lost herself again in the music. She didn't have spirituality to turn to. She had no God. No center. No belief. The child within her was somewhere lost and buried by layers and layers of responsibilities of adulthood. Her wellspring of creativity sat sadly with a dry well bucket swinging on a rope-string stitched by a thread. She knew something was a miss. She tried to write about it, but the only way she found words to express herself was, "My passion is gone." She even expressed as much to William, but he didn't know what to do or say. The losing or finding of passion is a personal struggle – it's a pathway of self-identity – a myriad of vast networks of tangled crosses that lead toward one simple way that lights the networks and connections in beautiful unity. So, the time with her sister and mother gave Sarah time to think, to reflect.

# Chapter Forty-Five

*A true friend is one soul in two bodies.*

**Artistotle** (384-322 BC)

When she returned to Garden City County after the Christmas holiday, she was so happy to see William, and he was equally as happy to see her. They spent the next few days experiencing each other again, and Sarah returned to work, and William returned to the business school.

William's birthday was fast approaching, and Sarah wanted to get him something special. She noticed that he had been a little forlorn as of late. He attributed it to business school, and the people that he came in contact with on a daily basis. He didn't quite like the way the classes were structured, and he felt as if it was a social-business etiquette school, which he wasn't really too keen on learning. And

Sarah even surmised that he was having a bit of the travel itch, as it had been a while since he had been on a journey.

So, Sarah decided to enlarge one of the photographs from his trip to South America, and frame it, to add to his collection of travel pursuits and mementos that already kissed the house. She couldn't decide between a close-up shot of a little boy who worked as a shoe shiner in Central America, and an aerial shot of Plaza Bolivar in Merida, Venezuela. The picture was taken from the balcony of his apartment where he stayed with his four international friends. In the end, she chose the latter, picked a beautiful black matte and frame, and wrapped his special memento. It seemed strange to her that he never displayed the photos or mementos from this particular trip. Perhaps he didn't want to offend Sarah, since she wasn't there. So, Sarah wanted to assure him that no matter the separation, she supported it, and still felt like she was a part of the journey, as they both needed to go through their own respective struggles to connect again. Somehow, they made it through, and she didn't want him to hide his feelings on account of her.

Well, a day before his birthday, as they were drifting off to sleep, they talked to each other about how close they had grown, and how surprised they both were at how smoothly things were happening. William brought up the subject of ex-girlfriends, as he often compared Sarah to his last, and sooner or later the conversation led to Sarah's ex-boyfriends. And William asked, "When was the last time you saw your ex-boyfriend?"

"Before Christmas," Sarah replied.

William was stunned. That was not the answer he was expecting. He expected two years, three years, maybe. But two weeks? That meant that she saw him while she was living with him. His silence grew, and Sarah explained.

"I knew you smelt different," was William's reply, and he then became convinced that Sarah had cheated on him. Sarah tried to reassure him that nothing of the sort happened, but he did not believe her. He said he did not want to discuss it further, and they slept very far apart that night. He did not touch her, or even move during the night.

The next morning, his birthday, was equally as unbearable. He arose without saying good morning to her, and began to make breakfast for one. She dressed and entered the kitchen where he stood with his back to her the entire time. She pleaded and explained everything the way it had happened but he was suspicious because she hadn't told him about the car ride even after he returned from New Jersey. He had a point, she knew it, and she knew she was wrong for not telling him up front, but she still stood her ground that she did not cheat on him, as she truly didn't. But the deed was done, and from that day forward, the bubble that had protected them was burst. That evening, they walked to the plantation home silently. William walked far ahead of her, to leave her trailing behind, holding the gift she had especially chosen and wrapped and framed for William. He hadn't spoken to her all day, even at her numerous attempts to talk about spirited or happy topics. It was torture for her. They ate a birthday dinner with his family, ate cake and ice cream, and all the while he did not look at her, much less talk to her.

They retired to the living room to open gifts, and when he saw the photo, he said, "You went through my things," with eyes of steel.

Sarah had hurt him. And now, things had become mine and yours, as he knew that would hurt her.

After a week or so, William began to talk to her, but things were never the same . They were now roommates, not a couple who had a future together. He hung the photo on the living room wall, and Sarah was pleased that he made that effort, but it wasn't the same, particularly from the comment he made. The photograph was his, the trip was his. She had no part in it, in his eyes. She always looked into that photograph on their living room wall, into that faraway place that she didn't know, the view that he saw everyday when he woke up in the morning in Merida, Venezuela. It looked so brilliant, so tranquil, and yet vibrant with activity. What was it like for him? What was the apartment like? What were the people like? She could only look into the photo and imagine . . .

The next several months following the Christmas holidays moved quickly. The crack in the wheel was felt by both Sarah and William, and they struggled to help the whole wheel spin smoothly for a while, but after a time, the small chasm was filled by love, by the other's reassurance, and they seemed to regain each other's trust. But there was more happening beneath the surface.

William was discontent and marred in business school tasks. He spent more and more time behind closed doors in his study, reading case studies, learning IT programs and creating spreadsheets. Sarah continued working, but the free time she had now, as William seemed to be more engrossed with school, was spent running from the memories that she hadn't quite recovered.

William knew that Sarah had a past. She alluded to it, in so many words, now and again, but she never spoke about it in detail. And when she did happen to mention it, and William probed further, she retreated quicker than a British army on a Yorktown battlefield. So, William didn't press her. He figured she would tell him when she was ready. He tried to reassure her that people's pasts are just stories that make up the events of their lives, and that they are nothing to be ashamed of, but she didn't quite know what she shouldn't have been ashamed of at that point. She was floundering in gray space, doing summersaults and nosedives throughout her temporal and occipital lobes. Her left-brain capacity- where emotions, imagination, dreams and language are all stored – had just about died. And the only comfort she now seemed to have was listening to William talk, as she was muddled somewhere in a befuddled state of bewilderment and seemed to have lost all ability to communicate emotions, feelings or thoughts. She continued to function at work, as the business world has its own functional lingo that is easily mastered, and she had been in a public relations role for long enough now that it was old hat for her. She repeated words that she had always repeated with no emotionality, no sincerity, and no heart. She was a walking robot, repeating her lines, serving as a puppet at board meetings, somehow mustering energy to survive meetings with her boss, the executive director, but she didn't feel anything. She was numb.

258

Her employer was paying her quite well, which was a rationalization, for her, to turn a blind eye on some of the events that were happening within the organization.

All of her energy was spent on work, and when she came home to Garden City County, she could barely stand. She often took naps when she got home, and couldn't provide much stimulating conversation or support for William. He talked to her, tried to illicit a response, but it was like shining a light on a dead amoeba. She didn't even flinch.

# Chapter Forty-Six

*There is nothing nobler or more admirable than when two people who see eye to eye keep house as man and wife, confounding their enemies and delighting their friends.*

Homer (800-700 BC)

William further retreated into his study, spent more time at the business school, and Sarah spent more and more time rekindling her friendship with Sara in Richmond. William knew that Sarah and Sara had been childhood friends, but didn't quite know the whole story, nor did he have all the pieces to analyze why she would do such a thing at this point in her life. Sarah and Sara went to parties, went out to nightclubs, and went to the outdoor concerts and festivals. Sarah asked William to go to these events, but he was always too busy with schoolwork. Sarah took this as a sign that he did not want to go at all, did not particularly want to spend his time with her, so she spent more and more time with Sara in Richmond.

William didn't understand why she was acting this way. He had experienced the whole dance club and bar scene many years ago, and was over it. Maybe once or twice, he would partake, but he usually left the evening loathing it, reminding himself that THAT was the reason why he hadn't been in months. He went more than he would have liked only because Sarah wanted to, and whatever she was going through now, he wanted to support. They seemed to support each other through everything else, so why not this? Plus, it wasn't half bad when he was there. He liked to be around Sarah when she had a couple of drinks in her because as of late, she had begun to retreat into herself, and sometimes didn't even talk at all. And a few drinks seemed to open her up again into the old Sarah he knew so long ago.

So, as the months moved into summer, the only times William and Sarah seemed to connect was when Sarah had a few drinks in her. Sarah saw William's response to her when she had a few drinks in her, and her drinking increased. All the memories, the past lives, the stepfather, the stepsiblings, the creditors, Brownie, Lucy, Mindy, Shelley, Belle, Virginia Tech, Belle's bedroom, Patty, Curtis, Snuffy and Sheba, her backyard, weekend trips to Chapel Hill and Ocracoke, were long buried and long forgotten under the laughs and smiles that a few drinks brought.

This behavior soon got out of hand, and William spent more and more time at home, and Sarah went out. He was losing his best friend. She barely seemed to be there anymore, and he wanted nothing but to settle down. He had one year left of law school and his career to think about. He had been talking with an advisor at the College of William and Mary about internships abroad and had even asked them about job placement opportunities for spouses. He found a perfect opportunity in Madagascar, and sent his letter of application, along with information about his fiancé.

He mentioned this to Sarah one day, but the contents of his statement and the implication of its meaning was too much for her. She wasn't ready to get married. She wasn't ready to lose her life on account of his. She could barely keep her head above water at this point. She was tired all of the time, she went out drinking with childhood friends, her passion and imagination were gone, and she had a head full of memories that kept her lost at sea, most of the time.

These certainly weren't the best conditions to start a marriage, or start a new life in Madagascar, some far away place, she knew was somewhere near Africa, but didn't know much more than that. She went to work and came home, but William managed to do most everything else for her. And she still had a massive amount of credit card debt that had been pacified a bit, but was still looming. She couldn't expect him to marry her, only to acquire this debt, an act of irresponsibility on her own part. She had dug her own grave, and she had too much respect for him to drag him down there in it. So, she did the only thing she could respectably do at the time. She left.

♠

# Chapter Forty-Seven

*Gratitude bestows reverence, allowing us to encounter everyday epiphanies, those transcendent moments of awe that change forever how we experience life and the world.*

**John Milton** (1608-1674)

She went to her mother's at first, and lay in her childhood bed for days. She cried and cried. Her mother came in occasionally, tried to offer concern and conversation, but Sarah did not respond. After a week, Sarah had still not much moved from the bed, so Louisa pushed her toward getting an apartment in Richmond. She did, secured an apartment the next week, and she moved all of her things out of Garden City County.

The separation was excruciating. The pain was immeasurable. She didn't know her head from her ass. She went to work some days, and the days that she *was* there, she went through the motions, and scheduled many out of office appointments.

Her boss still had frequent meetings with her; she met with the board of trustees and committees. She managed to plan their centennial celebratory events, and performed all of her job function, but she was dead inside. She talked with William a few times by phone, mainly to discuss all of the mail that he had been receiving at his house, mainly from creditors and student loan offices, which were looking for their payments. She collected them, and knew she would have to face them at some point, but only had enough energy at that time to get up every morning without William by her side.

In a few months, she began to feel somewhat ready to face some of the contents in her life. She knew she needed to be with Nature to do so, or to be with something spiritual, as she had just begun to go to church again. But she didn't feel comfortable hiking by herself, and she didn't want to go with friends or other people, because she was embarking on a spiritual journey, which can only be done alone. So, she bought a Boxer, and Bailey, became her new best friend.

She took to Appalachia and Shenandoah National Forest every weekend. Bailey went on his first hike when he was two months old, and she will never forget that first time when she crossed a stream on a fallen log and looked behind her to find Bailey whimpering on the other side. He had never been that far away from her, and he didn't know how to cross it. She walked back over to his side, and patiently showed him how to pass over the rocks, slightly off to the right of the fallen log. Because he had grown accustomed to only looking at her, he didn't notice other ways to cross the stream. Every time after that, he bounded with glee over and through streams, scaled steep rocks with his front paws, and taught Sarah a thing or two about hiking. They seemed to grow together, in those woods, in that beautiful expanse of Virginia's heartland, and as the months progressed, she began to notice the subtle changes in the forest with the changes in the seasons—the colors of the tiny wildflowers, the majestic and calming nature of the laurel bushes, the warming smell of the ferns, which reminded her of the smells from her childhood backyard. She saw the stately run of a white-tailed deer as flew gracefully down a leaf-lined valley. She startled a small, brown bear that found lunch in a patch of blackberries. She found streams and clear pools that she swam in, with only her bare skin, as there was no one else around. She watched butterflies dance and dart, and play games with one another as they flit and circled in a dance like an offering to the sun. She reconnected with herself, with her center, with her inner child, and with God. And all the events, the past, her dreams, her fears, her values, her morals, her integrity, her character, came flooding back.

About this same time, the things at her organization that she was able to turn a blind eye on in the past, seemed to grate on her. Their unethical nature seemed to go against the current in the river that she now found herself. She was asked to change financial figures on annual reports, she was asked to fudge numbers, and appease many of the board members' hearts with blatant lies about the progress of the programs or community activities. She needed an environment that was ethical, and she needed a role model, someone to shape her life in a positive direction. She needed a leader to help her be a leader, to form her into the person she wanted to be, the person she needed to be for the future. She didn't see a future in this environment. It was toxic for her soul.

So, she up and quit. She had no job, and no prospects of one. Her family and friends thought she was crazy. Brownie was in a panic, as she had never taught her to do such a thing. Her mother was in a panic, "What?? You have no job??"

The only one who offered some sense of normalcy was her father. Sarah knew she could survive financially for about two months. She sent out resumes, which was all she could do at that point, and wait. But her father simply said, "Well, now is the perfect time for you to attend a Vipassana Meditation Retreat."

Sarah's father, in his quest to discover the cosmos and spirituality, found peace and serenity in Vipassana, a branch of Buddhism originating in Burma. He volunteered his time at a local Vipassana Center in western Massachusetts, and meditated religiously on his own. Sarah signed up and soon found herself on a ten-day silent meditation retreat. She had worked so hard thus far to get to know herself again by uncovering all of the layers that had clouded her heart and soul, but nothing prepared her for this moment. It was like prison, as she was forced to face the contents of her own mind. They arose at four o'clock every morning and meditated in a large pagoda hall on small square mats. There were sixty men, and sixty women in attendance, and it was led by two Vipassana teachers from California. The meditation practices and techniques were introduced slowly over a four-day period. Day Four was the most excruciating, and many participants actually gave up and left. Sarah thought about it, but the only thing that kept her there was her father, whom she knew was there every day volunteering or meditating. But although it was difficult work, it was one of the most rewarding and enlightening experiences for her. At this state, in silence, and in complete rhythm with the universe, with one's pulse, with one's breath and heartbeat, one begins to enter into a peace that is heartwarming. One becomes sensitized and completely aware of all the little nuances of the body. Sarah remembered the traumas of her scoliosis in her youth, as her posture and maintenance of such a rigid sitting position for long periods of time, was paramount. But her practices with her own self-discipline in maintaining that position, told her a lot about herself, and the way that she reacted to certain situations in life. By day five, she could comfortably maintain the hour-long sitting positions, without breaking her posture, or opening her eyes. It was truly a lesson in self-discipline. And when one is in that state, in complete awareness of one's body, the act of eating becomes a spiritual experience, much like sex. One is aware of all the subtle tastes, and spices, and herbs, and the way it feels on the tongue, and the way it feels as it travels through the body. And the way one feels a minute after ingestion, and the way one feels an hour after digestion. Sarah had a cup of herbal tea on the last day, and included a spoonful of sugar. Her body had not seen refined sugar in that ten-day period, and because she had become so sensitized to any changes, she felt her pulse quicken, and felt the sugar traveling through her veins minutes after the ingestion. Those types of observances are important, and make one aware of the mystery and beauty of one's body.

They slept in cabins, with small, cot-like beds. Others slept in tents with three other roommates. Everyone walked solemnly and calmly in between the pagoda hall, the walking grounds, and the dining hall. Everyone was on their own respective journeys, in their own respective worlds. Sarah didn't know any of them, they all came from different states and areas of the country, but they all seemed to hold a common bond, in that, they were enduring this ultimate test of self-discipline together, to get to that final destination, that final moment, when they could release and share with one another about their experiences.

Throughout this entire year, Sarah wrote letters to William, to tell him of her experiences, and her longing to return to him. She didn't want him to forget her, as she did not leave him to hurt him, but to heal herself for him. She heard from him twice, and the letters were not at all receptive. One was written expressing regret that things did not work, and the other expressed anger for enduring the wait. Sarah wrote frequently, even though she rarely heard any response. She always promised she would return. She even showed up, back at their house, on an April, sunny afternoon, but Sarah was still hurt and angry, and he turned Sarah away.

Before Sarah left for the Vipassana retreat, she penned William a letter to tell him of her plans. He wrote a short and angered reply that he was embarking on his own journeys, and he wished that Sarah would let go of him. Sarah was crushed, but proceeded with her life. What could she do? He was not ready to accept her again. He didn't understand all the reason why she had to leave. And he was still hurting from her departure.

When Sarah returned from Massachusetts, a job offer from the University of Richmond awaited her. It was a job as a research assistant, and was a step down for her professionally, but after talking with its ambassadors and employees, Sarah knew that it was the right fit for her, as its foundations were based in morals, values, ethics and integrity. She was under the direct supervision of a woman of a strong character and a patient spirit. And the whole staff seemed to blend together as a family. She began taking classes and actively involved herself in all of the campus activities – plays, music, performances, lectures, art exhibits and student groups. She frequently visited the Music Department, where the Chair allowed her to use a piano room at any time, and it was here where all of her piano knowledge came flooding back. She participated in a departmental chorus for the Christmas holidays and her confidence in singing alto came back. Her thirst for knowledge was never quite sated, as she learned more about the law from the Law School activities, art from the visiting artists, politics from visiting politicians or visiting professors from other universities, but most importantly, she began to learn more about History, with the roots of the University and the roots of the State of Virginia, which were closely related. And as she studied the University's history and the genealogy of many of its alumni, she noticed that the Gardner name began to appear everywhere. She hadn't quite concerned herself with this before, as it didn't quite matter to her then. She wasn't ready for all it entailed, all it represented, all it expected, and all it demanded. It wasn't something that one chose as a lifestyle, but rather, it was something that chose the one who was most worthy. Because only one with impeccable morals, integrity, strength, perseverance, self-discipline, character and faith can live to represent such a legacy. And one cannot own it, until one claims it.

# Chapter Forty-Eight

*Gray skies are just clouds passing over.*

**Duke Ellington** (1899-1974)

But one day, the University of Richmond had an extra ticket to a drum concert at one of the local venues in Richmond. Sarah didn't have any plans that night so she took the tickets and invited a friend. Sarah had continued her weekly letters to William, even after she returned from Massachusetts, but hadn't heard from him. He had since graduated from Law School, passed the bar, and began working for one of the top law firms in the City of Richmond. During intermissions at the concert, Sarah walked to the bathroom, and as she walked across the top floor of the intermission area, the same place where William and her had seen the Nutcracker, almost a year earlier, she saw William.

They locked eyes, and her heart dropped to her stomach. He was with a girl with long dark hair. Sarah was crushed, looked toward the ground and proceeded to walk past him toward the bathroom. She couldn't quite think for the rest of the performance, as she knew that she was in the same room with William and another girl.

At the end of the performance, they happened to leave the theater at the same time. He walked with his arm around her. When he saw Sarah, he let go of the black-haired beauty, and hugged Sarah. His cheek brushed up against hers, and she could tell he hadn't shaved that morning. It was only a two-day stubble, and he was wearing the Gap corduroys that she had bought for him over a year ago. But he was wearing a new sweater. It was made of cashmere, and was hunter-green. It felt nice against her skin as he hugged her and she reveled in the fact that she had a similar sweater: cashmere and hunter green. But the hug was brief, and he returned to the foreign girl-foreign, at least, to Sarah, and locked hands with her. Sarah watched them walk down the street and William seemed to circle her, as in a protective gesture, and Sarah could do nothing but watch it, as they slowly faded into the distance.

Who was this girl? Did she work at the law firm? Did she live in Richmond? Where did they meet? It couldn't be serious, who ever it was. Sarah was certain of William's love for her. How could they have experienced what they did, only to start a relationship with another person? Sarah certainly couldn't. She had gone on a couple of dates, but they all ended flatly, and Sarah only thought of William the entire time.

This latest piece of information required immediate action. Sarah drove immediately to Garden City County, to talk with William. She entered their home, and William was in bed, and not at all happy that Sarah was in his living room.

Sarah wasn't sure what she was doing in there either, but seeing him with another woman was something she could not bear. She had taken up her cross, walked up Mount Calvary, and seemed to be progressing toward a resurrection, but this latest blow seemed to put her back in the Garden of Gethsemane.

270

And to make matters worse, she discovered that the black-haired beauty was a Mexican, whom he had met on his last trip to Mexico (when Sarah went to Massachusetts). The girl was visiting for the weekend, and was next door in his bedroom! Their bedroom! The bedroom where they had talked and all of their dreams! This Mexican girl was naked in the same bed that Sarah had slept and opened her soul to William! Only a wall stood between them – the same wall with the black and white photographs that his mother had framed years before.

"You're not thinking," Sarah said sternly to him.

"I'm not thinking?!?! You're the one in my house!" he yelled.

He had a point. But Sarah never expected that another woman would be there! So many thoughts were swarming in her head. She thought back to that day when they laid in that same bed, after William had made the decision to go to South America. Sarah was nervous that he would find another girlfriend down there. At the time, William reassured her, "I am not going down there to look for a girlfriend." This conversation came back to Sarah as she stood in front of him with his naked girlfriend in the next room.

"So," Sarah quipped, "You found yourself a Mexican girlfriend."

William looked her dead in the eyes and said, "Yeah, I did."

This was not about the circumstances anymore. He only wanted to hurt her. And he did.

Sarah left the house and went back to Richmond.

# Chapter Forty-Nine

*It takes courage to push yourself to places that you have never been before... to test your limits... to break through barriers. And the day came when the risk it took to remain tight inside the bud was more painful than the risk it took to blossom.*

**Anais Nin** (1903-1977)

In the past two years, Sarah had grown by leaps and bounds, she had completely annihilated her debt, taken back control over her life, formed her character and foundation in such a way to be acceptable to William. And, William could not wait for her. He now had a Mexican girlfriend with prospects of a future wife.

Sarah was destitute. How tragic a tale her life had become. How difficult it was to leave him, but how unfathomably wretched it was to know she couldn't go back to the home she adored, to the soil she loved, to the endearing nuances of the county, of the sun, of the air that made her heart swoon when she neared it. It had caught her long ago, and she remained, trapped in its web, without the ability to legitimately feel it.

She was crushed. "Well," she thought, "I suppose it is my time to go out in the world, with or without a soul mate. Now is my time to travel." She thought this with a heavy heart, as she couldn't bear to think of traveling without William. There was no hope of reconnecting again with him, as he had moved on to other pursuits. Her heart and soul were irreconcilably shattered. She made all the preparations and arrangements, half-heartedly, and without much zeal, and flew to Buenos Aires, Argentina.

She made her way northward through the continent, traveling to all of the places she had wanted to travel with William, and all of the places she only knew about from a few short email messages. She snowboarded the Andes in Argentina with the snowboard he had bought her for her birthday. She hiked through forests and island in the Lake District of Argentina. She toured and hiked through the islands of Lake Titicaca off the coasts of Bolivia and Peru. She visited the ruins near La Paz. She hiked Machu Picchu in Peru. She saw the coast of Peru, and crossed the Peruvian Ecuadorian border, where William had his near-fatal fall. She went to the town of Baños, Ecuador and saw looming volcanoes. And then, she crossed into Colombia. She hadn't had much trouble in her trip until this point. She had planned to cross through Colombia and go directly into Panama, making her way through Central America, but she encountered trouble on the Colombian border, and was only given five days in the country. So instead of traveling quickly through the country to make it to the Panamanian and Colombian border- with little reassurance that five days would be enough, she retreated into Venezuela, with the intentions of crossing into Colombia on another northern border with more luck. But since she was in Venezuela, she decided to visit the old Colonial Caribbean coast town where she and William had spent a four-day Easter weekend so long ago. She sat on the same stone wall, where they had sat five years earlier, when she was, emotionally, in a sea of desperation, buried beneath layers and layers of undecipherable memories. She sat on that same stone wall, now alone, with only detailed memories of a love gone by.

Throughout her journey, she sent William daily emails and accounts of her whereabouts. She had never shut herself off from his life, and always kept the door open in case he was ever ready to forgive her. She never knew if he read them, or deleted them. She never heard any response, but always lived with the hope that she would.

She was growing weary at the end of her travels through South America, and had decided she would fly back to the States from Caracas. But, there was one more place she needed to visit.

She arrived in Merida on a sunny afternoon and checked into a hotel. She walked around the city as she always did in every city she had been in since Argentina, sent a few quick emails to family and friends, but most importantly, to William. She had sent him a message the previous day to tell him she would be in Merida. But she never put much thought into these messages. She wrote them, sent them off into cyberspace, and that was the last of it.

She walked toward Plaza Bolivar and recognized it immediately. This was the black and white photograph she framed, this was the black and white photograph she had stared at so many times, and looked at ominously---the one that hung framed on William's living room wall. This was the far away place she didn't know. And it served as a symbol for the delineation between mine and yours, as William made it perfectly clear that this was his trip, not hers. She looked at its palm trees, the statue of Simon Bolivar in the middle, and was flooded with emotions. This wasn't the ominous photograph anymore, but the real thing. She felt as if she was living a dream. She began to walk toward its middle, toward the statue, and she walked slowly, as she felt like she was walking in the middle of a photograph, the photograph that had always looked at her from their living room wall. And here she was walking through it, in Merida, in Garden City County, Virginia, on a living room wall that William had built. The sun was shining, just as it had been in the photograph, and tears began to stream down her eyes. She thought of William, how far she had come, how their lives had been shaped, molded and perfected by those strange phenomena in life called space and time. The great philosophers talk about them, the great mathematicians talk about them, and the physicists and poets talk about them. But what exactly do space and time entail? Can they be measured? Can they be claimed by an individual or a thing? Can space and time claim an individual? Why do they exist in our world, if they are so intangible, so unfathomable? But, whatever they are, they move silently and knowingly, forming a concentric wheel that somehow spin the axis of this great universe in perfect harmony. They work lovingly to create the best conditions and best formation of individuals so that they may best provide the light of love to the world. Space and time can be spoken of in so many terms – philosophical, scientific, mathematical, and poetical – but in whatever form they take, they always lead toward love.

Who knows why our lives take the course they so, and why others' lives take the course they do. And who knows why two people may collide and walk together for a while, and then separate, only to meet each other again, as newly perfected souls, shaped by the hands of space and time.

Some call it God. Some call it a universal force – the cosmos. But whatever it is, it is powerful, IF YOU BELIEVE.

# Chapter Fifty

*Life is either a daring adventure or nothing.*

**Helen Keller** (1880-1968)

All these thoughts ran through Sarah's head as she walked across that photograph, that reality.

She walked toward the statue, deep in thought, and looked up at the massive bronze figure before her. Suddenly, she felt a tap on her shoulder. As she slowly turned, in deep reverie, there, in front of her, in the photograph, on the wall in Garden City County, and in Merida, Venezuela, was William.

# EPILOGUE

So, what happened to everyone in the end? We have created this lovely cast of characters that encompass Williamsburg, and the roots of the United States, but span continents. Where did everyone end up?

Sarah's mother worked to polish the twinkle in her eye and the youthfulness that everyone from her youth forward had grown to know and love. She eventually healed her heart, said her goodbyes to the beautiful town where she raised her children and moved to Lexington, Massachusetts, where she took a job as an archivist and reference librarian. She left the birthplace of America and the location where the last battle of America's quest for freedom was fought and won, to move to the battlefield where John Parker fired the first shot against the British. What American women will do for History!

She reconnected with her family, her brothers, and the countless cousins she lost contact with over the years and embarked on a massive genealogy project that led her and her sister, Mary, to Ireland. She purchased a summer camp on a pristine, evergreen-clad lake in the Green Mountains of Vermont, and spends her summer weekends near Mary and "at camp" with the loons, the moose and the beauties of Vermont life. When asked why she made the purchase and move to Vermont, she replies, "It has always been my dream."

Sarah's father became the one foundational stronghold in Sarah's life, as he never moved, and never wavered in his strength and support, in his distant and peaceful way. He plays the piano daily, volunteers for the Vippassana Center, takes daily walks with Sally, and makes batches of the best damn granola this side of India, which he not frequently enough, sends to Sarah.

278

Meghan reunited with the love of her college years in Williamsburg, and had a daughter of her own, who she is now raising to heartfelt perfection. She is now a mother with the same heart, soul and passion that her own mother formed, but with the same determination that she formed herself in the gravest of situations in her youth. She moved back to Williamsburg and became a professor of sociology and race relations at her alma mater, the College of William and Mary, authored two books, and teaches in the beautiful town that somehow worked together to form her life's passion: fighting against racism. She attends social protests against racism, social injustices and other politically-minded activities, and now, carries her one-year-old daughter along with her to carry the light of the legacy.

And Sarah and William? You'll have to wait until the next book . . .

Life sometimes throws the almost unbearable circumstances and situations to certain individuals for several reasons. Firstly, these trials prepare them for a life that will be continually tested, and a life of renewal. Someone who is bound for greatness cannot automatically reach the top, and stand fiercely and boldly on two feet in the strong open winds. He will most likely inevitably fall, as he has not endured the sufferings and pain that would prepare him for the severe conditions at the top. Secondly, these circumstances strengthen faith and hope, which are life's most powerful defense and offense weapons. It takes a certain kind of person to be continually beat down, time and time again, and each time to rise, simply on the laurels of faith and hope. And thirdly, these trials test the memory. The mind is a powerful thing, but the heart and body are much smarter. If you ever find yourself in a struggle between your head and your heart, always, always listen to your heart. The mind can easily repress things, and forget things and play tricks on your memory. But it takes a certain courage and bravery to look at those memories, dead in the eye, and reclaim the power that they can take after years and years of repression. Once you have taken back what is rightfully yours, you have an incredible power to give to the world. Giving, no matter who the recipient, nor the cost, is a powerful phenomenon when it is accompanied by good and expectation-less intentions. And when one is free of all blockages of the ability to freely give, one has full access to one's memory.

And with that, I leave you with a few quotes about memory by Samuel Johnson (1709-1784):

*"It is ... the faculty of remembrance which may be said to place us in the class of moral agents. If we were to act only in consequence of some immediate impulse, and receive no direction from internal motives of choice, we should be pushed forward by an invincible fatality, without power or reason for the most part to prefer one thing to another, because we could make no comparison but of objects which might both happen to be present."*

*"Memory is, among the faculties of the human mind, that of which we make the most frequent use, or rather that of which the agent is incessant or perpetual. Memory is the primary and fundamental power, without which there could be no other intellectual operation."*

Printed in the United States
119905LV00007B/1-48/P